SLEEPING FUNNY

Miranda Hill

Sleeping Funny

Stories

 DOUBLEDAY CANADA

Doubleday Canada and colophon are registered trademarks

Library and Archives Canada Cataloguing in Publication

Hill, Miranda
Sleeping funny / Miranda Hill.

Short stories.
Issued also in an electronic format.
ISBN 978-0-385-67683-0
I. Title.

PS8615.I419S54 2012   C813'.6   C2012-902360-4

This book is a work of fiction. Names, characters, places and incidents are products of the author's imagination or are used fictitiously. Any resemblance to actual events or locales or persons, living or dead, is entirely coincidental.

Cover and text design: CS Richardson
Cover image: © Academy of Natural Sciences of Philadelphia/CORBIS
Printed and bound in the USA

Published in Canada by Doubleday Canada,
a division of Random House of Canada Limited

Visit Random House of Canada Limited's website: www.randomhouse.ca

10 9 8 7 6 5 4 3 2 1

For Larry, who loves my ideas.

CONTENTS

THE VARIANCE

—

THE LICE MOVED THROUGH the neighbourhood with the precision of a military campaign.
An infrared map of Glenmount Crescent would
have shown a pattern so complete that even the houses
that were spared seemed part of the strategy.

By Monday of the second week, a third of the students at Forest Glen Elementary School were away,
along with two teachers and even the well-coiffed lady
from the front office who never touched anything that
had been handled by a student without dispensing a
squirt of anti-bacterial gel.

By Wednesday, the Johnstone, Clark-Mayer,
Banerjee-Blum and Stein houses all had children
affected, and the nannies were spending their days
laundering and combing, while the mothers went to

work with their smooth hair pulled into tight ponytails over sharp collars.

Imogene Clark had three children and had tried all the treatments, beginning with the most benign, a Vaseline-smeared head wrapped in scarves, so that Owen and Oliver and Mathilda looked at first like small cancer victims or a tumbling troupe gone awry, the dress-up box having been pilloried for one child after another. By that afternoon though, they had come to resemble dishevelled mummies, running around the house in greasy tatters, and Joy-Anne, the nanny, had stripped them of their ruined costumes and called Imogene at the university, where she was provost. Imogene sent a message back through her secretary, saying she'd bring home some tea tree oil.

The oil made the children's scalps tingle and got in Oliver's eyes when he rubbed them, so that that night when he laid his head on his once-again laundered sheets he also had chamomile tea bags dripping onto his pillow, Imogene having remembered that chamomile was meant to soothe something eye-related and not recalling that it was sties her own mother had used it for.

When the lice showed no sign of surrender after four days of treatment and with Joy-Anne tired of being asked again and again if there weren't some remedy from Jamaica she could recall, Imogene marched to the pharmacist and got the hard stuff.

At the counter, she met Lesley Banerjee, who was asking for tea tree oil. When Lesley saw Imogene she blushed and stammered an apology as if the lice were an indication of her own moral failure, and Imogene told her to just skip right to the chemicals and maybe they'd all be done with it.

Standing on Imogene's lawn with Imogene, Lesley and Adelaide three evenings later, monitoring the children's turns on the tree swing, Kate Johnstone held that the lice epidemic was worse than the attack of pinworms from when the children had all been in training pants and they'd gathered in the cesspool of a playgroup three mornings a week. The pinworms had moved back and forth between the children with disheartening regularity as if it were a game of hot potato, until one day they petered out altogether. Perhaps the children had just grown out of it. No one really knew, but the pinworm problems had certainly been a factor when Brian Johnstone told his wife that what he'd really wanted was a girl and couldn't they try just one more time and Kate had looked at Caleb and Campbell, scratching in their footed jammies, and said not on her life.

Yes, lice were worse. Lesley Banerjee was sure of it. There was the bedding, stripped and washed and bleached each day, then into the dryer for a sterile spin, but there were also the missed classes and the missed days of work when Edna the nanny had contracted them herself and had to stay home to do her own treatment and sterilize her apartment, and Lesley had not known what to say to her fellow partners at Gordon, Banerjee and Yates, until Vince had said, Oh you're on Glenmount, aren't you? My sister's daughter teaches at Forest Glen, but on the side she's studying entomology.

Of course, it wasn't just Glenmount. It was also streets like Park and Collingwood and Cedar Grove, where the houses were that much smaller, the gardens closer and some families without nannies and regular cleaners. Places, Lesley Banerjee reasoned, where the phone calls made to employers were perhaps not so tortured as those the mothers on Glenmount were making to law offices and head surgeons and deans of departments. Places where sometimes no one had to make any calls at all, the mothers simply giving up their days to hours of washing, scalp scrubbing and fine-combing for nits.

What about the chicken pox? asked Adelaide Stein, who was always late with a contribution until the conversation was almost over. The chicken pox was terrible, and there were all those scars.

Imogene said that the chicken pox were oh-so-different. There was a sense of legitimacy with chicken pox. Chicken pox was something that you wanted the children to get, to build up their immunity, unless of course you were one of those mothers who felt that your child shouldn't ever be sick and went out and got the vaccine.

Well, there was the question of secondary infection, said Lesley, and secondary infections could be deadly; a lot of pediatricians nowadays were highly recommending—in fact, practically insisting—that parents choose the vaccine. They acted like it was child abuse not to.

Doctors think they know, said Imogene, with a force meant to leave everyone thinking or trying not to think about Kate being a plastic surgeon and Imogene's own husband Paul's position as head of emergency services at the university hospital.

Now that the lice had made their way through the neighbourhood and down most of the street, there might have been an air of cleansing about it. After the chemicals had been applied to each of the children in turn (God knows what we'll find years from now, a brain tumour or skin cancer or something, said Adelaide to her husband David, who replied that if it could make Charles qualify for Mensa it would be more surprising, referring to their only child, whose favourite activity in grade four so far had been hoarding his classmates' pink erasers and nibbling them alone in his room), sometimes twice, and after they had been subjected to the humiliating—and excruciatingly boring—head check before being permitted re-entry to school, the lice decamped from Glenmount Crescent, appearing not to leave a trace. It was fall, and other things should have been on the adults' minds: parent–teacher interviews, and increased homework or lack of homework, and whether the older girls should be allowed to wear those jeans so tight that there were zippers on the sides as well as in the front. The leaves were turning on the oaks and maples and beeches, the crabapples falling into the street and attracting the wasps before garden services or intrepid fathers scraped them from the pavement.

Soon, the neighbours on Glenmount Crescent would be in a position to shake their heads and give a small, clipped laugh about "the epidemic," whenever someone brought it up, almost accidentally, as a reference point for the other things that happened that fall, like Owen Clark-Mayer's broken arm or Charles Stein's eye surgery or that business with the Banerjee-Blums. Indeed, maybe it all would have been different if they had just gone back into their stone or brick and stucco houses, walked out of that late-September evening and into their granite-countered kitchens to the smell of the housekeepers' cooking. Moved away from under the old beech with the tree swing in front of the Clark-Mayer house. And if Adelaide hadn't, at that moment, said, "I wonder where it all started," then turned and looked up and across the crescent almost to the place where it bent, at Michal Revivo, standing in her garden, her mass of frizzy white-blonde hair flowing out like meringue from under a red kerchief, and said, "Can you imagine pulling a lice comb through that? You know, if I had hair

like that, I don't think I could comb it at all." And each
of the women watched the words form into a cloud
before them that might just have been the first frozen
breath of the season.

The Revivo-Smitherman clan had moved into one of the
homes on the street that everyone knew, from their visits
during the real estate open houses, needed a good deal
of work. Not gutting, but some serious repairs that
would probably require dumpsters, permits, and a long
sacrifice of a family's days to the trades. In fact, it was one
of those houses that really required renovations before
anyone moved in—shag carpet and ochre paint and a
smell of Mrs. Anderson's cats on the back porch (which
could eventually become a lovely sunroom) and made
the low-for-the-area price seem less like a deal. But
Michal and Luke had moved in last spring, and the only
sign of work had been the very visible attack on the lawn.

They had arrived just before the birth of their third
child, Andreas (Romero and Sasha before him) and had
promptly ripped up the grass in front of the three-
storey Tudor and replaced the entire area between the
sidewalk and the flagstone with echinacea, black-eyed
Susans and three-foot grasses. I'd rather dig than mow,
laughed Michal, her frizz bouncing. To the rest of the
Glenmount set, whether one liked to mow was not a
consideration. Daily, trucks parked in front of the

crescent's houses, delivering young men and lawn mowers, edgers and stiff brooms to various properties. But all summer, Michal Revivo had stood in work boots and baggy pants with a baby sling across her back, Andreas bobbing in it, the top of his head covered in a man-sized fishing cap.

The women had made the usual forays at first, enquiring about Michal's origins (Ontario, Tel Aviv, wanderer, San Francisco, here) and Luke's practice (he was a lawyer, but only legal aid); the nannies had brought the children by to play (Sasha was usually reading and Romero showed a fascination with archery that was at first exciting and then bordered on the obsessive, soon being abandoned by other boys playing Star Wars in between the houses or soccer on the lawns). But soon, the Glenmount Crescent residents had fallen back into their old allegiances, merely averting their eyes from the wild meadow of the Revivo-Smitherman yard, and when, at the end of the summer, Adelaide had mentioned to Lesley that she'd only ever seen babies worn like that in *National Geographic* and wasn't that going to lead to chiropractic problems in the future, Lesley hadn't answered her at all.

The residents of Glenmount Crescent had things they embraced and things they ignored, and the Revivo-Smithermans fell firmly into the second category with the thunk of a child's wooden block through a sorting toy. If anyone happened to mention the house with the straggly-hair lawn or the strange yard that stretched out to the side, maple tree leaning over an old fence, most of the other Glenmount residents would just wave their hands as if they were swatting away one of those late-summer yellow jackets that moved dozily round picnics, and leave it simply with, Well.

All summer they had approached their houses from either side of the street curve, the Johnstones and the Clark-Mayers from the left, the Steins and the Banerjee-Blums from the right, and because of the cottage trips, because of the children congregating first at one back-yard pool then another, and because of the special programs and the tutoring (for some), the Revivo-Smitherman house had become something that didn't register on their internal maps of the neighbourhood they all loved. But now that Adelaide had pointed their way, because there were four of them there to see it, because there were witnesses, it seemed they could see nothing else. Now that their attention was drawn to it, they saw the place blowing and flowering, spores tossed from lawn to lawn, blooming and seeding themselves along the block, and they became aware, like an itch that passed between them, that they couldn't help but be affected. They could no longer look away.

—

Now, Michal was everywhere. Kate Johnstone saw her weighing grapes at the grocery store, Lesley Banerjee saw her pedalling through the intersection at Cedar Grove and High Field, Imogene Clark saw her striding, cargo pants and canvas bag swinging, around the corner between the Continuing Studies building and the art gallery. Michal Revivo was now a permanent fixture in their landscape.

Nowhere was this more apparent than on the morning walk to school. On the Tuesday following Adelaide's observation, Imogene ushered the children and Joy-Anne onto the stone porch, closed the oak door behind her and looked out across Glenmount Crescent just in time to see Michal and Luke step down onto their own, wooden steps. Romero wore a black toque pulled low over his blond ringlets and Sasha held a book before her like a monk's tablet. Luke had a knapsack slung over his jacketed shoulder and Michal had one hand draped across the sling—in front this time—as if she were resting an arm on a table. At the bottom of the steps, Luke and the children waited for Michal, and then the four of them merged into the passing foot traffic of children and nannies and mothers.

Imogene tightened her hand along the handle of her soft leather briefcase. She blamed herself, of course. In the flurry of spring graduation, the arrival of the new chancellor, the conferences in Zurich and Dubai,

she had looked upon Michal and her litter as a temporary nuisance, an eccentric visual distraction that would
eventually fade into the background. But she had made
a tactical error. She saw that now. Michal was a rogue
element. Sure, she had looked innocent in her gardening clothes and Imogene had thought that her insis-
tence on adding whimsy to her property was as much
a result of lack of funds as lack of taste, with her packs
of assorted seeds sprinkled by children from the porch
railing in random handfuls, throwing out poppies here
and bachelor buttons there, but Imogene had surmised
that soon Michal would grow bored and turn to rag-
rolling the dining room some hideous purple and
they'd see little of her.

As the Revivo-Smitherman children went ahead of
their parents, weaving in and out of the other neighbourhood walking parties, Imogene wondered how she could
not have understood. The children reached the road and
Michal called out to them, something almost inaudible
that seemed to draw no notice from the other walkers,
but that caused Sasha and Romero to turn to her—his
toque pushed up and her book held down—until she
released them with a similarly silent command, so that
though they crossed between two parked cars instead of
at the corner, they looked carefully before Romero
shoved the toque lower over his eyes and Sasha turned
the page and brought the book level with her face again.

Adelaide was right. Some threats were pervasive, dangerous precisely because they seemed of no consequence. Like purple loostrife and zebra mussels, non-native species that floated in little by little until the entire ecosystem was changed. Though the landscape might remain something you recognized, it was irrevocably altered. The lice had been merely a warning.

Imogene put her keys in her purse and looked down her own steps for her brood and their nanny, but Joy-Anne and the children had gone on without her, without saying a word.

Lesley Banerjee was due in court at nine-fifteen. The children knew this. It wasn't as if she hadn't told them, eleven times, that she was going to be late. That this was only going to work if they all pulled together, that just because Edna had to go to the dentist this morning didn't mean that they could be late for school. No, mommy was perfectly capable of getting them there—though that, of course, was not what she had said to Marty, hissing in the bedroom that morning, "Well, couldn't you just move your meeting, for once? You're the head of the division, after all. I can't just tell the judge I won't be there"—but they would have to hurry and there was no reason they couldn't hurry, was there? Lesley was twisting past the steering wheel, flinging the car door open in the bus loading zone, making a brushing motion with her hand as if the force of the wind past the children's knees and knapsacks would propel them out and her forward on a hurricane gust—Shut the door! Harder, Maya, you know it won't close—when she saw Michal and Luke. They walked out of the school-yard, pausing to look at the late Rose of Sharon in the neighbouring temple garden, and Michal held the baby against her forearm as she swept forward to pick up a shrivelled blossom. She crushed it in her palm and unrolled its petals. She brought it to her nose, and then let it fall to the ground again.

Lesley watched Michal and Luke walk back toward the stop sign and the crossing guard. On the other side of the crosswalk, they looked as if they were about to part, Luke turning toward the bus stop, now to Michal again, but then they faced each other for a moment and together they turned back in the direction of Glenmount Crescent.

Lesley angled the rear-view mirror to take in the corner where they would turn. They were moving too slowly to have forgotten something. It seemed only that their plans had changed. As if today were a meandering Sunday and not a workday morning.

It was as bad as if David Stein had stepped out that morning, his pockets bursting with thousand-dollar bills. Michal and Luke were flaunting something that no one else on the block could lay claim to. It was as if Michal Revivo possessed all the time in the world.

—

Kate didn't have a patient till noon. Usually on Tuesday mornings she was in surgery, tucking a tummy or reworking scar tissue, but she had booked herself off the schedule to finish an article that really should have been completed in the summer, but which, like so many other things, had slipped into September, the deadline barely insistent, lingering like warm weather that was bound to change.

From her office on the second floor of the house— a room that had probably held a crib once, or a narrow servant's bed, but was much too small to call a real bedroom—Kate had a view of the street from the corner to the bend in the road. Her perspective was framed on the left by a tall cedar hedge and a stop sign, to the right by the crooked fence and old maple on the Revivo-Smitherman property, bordered by Michal's grassland. Kate limbered her fingers over the keyboard and tried think of a word for it. *Tundra?* No. Tundra was something flat with low-lying life. This was more assertive. Defiant. *Serengeti?*

Kate opened her long-dormant document: a description of a complex reconstruction of the face of a burn victim—airlifted twice to bigger hospitals, then brought to Kate at the university hospital, where she had led a team that built the woman's tissue anew. A precedent-setting case. Something that should inspire precise words.

Triumphant words, despite the academic nature of the article and the medical journal that awaited it. A "tundra" type of word. A "Serengeti" in medical language. An article that not only relayed the procedure, but replayed it. Kate looked out the window again.

Michal and Luke were turning up the driveway, walking with their heads tilted toward each other. Kate saw how Michal's hair slid down her sweatered back as she lifted her head to laugh and how Luke caught his wife by the belt loops and pulled her to him, so that their hips bumped together and stayed connected as they walked toward the steps, their bodies coming apart only when Michal sidled in front of him and lifted a foot to the step. Then he slid in close behind her, lifted her (and the baby), her backside cradled by his thighs, and carried her up the steps to the door, where he set her down and threw the door open, and the three of them tumbled inside, the green screen slamming shut behind them.

The entire scene took fifteen seconds. It was the sort of thing one might not have noticed at all. But Kate did. Just looking out her window, innocently. What did it matter? They were only neighbours. Mildly out-of-sync neighbours. No wild parties. No cars parked on the lawn. They hadn't known she was looking.

Kate pressed down hard on the keys, as if they were typewriter-stiff. She hammered out a description of the pre-op procedure, the patient's condition. She read it back, aloud. How the skin had been moistened. Separated. Elongated.

Kate looked across the road again, at the closed door. At the daytime windows that revealed nothing to the street.

For Adelaide Stein, Michal had been everywhere since the end of June. While the others had come and gone to cottages, on European trips, Adelaide had sat in her backyard, listening through the fence to the Revivo-Smitherman children playing. David had booked a summer of takeovers and acquisitions and long business trips and so Charles had been enrolled in day camp after day camp. But by the second day of every program, he was disinterested and making trouble. Not the sort of trouble for which he had managed to recruit other children to his cause, just a disruptive resistance that got him sent home with notes and ultimatums until, on day three of each camp, Adelaide had pulled him out and brought him home to lie in the hammock or stare at the TV screen, face close and slack.

It was true that the neighbourhood children had not warmed to Romero and Sasha, but as Adelaide had listened to their inventive games in the backyard, their father sometimes joining in with a cardboard sword or helping them to do something that sounded much like ripping apart old VHS tapes and measuring the black ribbon spread out on the grass, she knew it was only a matter of time before the Revivo-Smitherman offspring were no longer at the bottom of the social order, and that the position would return to its rightful owner: her son, Charles.

Charles Stein, her only child, was a boy who seemed destined never to live up to the grace of his formal name, nor to become athletic and buff enough to be a "Chuck," or popular and easygoing enough to be a "Chip." Charles was born to be "Charlie," and everyone seemed to realize this long ago, with only his parents adhering to his given name, and Adelaide frequently lapsing into a reverie in which she had named him something easier, with built-in possibilities: something apostolic, like John or James, that instantly gave him a group. Made him a follower.

Charles had developed lice for the first time at the very beginning of the school year. Perhaps they were even a result of his final camp failure, Introduction to Orchestra, which took place in the community hall near the city centre and had a large number of subsidized spaces. Adelaide had spotted the lice herself, before the notes had come home from school and the public health nurses had been called in to go through the hair of every child from kindergarten to grade six. Adelaide had seen him scratching his head one night and sucking on his arm, bringing up a big, purple hickey (David would say it was the only way the boy would ever get one), sitting within a foot of the big screen in the brown brocade family room on the second floor, watching a rerun of *Survivor*.

"Don't you know how this turns out?"

"'Best of,' Mom."

"Oh, Charles, just look at what you're doing to your arm!"

And as she pulled the bruised and slick arm toward her, she got a glimpse of something pearly under the reading lamp, shining out against Charles's limp brown hair. But only for an instant, before he put his hand up to scratch.

That first round of lice Adelaide had kept secret. She went for the chemicals right away, driving to the pharmacy on the east side of town. It was a crowded night, and after a half-hour wait, she drove home, roused Charles from his bed, scrubbed his hair clean, took the sheets and put them in a black garbage bag, washed the fleece sweaters hanging in the closet, washed and folded the remainder of the towels and face cloths and stripped her own king-size bed and washed those sheets too. It was nearly three by the time everything was returned to the linen closets and Adelaide went to sleep, leaving a note for the housekeeper to call the school and let them know that Charles Stein was experiencing a fever and wouldn't be back for a day or two.

It wasn't till she woke up the next morning that she wondered about something she had seen out of the corner of her unusually distracted eye. The back of a tall woman

in overalls and a bohemian hat, white-blonde hair spring-
ing out at the corners like the wig of a laughing clown.

She should have asked Edna. She could have asked Edna.
Salads were in Edna's repertoire and Lesley paid Edna and
therefore Edna's salads were her salads and why, why did
she do this to herself every time and make herself late with
the salad to the Home and School fall barbecue? Her children Maya and Simon were already there, with her husband Marty—I don't know why you bother, everyone only
eats the burgers anyway—and now there was barely room
beside Adelaide Stein's Chinese noodle salad and Imogene
Clark's three-layer Mexican and Kate Johnstone's killer
Caesar for Lesley's faux cut-class bowl with *Banerjee-Blum*
written across the bottom in Sharpie on masking tape.

Lesley edged the bowl onto the table and reached
back into her canvas bag and found, instead of servers,
crumbled bits of old broccoli.

Imogene straightened the tablecloth where it had
rippled and pulled a pair of metal tongs from a box
underneath the table. "Someone always forgets," she
said. "I found this pair in the staff room."

Lesley recognized the tongs as the ones she had forgotten to label and bring home two years ago.

Lesley looked up again, but Imogene was walking
toward the barbecues. Over by the fence, Lesley saw
Imogene's Owen and her own son Simon catching hold

of each other's T-shirts and swinging each other around like gladiators. Her daughter Maya was crying. Because of the fighting or because of the wasps or because they were out of orange pop. Marty was scanning the crowd of strollers and mothers and fathers and somersaulting children. Lesley walked in the opposite direction.

Kate and Adelaide were sitting at the table for the Home and School volunteer sign-up, coloured markers fanned out before them. There was clearly nothing for her to do, but Lesley took up the empty chair.

"I've never seen it so busy," she said.

"At the burger lineup, yes. Slower than ever here," Kate said, indicating the still-white sheet in front of her.

Lesley could not understand how, despite her job as a plastic surgeon, Kate managed every year to walk the school children to the pool, six Thursdays in a row, for swimming lessons. Of course, Imogene would never have the luxury to do such a thing midday, so instead she chaired committees. The same committees that Lesley merely sat on, deciding her vote on every issue based on Imogene's précis during the walk over to the school.

"It's always the same people, isn't it," Adelaide said. "Doing everyone else's work."

Adelaide was down to teaching one class a semester at the university, just your basic first-year world religions, and Lesley knew that she spent every Tuesday and Thursday helping in the Forest Glen office.

Lesley looked at her hands, which were badly in need of tending. There was a raw spot beside the nail on both thumbs, as if she had been chewing them. She didn't remember putting her nails to her mouth—something Edna, uptight and British, cautioned the children against hourly. She must have bitten them in her sleep.

"Well, well . . ." Adelaide said, low and in Lesley's ear.

Lesley tucked her thumbs inside her fists, expecting a rebuke. Then she saw Michal coming across the schoolyard, directly toward the sign-up table.

Lesley had never seen Michal walking without the baby, and freed of this encumbrance, Michal seemed even taller. She swayed side to side like one of the fuzzy grasses on her lawn.

"Art enrichment." She said it like an answer to a question they had posed. "Three lunches a week. Pastels, clay, and maybe—depending on their patience—stained glass."

Lesley felt a movement to the left of her. Kate had leaned back in her chair. Adelaide was pursing her lips. No one spoke.

"Well?" Michal looked from one to the other of them, her gaze finally landing on Lesley.

"I don't think any of us is up to that," Lesley said.

Michal laughed. She had lovely teeth, white and all perfectly straight except for one on the top front that protruded ever so slightly and gave her smile a stuttering quality, so that the process seemed to last longer than in most people.

"No, no. I'm offering to do it. Do I sign up here?"

"You do," said Kate, and with a minuscule shrug to Lesley she handed Michal one of the coloured pens.

"Hello, women."

"Oh, Imogene, Michal is just offering to provide lunchtime art classes!" Adelaide sounded nervous and simultaneously relieved.

Lesley had never seen Imogene look short before. Certainly she was not the tallest woman Lesley knew, but now Lesley saw that she was really not that much taller than Lesley herself, not even that much taller than average, as she turned and looked up to meet Michal's eye.

"Oh, goodness. I wouldn't think of it. It's too much. You have the baby and your incredible garden," Imogene said, and she plucked the blue marker from Michal's hand. "Really, we plan these things in the spring. Come see us if you still have this wonderful enthusiasm then."

In the space between Michal and Imogene, Lesley saw the people at the barbecue move, flat and two-dimensional, like a film projected on a wall. Michal dropped her hand, the one that had been holding the pen, into the wide front pocket of her overalls.

"One bit of business, then," Michal said, and she pulled out several unmarked envelopes, handing them one by one to each of the women. "We're building my

studio, and we'll require a few variations to the zoning."
She smiled again, but this time the smile caught on the
tooth and went no farther.

It was almost dark. Kate was emptying the last of the
barbecue garbage into the outdoor bins with Mr.
Carmichael, the school janitor. She didn't have to do it.
He had urged her several times to go home. It was not
the sort of job she would usually volunteer for, but
tonight, in the empty gym, she revelled in crushing the
cans and hearing them avalanche into the recycling bins.

Was it how Luke said to her "Darling?" Or how
Michal answered, her voice like the clasp on a necklace
that opened and then fastened him to her?

It had been after the confrontation, if that's what it
was, at the sign-up table. Kate was coming around the
corner from the playground and Michal was walking
toward the blanket anchored by her husband and two
older children, a diaper bag on her shoulder, Andreas
in clean pyjamas in her arms. And then what? Luke had
stood and reached for the baby. Only that and then,
"Darling?" he had said. A simple word, but potent. And
Michal had understood his question and answered "Yes,
let's go home," her tone suggesting it was a nest they'd
made together, a bed they would lie in forever.

Kate stood quietly, watched them roll their plaid
blanket and strap the baby into his sling, watched the

children stand up and lead their parents in procession. She held very, very still, waiting for something more to be revealed. Then she felt her husband's hand on her arm.

"You coming or staying? I'm going to take the boys home," Brian said. Kate shook her head. And when he leaned forward to kiss her, said, "Okay, see you soon," nothing had budged in her at all.

It was two weeks later, a Thursday, when Imogene arrived at her office to find the morning paper folded atop the interdepartmental mail. It was only nine-twenty, but already there had been calls. Imogene's secretary had put a sticky-note beside the headline "Major Gifts wants to chat about possible art gallery donation."

Imogene slid the inbox to the side and stood for a moment, as she did each morning, looking out the window onto the campus below. Across the quadrangle students were entering the library in fall jackets and striped scarves, warming their hands around travel mugs of coffee. Only two weeks ago, they had still been moving with early-term enthusiasm across the same square wearing flip-flops and ridiculous surfer shorts, mentally extending their vacations, ignoring all their professors' suggestions that they pace themselves and not leave their reading and research until too late.

Imogene moved her plants a little farther away from the drafty old window. To think it was only two weeks ago that Imogene had organized the school barbecue. Now there were Home and School meetings to chair and the inevitable complaints from parents unhappy with their children's teachers. Fall had truly begun.

Imogene turned on her computer and considered the pile of paperwork while she waited for the screen to brighten. She lifted the flagged newspaper. And there it was, on the front page of the Arts section: "Artist Takes Manhattan, Berlin . . . and Forest Glen." The article quoted from reviews: "Paintings that defy two dimensions" and "Revivo's work has become a symbol of restraint-encased passion." Behind Michal in the half-page picture, and close up on pages 4 and 5 where the article continued, were paintings in deep reds and purples with a veiny blue streak that Imogene, overriding the art-speak, could only interpret as placental.

The reporter had asked her how she found Forest Glen for inspiration and she said that she hadn't been doing much painting lately, just working on her garden and caring for her children. "But big changes are coming. I have to get a sense of a place before I know what I want to do in it. I let the space work on me, and then I work on the space."

Imogene read about the studio. And then she read it again—the description more immediately revealing than the blueprint on the single sheet of paper Michal had provided. They were planning a four-storey glass structure that would "let in sufficient light and have enough space for the giant canvases the celebrated artist often favours." What about what Imogene favoured? What about old growth, definite borders, and the neighbourhood's shared sense of appropriate conduct?

Imogene held the paper at arm's length so that Michal, eyes sultry and downcast, looking over a bare shoulder above a bright orange evening gown, was in crisp focus. This was no different, she thought, than the time the neighbourhood had successfully argued against the giant, impersonal postal boxes or fought the building of the new undergraduate residence a mere two blocks away from Glenmount Crescent (Imogene carefully staying behind the scenes and publicly neutral while Kate and Adelaide delivered the PowerPoint presentation Imogene had helped them prepare).

Imogene led. That's what she did. Her leadership being born, not of any egotistical urges, but because no one else was really capable. She had marshalled her brothers through everything from capture-the-flag to her parents' sixtieth anniversary. And though her private school roommates had complained that there was too much work and not enough gossip and chocolate at her study groups, hadn't every one of them maintained an A in senior year? Collette was a professor now at Harvard, Janine was studying something microscopic and not quite unfindable on the bottom of the

Great Barrier Reef, Snooky was the investment banker of the moment. And on it went for Imogene: best girl, proctor, valedictorian, head of class, don, valedictorian (again), head of department, dean, provost. It wasn't just her role, it was her very nature: born in her boots and marching on.

Imogene folded the article into the front pouch of her briefcase and carried on with her day, which ended after 9 p.m. with the official welcome dinner for the chancellor. But before she went upstairs to bed, she took the newspaper from her briefcase, clipped out the article and hung it on the fridge with magnets of the old masters— van Gogh, Cezanne, Matisse—beside the application to appear before the Committee of Adjustment.

Adelaide had been matching children to their pre-printed envelopes all morning, tucking the invitations to next week's parent–teacher night inside and listening to the crisp *pffit* of the papers as if they were the final breaths of individual oracles. On every page was printed, *Please come to discuss,* and a handwritten comment followed: *Simon continuing his excellent progress in science with additional exploration at home; Cameron's kindness to his fellow students and teachers; Owen developing his leadership qualities in the classroom as well as on the playing field.* It was a veritable parade of the attributes and accomplishments of the children of Forest Glen.

Except, of course, for Charles. Before tackling the stack left for her on the extra desk in the Forest Glen office, Adelaide had waited until the school's officious secretary answered the phone, then she surreptitiously eased Charles's note from the middle of the pile. *Please come to discuss: Charlie practising his times table, remembering all clothing items for gym days, checking agenda for assignments.* Rote and bland, as if, like Charles himself, the teachers could think of nothing to say. Now, forty or a hundred papers in, Adelaide's fingers no longer throbbed with paper cuts. She had worked her breathing back to a shallow rhythm, returned her heart to a slow and regular pace. After reading the name at the top of each page, Adelaide immediately flipped the page over without reading farther, so that she was staring only at its blank, white back. The relief was profound, the predictability of the action inducing a comforting catatonia.

The bell rang for the children to come in from recess and the hall filled with the sound of shuffling feet and voices. Then Owen and Simon, their cheeks rosy, their fall jackets askew, entered the office. They were followed by a couple of boys that Adelaide barely knew, then finally by Romero, blood gushing from his nose. But not finally, because, behind them all came Charles, looking as if he were an understudy struggling to remember the lines.

"Goodness!" the secretary said with a shudder. "I'll get the ice. Could you—" She handed Adelaide a box of Kleenex and rushed off in the direction of the staff room.

The boys arranged themselves in the row of chairs as if they had bought tickets, all except Romero, whose nose was staining his shirt and making a puddle under him, and Charles, who stood just inside the doorway, his expression unreadable.

"Simon, get up," Adelaide said. "Romero needs that chair." She guided Romero by the shoulder and got him to put his head between his knees and hold a clump of Kleenex to his nose.

The door to the inner office opened and Mrs. Trask, the principal, stepped into the reception area. She stood for a moment, a general surveying the sorry state of her troops. "Mr. Clark-Mayer," she said, with the weary tone of one assigned to an outpost that would never see real combat, "could you enlighten me?"

"He got hit by a ball," Owen said.

"I kicked it," Simon said. Clearly, there were points to be won for participation.

"But we were all playing," Owen said. "Well, all of us except Romero. He was only watching."

A phone was ringing, but Adelaide didn't move to answer it. While she had been here, sizing up her son's failure, he'd been on the field with the other boys. Charles, playing soccer! Adelaide stood frozen until she was shooed aside by the secretary, who pressed an ice pack up against Romero's nose, removing the wad of bloody Kleenex with a hand encased in a latex glove.

"I'll call his mother," she said.

"All right," said Mrs. Trask. "Back to class, the rest of you."

The boys stood and walked through the door, their voices picking up one-by-one in the empty hallway as they crossed the office threshold. Charles trailed at the end, and as he turned the corner, Adelaide readied herself to strain for his particular timbre, to hear it blend in to the chorus of secrets and retellings, the real story revealing itself and being remade into legend even as the boys pushed and shoved their way back to class, but then—

"Charlie!" Mrs. Trask called him back. "What exactly were you doing when all this happened?"

Charles turned slowly to face her. "The teacher outside said to come. He said, 'You too.'"

"Charlie, you weren't playing soccer." Mrs. Trask wasn't asking questions any more, just stating facts for the record.

"No," said Charles, and Adelaide saw Romero look up at him, as if noticing him there for the first time.

"Well, then don't come to the office, Charlie. Do you think your mother is happy to see you here?"

Charles shrugged.

"Go back to your class," Mrs. Trask said, and Charles

looked for a moment as if he didn't know where or what that was, before he exited in silence.

Mrs. Trask turned to Adelaide and gave a little smile. "A straightforward case of mistaken identity," she said, stepping back into her office. "Oh, if you wouldn't mind, Mrs. Stein, could you sit with Romero until his mother gets here?"

Adelaide sat down in the plastic chairs. She watched the secretary pick up the envelopes Adelaide had stuffed, and then seal each of them shut.

Lesley curled her shoulders forward and collapsed her chest away from the safety pin that she was using to pull together two pieces of black silk at her bodice. It wasn't the dress she would have chosen—that dress had been on the floor of the closet, forgotten since the last harried occasion. This dress Edna had fetched from the cleaners this afternoon, using a crumpled pink ticket that had appeared like an answer at the bottom of Lesley's purse. But though Lesley recognized the fabric and the style, it was like the dress belonged to someone else. The fit was all wrong, loose across the hips instead of clinging, and coming open at the chest, as if she were offering someone a particularly good shot at her heart. Lesley closed the pin and straightened her shoulders in front of the ladies' room mirror. Under the circumstances, it would have to do.

That morning, Maya had announced that Lesley was expected at parent–teacher interviews that night.

"They're not tonight, honey," Lesley said to Maya, "that's on the nineteenth."

"It is the nineteenth," Maya said. She put two puddings into her lunch bag and Edna took one back out.

"They can't be tonight, Maya," Lesley said, "because I have a meeting with Jackson Cullen—our biggest client. And I know I wouldn't have scheduled your interview at the same time." Even then she should have been at the office preparing, not standing behind Marty at the counter, waiting her turn with the milk.

"No, they can't be tonight because we have that thing with my president at the gallery," Marty said, pouring the last of the milk into his coffee.

"But it's on the fridge," Maya said, which Lesley could plainly see, now that Edna had refilled the milk jug and put it away, even though Lesley's cereal was dry and her coffee still black.

"Les, don't look at me like that," Marty said. "You said you'd put it in your calendar."

"No one goes to those things," Simon said, "unless their kids are stupid."

"You'll never get anywhere in life with an attitude like that," Marty said, picking up his laptop. "Six o'clock. Black tie," he said.

In the end, the client meeting could not be postponed,

because the clients had brought the big cheese in from out of town, and the interviews could not be moved because priority had been given to those who had responded first, whereas Lesley, apparently, had not responded at all. She had made her excuses at the meeting, when she ducked out early, she had made her apologies at the interviews when she arrived late, and she had smiled in a way she hoped was gracious when she took her seat beside Marty and stared down at the five-hundred-dollar meal that the waiters were just beginning to clear away. So she was late. She was here, wasn't she? Or she had been, briefly, until she saw Marty staring at the gap at her breast in a way that was not at all admiring, and she'd had to excuse herself. Lesley took a last look in the mirror. Maybe it was just the bra that was wrong, she thought. Next time, she would definitely wear one with padding.

Back in the main exhibit space, the waiters were bringing out coffee and dessert. Lesley wound her way through the post-dinner chatter, back to table 16, but halfway there she felt someone grab her arm. At the end of the closed hand was the vice-president of operations at Jackson Cullen.

"Is this what you abandoned us for?" he said, laughing. "What, had to get your hair done first?"

"Steve, no"—his grip softened, but he kept his hand around her arm—"I trust you were in good hands while I was gone."

"But they weren't your hands, were they, Banerjee? And that's what we're paying for."

"Yes, I know, and I apologize again. The team will brief me in the morning. It's just—I had to go talk to my kids' teachers."

Across the room, Marty was trying to catch her eye.

"I'm sorry, little ones having a problem?"

"No, it's just—"

Marty's smile was widening to dangerous proportions. The older couple standing next to him were beckoning to someone else to join them.

"Excuse me, Steve," Lesley said. "I believe I'm wanted elsewhere."

"What, can't talk when you're not on the clock?"

Lesley looked at Marty, then at Steve. She felt the safety pin poke the skin at her cleavage, and willed herself not to look down to see what was revealed.

"Lunch," Steve said. "You and me. Tomorrow." He lifted his hand and her arm went with it. "Okay?"

"Sounds wonderful," she said.

"Here she is," Marty said. "Bob, Evelyn, I'd like you to meet my wife. This is our president, Bob Matheson, and the much more beautiful Evelyn Matheson. Bob's on the board of the gallery."

"Ah, Mrs. Blum, wonderful to finally meet you," said the president. "I was beginning to think Marty made you up."

"Lesley Banerjee," Lesley said, shaking hands. "But just Lesley is fine."

"I understand you've already met our featured artist," Bob said. Michal was making her way through the crowd between tables. Her dress clung as if it were a tattoo instead of a garment, tight and still managing to be tasteful, her usually unruly hair rising up like spun-sugar. "How lucky you are to have this talent in your neighbourhood. Raised the tone a bit, I imagine." Bob laughed and Marty joined in with too much approval.

"Hardly," Michal said. "I'm working on dragging everyone else down."

Michal gave the briefest of smiles, but Bob and Marty laughed again, Marty panning the assembled group to show each of them his bonhomie. And then, while the men's heads were thrown back and turned away, Michal winked. Lesley glanced behind her to see who Michal had meant the wink for, but only waiters were passing. Beside her, the tiny Mrs. Matheson seemed to be studying the carpet. Through her thin white hair, Lesley could see the pink of her scalp. Another tuxedoed man joined the group, and Marty and Bob closed in around Michal, nudging Lesley and Evelyn into satellite positions.

"Bob's very excited about Miss Revivo's commission for the lobby," Evelyn said to Lesley.

"Oh," said Lesley. Over the little woman's head she could see a wall of black shoulders, punctuated every now and then by a sparkle from Michal's gown.

"Yes." The old woman sighed and fiddled with an earring, and Lesley saw that it was the kind that grandmothers used to wear before piercing came into vogue, a button that clipped tight to the lobe. "It's a good life, my dear, and I know you'll agree that children are the most important job in the world."

Lesley smiled at the waiter, nodded for coffee instead of tea.

"But there are times when I look at someone like Miss Revivo and I can't help wishing I'd had a little more," Evelyn Matheson said. She shook her head. "Silly, I suppose. Maybe women now don't think of such things."

"But I do, Evelyn," Lesley said. How people could surprise you, Lesley thought. "That's why I'm a lawyer. I'm a partner at my firm."

"Are you? My." Evelyn was looking into the distance, as if she could see right through the predictable cut of her husband's tuxedo, the waiters' serving jackets.

Lesley bent down so that she could meet Evelyn's eyes. "What I'm saying is, I don't think it's silly at all," Lesley said. "A career is important."

"Oh! That's not—" Evelyn laughed. A diminutive tinkle that matched her stature. "I mean, that's lovely if you can manage it. But I wouldn't call painting a career." Evelyn's smile was gentle, as if she were speaking to someone who'd have trouble grasping more nuanced concepts.

Suddenly Lesley was aware of a chill on her chest. She put her hand to her bodice and held on. "What would you call it then?"

"Why, dear, it's a calling."

Coffee spoons tinkled, stirring in cream, stirring in sugar, but Lesley was back in the classroom at the parent-teacher meeting, listening to the scrape of desk chairs along tile. What was it the English teacher had said? "It is important, Mrs. Blum, to talk about how the year is shaping up for Maya. We feel that the earlier you catch a problem, the easier it is to fix it."

"I'm sorry," Lesley had said. Her nylons were scraping up against the underside of a generic desk, halfway back in the middle row, that the teachers had assured her was Maya's. "I wasn't aware that Maya was having any problems."

"Not problems, per se," the French immersion teacher said. "Not yet."

"Right now, she's doing fine," the English teacher said.

The clock on the wall announced the passing seconds in audible clicks. Marty would be fuming.

"I'm afraid I don't understand," Lesley said.

"I guess what you have to ask yourself," said the English teacher, "is whether that's good enough." She unfolded her hands and held them out to Lesley. "Or could she do better?"

The sky from the window of Kate's office at the university's teaching hospital was that deceptive autumn blue, its intensity in direct correlation to the bite in the air. Passing through the revolving doors at the rear of the hospital, Kate inhaled sharply at the chill, and her throat filled up with cigarette smoke.

A group of young nurses were smoking just outside the door, savouring the building's escaping warmth. Pretty lips, still rosy, pursed around yellow filters, slender fingers waved sticks accumulating ash. They were old enough to know better. Even if they'd tuned out the public health campaigns that permeated their childhoods, ignored the warning labels on the packages, their profession had schooled them in the long-term effects of such behaviour. No, it was the concept of *long-term* that evaded them, Kate thought, Saturday being far enough away to require a leap of imagination, never mind the idea of twenty or forty years of this or any other habit. And twenty years was probably what she had on them.

Kate breathed in deeper and felt a mild burning in her lungs. Smoking. Just another of those things she'd given up, along with red meat and real cream and drinking too much. Or parties that kept you out past midnight. Those too were a thing of the past. Lying on the lawn with Brian, one step from passed out, watching the sun come up and seeing the morning paper arc up and over her head and hit the porch behind her. That was gone. No, people like her needed to relieve the baby-sitter, and if you weren't worried about waking your own kids, you were concerned for waking the neighbours, the neighbours' children. Gone were the days of looking across the room at a party, or a bar, the edges of her vision growing hazier as the night and the drink wore on, and catching Brian's eye, knowing he was remember-ing what she'd told him, that under her short red dress she wore no underwear. Even to remember it was fool-ishness, Kate thought, the memory becoming the dress itself, an outfit she'd once fit into but was embarrassed now even to contemplate. It seemed to belong to some-one else, a person with taut muscles and smooth skin and the confidence in her sexuality necessary to throw out such a come-hither stare. Not that she was doing so badly. It's just that, well, she was forty-three, after all.

And yes, there were things you could do about that. She'd been saying just that, a few minutes ago, to a patient. Every day, women came to her, wanting to erase the effects of time and gravity. But so far, Kate had refused to take advantage of the improvements made possible by her trade, adhering to a regime of underwire bras and eye cream. Was it a bizarre denial of passing time? Or perhaps some sort of morbid experiment pitting her own surgeon's skill against the gift of her natural beauty? As she judged her professional handiwork around the eyes of a fifty-year-old woman, she would compare it to her own untouched lids and encroaching crow's feet and think, Not bad. Still, not bad. But she had often looked at her older patients, women in their sixties and seventies to whom she had managed to give the look of tight and youthful skin (though the alterations required, stretched and moulded their faces in such a way that they never did emerge as the women from their yearbooks or wedding albums, but seemed like other people altogether) and wondered when the moment would come when she would cave to the pressure of improvement as surely as her cheeks would eventually collapse and her jawline melt into her neck.

Kate shook her head, exhaled and stepped onto the walking path that ringed the campus. She had fifteen minutes to get some fresh air before her next appointment.

A high-pitched bell rang out behind her, and Kate stepped back onto the frozen grass. A man riding a clunky bicycle was bearing down on her, and as he passed, Kate just had time to note the clip on his pant leg, the down vest covering his suit jacket, the empty baby seat behind him, before a second bicycle whipped by, overtaking him.

Michal's frizzy halo was exposed to the cold air, unrestricted by a helmet, so Kate saw clearly the look of playful triumph Michal threw at her husband before she lost her momentum and the bike wobbled and slowed. Luke pumped a fist into the air and took the lead again. Michal didn't fall, but had to stand on the pedals to get her bicycle moving forward again. As she worked her way back into the chase, she veered for a moment toward the bushes that lined the path and the end of her scarf caught in the brambles, and remained there as Michal began to pull away. Kate winced, anticipating the moment when the momentum of the bike and the knot of the fabric would pull in opposite directions, but instead the scarf spread out in a swath of colour between the bush and its departing owner, then fluttered down into the bare branches.

Michal and Luke rode across the road and around the corner. Surely Michal would come back, Kate thought. She'd feel the cold on her chest and realize the scarf was gone.

But she did not come back. The path was growing busier now, the classes in the nearby buildings changing. Kate looked around. There was no one to witness her obligation to retrieve the scarf and return it to its owner. No one was looking at Kate, in her shearling jacket, her tailored pants, her slim turtleneck. But as she stood to the side of the path, one or two female students did turn toward the scarf, draped tantalizingly in the bushes. If Michal didn't return soon, the scarf wouldn't be there to reclaim.

Kate walked against the traffic on the path to the bushes and reached up to grab the tassels. The scarf was thin and delicate and as Kate pulled on it, freeing one end, the weave snagged on the branches and the other end worked its way farther into the brambles. Kate reached farther over, but the branches scratched at the smooth surface of her shearling coat. Kate looked at her watch, the minutes of her short break dissolving. Well, she was committed now, wasn't she? Kate shrugged off her thick outer layer and dropped it beside her, leaning forward almost parallel across the bush, summoning every remaining stomach muscle to hold herself up so that she wouldn't pitch into the brambles. When she managed to reach the tassels at the other end, she closed her hand around them, took a breath and pulled. The material puckered up one side, then came free and fell to the path.

The fine weave was damaged now, but the colour was vibrant still, teal blue, like a sky over a café table on a summer night. Or maybe she thought of that because she was a little warm herself, despite the crispness of the day, despite her discarded jacket. Kate pulled at the cuffs and at the neck of her sweater, letting some air in against her skin. She didn't mind, really. She put her hands on her back and stretched her face up to the sun that was coming through the thinning branches. Skin cancer! Yes, but also vitamin D. It felt good. Kate bent a little farther back, raising her chin and her breasts skyward.

Kate felt someone's gaze on her, like fingers reaching up under the wool of her turtleneck. She straightened slowly and looked around to see where it came from. Over by the picnic tables at the side of the building was the young intern who'd once shadowed her on a shift in Emergency. He'd been watching her just now. And even as she met his gaze briefly before dropping her eyes to the path, he was still watching. How must she look? Throwing off her coat and scrambling around in the bushes, and then contorting her forty-three-year-old self like a cat in the sun? Kate picked up her coat and walked quickly back toward the hospital. She felt his eyes follow her, and as she passed him on the way to the hospital doors, her blood rose to the surface of her skin as if every inch of it were exposed. She threw Michal's scarf up and around her neck. She had meant only to cover herself, but as soon as she did it, the gesture seemed painfully beckoning.

Inside, the heat stayed with her. Back at her desk, she couldn't shake it, even as she took out the apple and the cheese sandwich in Saran that she'd brought from home. Was it embarrassment, or delight? Menopause, more likely, she told herself as she carried a file into an examining room.

"Good afternoon, Mrs. German," she said. "That bruising is coming down nicely."

Was Adelaide actually twitching? It had been eight days since the article appeared and there was only a week until the committee hearing and Imogene wondered if

Adelaide might be coming undone. Tonight, she had the quality of a downed wire, veering erratically this way and that. When she leaned forward on Imogene's couch she jostled Lesley, sitting in the white occasional chair, and Adelaide very nearly spilled her glass of cabernet.

"Oh. Are you okay?" Lesley asked Adelaide, but it was Lesley who was left dabbing at her suit pants, while Kate put an extra cushion's distance between herself and Adelaide.

"It's about the 'unique character' of the neighbour-hood," Adelaide said, righting herself on the couch and quoting from the twenty pages of zoning bylaws she had dutifully retrieved from the city hall website.

Adelaide was good at this, Imogene thought, good at watching for the little details, making sure the boxes were checked. But not really a big thinker. It made her work at the university all the more surprising. She wasn't some-one Imogene could ever imagine doing serious scholar-ship, but then again, she might be the sort to find some previously overlooked document and hand it on to some-one who would know what to do with it. An assistant. She would have been a marvellous assistant for someone. Good at checking calendars, composing basic secretarial notes. Imogene bet that of all the women she knew, Adelaide was the only one who had ever achieved sixty words a minute, the rest being intelligent enough not to limit themselves by trying.

"It says right here that you can't alter the streetscape

by exceeding the height of the tallest building," Adelaide said. "When Kate and Brian wanted to redo their attic, they could raise the roof by seven feet, no more."

Kate uncrossed her legs and drew them up onto the couch in a lotus position. "I don't think you can really make that comparison," she said.

"Why not? It's the very same bylaw," Adelaide said.

"We didn't apply for a variance."

Kate's pose suggested ease and a natural flexibility, when Imogene knew it was the result of years of contortions on a mat in an artificially hot room. The Johnstone reno was a sensitive topic, since rather than ruffle neighbours' feathers the Johnstones had put their money into a very nice basement remodel, with a state-of-the-art laundry room and a playroom for the boys, leaving the attic, where they slept, virtually untouched.

"But you wanted a permit, and that's what they told you," Adelaide said.

"Easy, Adelaide," Imogene said. It wasn't much of a lineup, but this was the team she'd been given and Imogene was going to lead it. Adelaide was persistent, you had to give her that. Lesley would be fine as soon as she had her marching orders; she'd memorize the script and wouldn't deviate, though right now she was busy scraping cracker crumbs from the coffee table into an open palm and looking like an unprepared student avoiding the teacher's eye. And Kate—despite appearances, she couldn't hold that position forever. She'd remember soon enough that they were all on the same side.

"Kate and Brian didn't know their plans were in violation, and the second they found out, they switched them." Imogene leaned forward and poured herself a first glass of wine. "This is different. Michal Revivo wants a variance. This is someone saying, I know it's not allowed, but for me you will make an exception."

It was all about the language, Imogene explained. It wasn't called the Committee of Protection, but the Committee of Adjustment. It existed to justify what had previously been unallowable.

Lesley finally brought her glass to her lips. Kate returned both feet to the floor. But Adelaide slumped forward and picked at the cheese.

"Keep your enthusiasm, Adelaide, we'll think of something," Imogene said.

And Imogene would. It was impossible to imagine any other outcome. Imogene had loved Glenmount from the moment she first walked on it, ten years ago when she had come to the university as dean of arts. Hundred-year-old houses, hundred-year-old trees, old folks moving out and families moving in, people who could afford it and were willing to put their money into restoring the houses. Families with children committed to raising them here, in the way that children should be brought up: with tree swings and bicycles and frog-catching in the storm gutters, all at walking distance from the best schools.

But it would be a mistake to call this place and its magic organic. Imogene had always understood that, like all other systems, Glenmount Crescent's idyllic atmosphere had much to do with invisible planning. Want beautiful streets that the children can play on? Honour those original builders, the ones who laid out the roads in winding patterns rather than straight lines, by pushing for speed bumps. With the trees and the greenery, the children playing on the street and the old stone, Glenmount Crescent looked like the picture of natural order. But someone still had to maintain it.

"Well, it's a shame about that tree," Adelaide said into her chest. "Our third floor's going to be a bear to keep cool in the summer without it."

Imogene turned and looked out the window across the road at the conical beam of the streetlight, catching the silhouette of the maple tree to one side of the Revivo-Smitherman house. The tallest, broadest tree in the neighbourhood. The original plans must show it here, already mature, part of the forest from which they had carved the streets, this tree spared while others had to be replanted with fledgling versions of the same species. The street curved to accommodate it, the fence ran alongside to encompass it, the sidewalk lifted over its roots. And the Committee of Adjustment would bend to it as well.

—

Adelaide walked past the urns, down Imogene's gracefully lit steps, and paused on the sidewalk, listening to the night sounds. It had turned warm again, unseasonably warm for the end of October, the heat of summer hanging in the air while the trees rustled with dry autumn leaves. There was one of those breezes that sometimes carried with it the sounds of the campus, six blocks away. Someone was having a party.

It was only 7 p.m. but already it was dark. The time had fallen back. Adelaide looked up and down the empty street, an affectation of checking for cars that she developed for Charles in his kindergarten years—*look both ways*—that had never left her, while Charles now barely moved his head in either direction, leaving Adelaide miming for no one. There were never any cars here anyway. Wasn't that, she'd said to David, the whole risk, the whole danger? Children on busy streets got used to cars passing. Children on Glenmount Crescent simply assumed that nothing would be in their way. The path would always be clear. Well, it wasn't. Sometimes it wasn't, and what then?

As Adelaide stepped off the sidewalk and onto the road, the front door opened at the Revivo-Smitherman house. The foyer light flooded onto the porch, and in it, stepping out as if the light were following her onto a

stage, was Michal, her arm around Romero. Only not
Romero. And not thin Sasha. A rounder child, stooped
and looking smaller than necessary, walked out from
under the woman's arm.

"Bye, Charlie."

Adelaide stood at the end of the flagstone walk that
cut through Michal's grassland and watched her son
walk toward her. "Charles?"

"Hi, Mom," he said.

It was an accepted truth, even to his mother, that
Charles Stein was dull. Dull-eyed and dull-witted, dull
as a dusty rock. Adelaide had identified this quality
years ago and had tried so hard to push the words from
her mind that they had embedded themselves there.
She now thought of this dullness as a handicap, one
that she had worked to accept, until she found that it
seemed the only thing she really knew of him and she
loved the dullness as if it were his essence. But in the
light off Michal's porch, Charles shone like a stone
dipped in water.

"What were you doing, Charles?" His hands were
splattered with something dark and bloodlike.

"Oh, Adelaide." Michal came down off the porch
and onto the sidewalk. "He's a bit dirty. We were painting and Romero could see him sitting at his computer
and he thought—I hope you don't mind—that he might
like something to do."

"No, I—Go get cleaned up, Charles. Your dad will be home soon."

"Can I come again tomorrow, Mrs.—"

"Michal. Sure you can. If your mother says it's okay."

"Mom?"

"Your dad'll be home any minute, Charles. We'll talk about it then."

Charles rolled his shoulders forward as if he were peeling off a sweater, and shuffled toward their house.

"It's just—He's supposed to tell me if he's going somewhere."

"Of course. I understand. He said you were in a meeting across the road. I figured I'd catch you when you came out. Will you come in a minute?"

The foyer was strewn with rubber boots and little girls' umbrellas. In the dining room, Sasha was playing with Play-Doh at a long oak table under a bright light with no fixture.

"Sorry." Michal beckoned Adelaide through the house. "Nothing ever gets in order until my studio is ready. For now, we're working back here."

On the Andersons' old back porch, covered in green indoor-outdoor carpet, were three canvases. One a black and blue sketch of something that might have been a wave, or a dancer. A work in progress. A Revivo.

"Just playing around with ideas until I can really stretch out in the new space." Michal fluttered her hand away from it and pointed toward another two. One was a splattering of colour that looked like vomit or hotel carpet.

"Oh, not that one, that's Romero's. He doesn't have much patience for stuff like this. Look here. This is Charlie's painting."

"Charles did that? By himself?"

"I wanted you to see it. He was so intent, so focused."

"Charles?" Adelaide felt she would keep saying his name over and over again. Charles, her son, had made this thing. When she looked at the orange and red and white, she saw Charles there, a whole new Charles.

"Really something, isn't it?"

Adelaide did not want to gape and stare like a mean child in the schoolyard imitating Charles, that old Charles that people thought they knew. She wanted to thank Michal. But no words came.

"There's only one thing," Michal said. "He got up so close to it. And the same when he looked at mine." She reached out to direct Adelaide's attention away from the painting and toward her. "Adelaide, I don't think he can see very well."

It was that same night that Lesley stumbled and fell. It wasn't a bad fall, just the kind that might on another occasion have resulted in a bruised elbow, a twisted ankle, an anecdote for the office or dinner out with friends. The bump in the sidewalk had always been there, something that small children jumped their bicycles over, a little peak of excitement on an otherwise tame course around the neighbourhood. Lesley herself had pushed a stroller around it, examined ants beneath it with Maya in summer, and stepped over it countless times on her way to the library or home from the shops in the little village. But tonight, hurrying along the dark sidewalks, Lesley stumbled and fell and found herself unable to get up.

The maple syrup she had been carrying was oozing out of the cracked bottle and the plastic bag and down through the cracks where the Andersons' maple—that's how Lesley still thought of it, this giant tree to the side of the Revivo-Smitherman house, the one that forced the bend in the road—had, over one hundred years, pushed up the sidewalk.

She shouldn't have been there at all, except that when she'd arrived home late and depleted from Imogene's meeting, Edna had informed her that the children had been promised pancakes for tomorrow's breakfast, but there was no maple syrup and there wouldn't be time to get it in the morning, so somebody would have to do it tonight.

Lesley could have drawn herself up to her lawyering height, could have felt the authoritative drape of the finely tailored suit jacket on her shoulders and asked Edna to go out and get it. Told Edna to go out and get it. But Edna had been washing dishes and Maya and Simon were lying on the floor, legs thrown over couch cushions, pulling at the remote, and when Lesley came in, Maya had run over and plastered her cheek against her and said, Mommy, you decide whose turn it is, and Lesley had said she'd be right back, sweetie, as soon as she got the maple syrup. And now here it was, leaking out of the broken bottle, the thick glass fragments like jagged cups inviting some animal or child to dip their tongues in.

And wasn't her life a series of infractions, just like this? Stacks of parking tickets, and missed receipts at tax time, instant-win coffee cups for which she'd forgotten to roll the rim, arguments with Marty that burned themselves out but were never made up. No scores ever settled, all simply lost or added to, with Lesley wondering whether her own accounting was anywhere near the tally that her husband, her law partners, the nanny, the teachers, the meter maids, the other mothers were keeping. Sometimes she hoped that some rare moment of goodness on her part—homemade—homemade goddamn cookies for the Christmas party, the bouquet of flowers for her secretary's missed birthday—might be noticed, might be counted, but Lesley feared that she would always be in the red. Still, every day she tried to shut the ledger and go on, to do the things that must be done. The cases, the bedtime stories, the trips to the store.

She saw it then, the streetlight beaming onto the glistening shards of the syrup bottle, which she gathered into her palm one sharp, shining piece at a time.

"God, what happened to you?"

Lesley saw a dark totem beside her, adorned at the top with a platinum headdress, the light from the streetlight pouring between each individual coil. Michal knelt beside her and stared at Lesley's hand, and Lesley saw then that it was not only sticky with syrup, but also covered in blood.

Lesley wanted to tell her that she had no idea what had happened. Michal's question was so much more pertinent than the one people usually asked, "How do you do it all?" to which Lesley always smiled demurely, while answering to herself that she did it all by doing each thing badly. Handing the children off to Edna, but leaving herself with the most time-consuming and least important of chores, finding the time to finish her briefs by skipping the supper Edna had prepared for her, letting the names and situations of her clients slip her mind so that she had to excuse herself to the bathroom to consult her BlackBerry for the details of the meeting she was in the midst of, forgetting whatever it was that her husband was working on now, and knowing that he no longer expected to be asked. And watching her own ample salary be reduced to the pin money of a fifties housewife as she hired enough help to attempt to carry on.

Lesley felt something being wound tightly around her hand. It was Michal's kerchief. Lesley's hand rested inside Michal's cradling palm. Lesley had the urge to lean her whole weight against this woman. To put her head on Michal's shoulder and her mouth in the crook of her neck and simply to breathe her in. But instead, Lesley reached out with her other hand and held Michal's arm, keeping her there.

"It's all right," Michal said. "It's over now. It just takes pressure."

But still they stayed, crouched in the warmth and the dark.

Thank God the handyman hadn't put up the storm windows, Kate thought. Here it was the end of October and the room was stifling, even with the ceiling fan turning, even with the windows pushed up high. She looked at the clock beside her. She'd been lying awake for an hour, naked and with the sheets kicked back, the thick air wrapped around her like a blanket. Beside her, Brian was covered up and sleeping soundly, lumplike and indistinguishable from the bedclothes.

Kate got up and crossed the room, hoping for a breeze. As she pulled back the heavy curtains, the light from the street lamp outside the window spilled in across the floor and caught her in its path. If someone were out on the street, what were the chances that they would see her? she wondered. Look now, young doctor, I dare you, she thought. Her breasts settled against her ribs, her belly skin puckered from the pressure of two pregnancies, her feet spread wide against the floor. Uncovered, all the things held up and in through the day, relaxed in the night.

But over them all, the streetlight lit up a sparkling sheen of sweat. Turning in front of the window, it seemed to Kate that she was glowing. A breeze stirred the curtains. It cooled the perspiration on her nipples and arms, her belly and thighs and the skin underneath the somewhat thinning pubic hair. How good it felt, Kate thought. How good she felt. How close she'd come to missing this.

Kate went back to bed. Beside her, Brian sucked in air, let out a prolonged snore, then shifted and rolled toward her, the covers falling away. The skin around his mouth was soft, Kate saw, with the shadow of stubble coming up through it, and his neck was no longer taut. There was a new grey patch on the dark tuft of his chest hair, up in the corner like a star on a flag. It was sharp and wiry against Kate's hand.

A larger gust of wind came through the window and with it, a high, keening sound, ascending, falling a few notes, then ascending again, swelling in pitch and volume. From these old houses, so many still without air conditioning, Kate had heard teenagers' parties, couples' fights, babies' cries. But never this unselfconscious abandon.

The sound of a woman giving in completely to her pleasure. Forgetting herself. Letting herself go.

Kate rolled toward her husband, stroked his grey chest, brought her cheek against the grooves of his cheek to reach his ear. "Darling," she said. "Darling? Wake up."

He murmured and shuddered, answered sleepily, "What?"

"Shh. Just—listen."

The variance hearing was October thirtieth. Adelaide knew this. Lesley and Kate knew this. But Imogene found herself staring at a mostly empty room, with Michal's the only recognizable face. When she called Adelaide again from her cell phone, the call just went to voicemail.

How predictable it all was, Imogene thought. Michal pleading the necessity of the studio for work, offering as proof of her status as artist the recent article in the paper, causing the four committee members shuffling documents at the front of the room to pass the article back and forth. One of them even said, "Welcome."

When the time came for the public to speak, only Imogene stepped forward. She unrolled the original site plan for the neighbourhood. She spoke eloquently, she spoke passionately. She spoke as a woman who understood the truth and was willing to share it. It was about stewardship. It was about honouring what had been there before and what would be there after. It was about the tree.

The committee members thanked her. Then they offered a decision that Imogene considered a triumph. "We have decided to table this decision until we can consult with a heritage arborist. No work may begin to alter the site until this time."

While Imogene stood before the Committee of Adjustment and while the rest of the street was at work and school, the nannies and housekeepers of Glenmount Crescent saw Luke rip down, board by board, the fence that jutted out around the old tree, revealing a fully constructed graveyard, with tombstones and spider-webs and skeletons propped up against the side of the house and hanging from the eavestrough. By the time the children and the parents got home, word had gone round that everyone was invited for wine and candy corn and apple-bobbing.

Imogene arrived home too late to insist that her family stay put, doing homework and practising the piano. By the time she read the note on the table, her husband Paul, and Owen, Oliver and Mathilda, were already at the Revivo-Smithermans', standing with the other families, examining the tombstones sunk into newly turned earth.

"It's so obvious, what they're doing," Imogene whispered to Paul. "How can everyone be so naive? You can't just ply the neighbourhood with alcohol and sugar and win people over."

But that's what was happening. Kate was standing by the front porch, hand in her husband's jeans pocket, talking to Luke. Lesley was sitting on a plastic picnic table at the far end of the garden near a patch of overgrown rhubarb, but she stood when Michal crossed the garden and handed her an old sweater. The neighbourhood children, the very ones who had shown no interest in Sasha and Romero all summer, seeing their parents standing with wine in their hands—served by Adelaide Stein, who lifted the mismatched glasses off a workbench table covered in plastic as if they were her mother-in-law's good crystal—moved out from beside their parents like ripples from skipped pebbles before they broke away completely and shot across the yard. Sasha Smitherman held back Mathilda's hair so that she could bob in a tub of apples. Paul took Oliver's picture with a skeleton's plastic fingers around his neck. And Owen climbed a ladder attached to the trunk (criss-crossed with spray-on spiderwebs) of a tree. The Tree.

The tree was right in the middle of what it seemed only Imogene could see: markers in the grass for the proposed—now much more actual—structure. Indeed, Imogene thought she could see the bones of the building itself, boxed around the maple and stretching up beyond it, its four floors of beams and glass cutting through the leafy air in front of her. Then, in an instant, she saw Owen standing on its floors, before he fell through the space and out of her sight.

It couldn't be. It was all wrong, Imogene thought. She remembered a time, back before she had the children, when she had lived in another house, in another neighbourhood, and saw three children fall from a tree and then spring up again into its branches. How she stood and watched revolution after revolution before realizing that the children weren't defying all natural laws, but bouncing on a trampoline behind the fence. It was an illusion. A trick to the eye.

As this must be, she thought, as she saw Owen come down from the tree in this more predictable descent, his fall taking on an otherworldly fluidity. It agreed with gravity, but worked against everything else Imogene understood of her own world, her security in it. So that her eyes did not follow him to the ground, but paused at the middle point, waiting for him to spring back up into the tree, back into the place of safety, for her own solid world to return beneath both their sets of feet.

People surged around Imogene like waves around a rock. He's fine, really, he'll be fine, she heard herself insisting, even as Paul ran his hands over the body of the screaming boy, asking where it hurt, asking someone to call an ambulance. "Gene!" Paul's word grasped at her. She hesitated only a moment more, countering the anchors of her feet to move to take her place with her family. But she was too late.

Michal Revivo was striding to Imogene's son, bending to assist Imogene's husband, like a woman who has always known her course. Which left Imogene to turn her eyes to the ground and the fallen branch, two feet across and fifteen feet long, the severed end like a matted sponge, or the contours of a brain.

Rotten, all the way through.

Some nights, they catch a glimpse of her, hair pulled into her kerchief, thin shoulders thrusting forward like a fencer's as she smears colour on fresh canvas, conjuring pictures they believe their minds could never understand. When the shades are up, the light falls onto the street in sluices, illuminating the ground in snow and clear weather—the Steins' fence, the yards beyond. But most evenings the giant curtains, rigged like sails on winches and pulleys, are lowered and the studio is a lampshade that glows long after the other lights on Glenmount Crescent have been extinguished.

By day, some still avert their eyes: a matter of principle they say. But others say the steel girders, the slate roof, the walls that are divided like a quilt of uneven glass squares, have become a neighbourhood fixture, something that adds to the distinct nature of the street, befitting of a building where creation is taking place.

Some never comment at all.

On most days, Adelaide, driving her son to painting class or baseball practice, Kate pushing the twin girls in their carriage, and Lesley, when she picks the children up for a weekend at her small, downtown apartment, have to admit that it's like it isn't there at all. The upper squares repeating the clear or clouded sky, the middle squares floating the stone of the houses across the way, the boxwood, the cobbled drives, and the sports cars and station wagons rolling by the place where the curve begins, where the meter readers pass, and the letter carriers, and the children, taunting each other on their way home from school—those who are running and those who are laughing and those who are dragging backpacks or tugging the leashes of golden retrievers—and the nannies and mothers and fathers all going about their usual business, and reflecting it back to them, pane by pane, so that it would seem that there was an identical street running parallel to the crescent. Unless you turned your head a moment to consider the giant, moving painting, or like Imogene and each of them has had occasion to do, you have to look away, from the small, shifting part of it that is undeniably you.

APPLE

—

A S IF MY PARENTS' KISSING wasn't bad
enough, their hugging and all that groping.
How right now, Lewis is pinching Tina's ass
while they do the dinner dishes, and how I can tell by
the sound of her giggling. It's like I said to Norman this
afternoon: Who needs sex ed? My parents are enough to
scare a girl into a life of celibacy.

And now there's what happened last week in 8FS.

As an advertisement for abstinence, the 8FS experience was pretty effective. Definitely better than the
babies—plastic simulators designed to show us how bad
it would be to get knocked up. We had to carry the
babies around all day—on the bus, to class, in lineup for
a hamburger at the caf. Every few minutes they would
wail or piss, even in the middle of the night. Once, when

I had my head under my pillow trying to ignore the screaming, Lewis banged on my bedroom wall. "Apple," he yelled, "your son."

Lewis. Sometimes he thinks he's funny.

There were only three babies though, so while you were busy wiping your baby's plastic ass or sticking something in its hole of a mouth, Colin Jacks would point at you and lead the other kids, the ones who hadn't been assigned a baby yet, in making birthing noises—grunts and *he-he-he* panting. Even Norman did it once when I had to quit playing soccer and go back to the fence to stop mine wailing.

"Don't worry, Norman. You'll get yours," I said.

Only then he didn't. Because Farid Gill kicked one of the babies down the hall and once it was hurtling along the floor, four or five other guys started kicking it from locker to locker, until it got lodged under the water fountain outside the girls' bathroom.

I was just going in there when it happened, so I saw how when Andrea Fowler came out the bathroom door to see her baby's little plastic head against the brightly waxed floor, she actually cried.

The baby wasn't right after that. You could feed it, but no pee would come out. It got smelly and heavy and it never made a sound.

And just like that, no more babies.

That's how we got stuck with the plain old sex talk in

8FS—Family Studies. The class was a dumb idea from the beginning. They pretend it's all about child psychology and tell us it'll be good for our biology and social studies classes next year in high school, but we all know it's just to convince us not to screw around.

We all have to take it. Everyone from Farid, who's been hooking up with high school girls under the bleachers during football games since sixth grade, to little Laurel Delveccio, who would never do it because the only thing worse than getting caught by her hundred-year-old dad would be getting caught by Jesus.

Anyway, they brought in Mrs. Redimeyer. She's the teacher they call for the tough jobs, like teaching science to kids who would rather perfect their spitball technique. Once, after a particularly enthusiastic attack on Laurel in Monsieur Kale's class, Mrs. Redimeyer got Colin and Farid to examine the properties of their own saliva under the microscope. Then she gave them extra credit and put double bonus marks on Laurel's science average, for "inspiring investigation."

When we came in from French, Mrs. Redimeyer was drawing a chalk diagram of conception on the board, and getting right into it too, with pink chalk for the ovaries and fallopian tubes, green eggs and white squiggles for sperm.

Norman pushed his binder to the edge of his desk to show me his cartoon of an egg with arms and a mouth, saying, "Yes, yes!"

"Norman, you are a juvenoid," I told him.

Mrs. Redimeyer stood at the front and waited for us to shut up. She's better than those teachers that still dim the lights or clap their hands. She just folded her arms across her sweater, the one that looks like it's still being worn by the alpaca, and waited.

"Today, we are going to look at conception—how life begins. Now, each of you"—here she pressed her fingers to her lips, removing a bit of her frosted pink lipstick—"well, some of you, have had the opportunity to see what happens after conception, after fetal development, after birth. I am sure those of you who were lucky enough to have had the opportunity to make use of the very expensive baby simulators will agree that there was a lesson in that."

Even though she was two rows over, I could hear Andrea Fowler sniff.

"But today, we are going back to the basics," said Mrs. Redimeyer. "How do babies come to be? How are they made?"

"I'm pretty sure mine was made in China," I said to Norman. He smiled, but turned away before I could see if the smile turned into a laugh.

"Apple?" Mrs. Redimeyer said.

"Are you talking about sex, Mrs. Redimeyer?" I said. "Because I think we should just get that out in the open."

"Actually, Apple," she said, "I was talking about

conception." She pointed to the diagram on the board. "What we could call 'The Journey to Life.'" She wrote that in capitals under the drawing.

In the front row, Laurel stood up beside her desk. Laurel doesn't just raise her hand, her whole body goes along with it, as if she's levitating.

"Yes, Laurel," Mrs. Redimeyer said.

"Mrs. Redimeyer, I think it is just really important to remember that what we are talking about is original sin. Before Eve took the apple, Adam and Eve were happy and not embarrassed and had everything they needed. But now all of us are conceived in sin, and the only way to wash it clean is to make your apologies to our Lord and Saviour Jesus Christ through prayer."

Mrs. Redimeyer scratched at her skirt and said that wasn't really the interpretation we were taking in this class, but of course we all had to work within our own family value systems. I could hear her nails scrape right down to her black cotton tights.

Then she turned back to the board and all of us could see that she had pink and green chalk marks across her ass. Farid snorted, which started someone snickering in the back row. Mrs. Redimeyer looked over her shoulder and everyone went back to doodling on their shoes.

"This is the first step on The Journey to Life, in preparation for the essential moment, the start of being: fertilization." The little sperm squiggle at the end of

Mrs. Redimeyer's chalk was making its way up the tube toward the ovum.

"Go spermy, go spermy," Colin Jacks said.

I looked across the aisle at Norman. I could see that he was staring at me, even though his long brown hair was over his eyes. *What?* I mouthed. Norman looked back at the board.

One of the light tubes at the front of the class was blinking on and off, flipping the room from sunlight to blue and back again. One second, in the top-down light from the fluorescent bulbs, I could see the grade fives outside playing dodge ball. One girl was away from the group and kicking the tetherball post, making the metal ring. Then the bulb would go out and the sunlight flashed brighter, tilting in through the window. For a moment, the girl in the yard seemed far away, but I could still hear the ringing of her foot against the post.

The light show gave Mrs. Redimeyer's sperm a strobe effect. Its wavy white line jerked toward the egg. The egg shook, making its green outline blur. The chalkboard art flickered like film at the end of a reel.

"We each began our lives this way. It is the same for you, for your friends, for your parents, for me," Mrs. Redimeyer said, poking her white sperm right inside the egg. Then, flushed with the exertion of single-handedly creating life, she turned back around to face us.

Except, it wasn't Mrs. Redimeyer I saw. Mrs.

Redimeyer was there, all right, but it was as if she were standing behind the transparent curtain they used in the spring play. In front of her I could see a man and a woman screwing. The woman had a miniskirt pushed high up her hips and on top she was stripped down to a bright red bra. Her back was sliding up and down some black and white patterned wallpaper. The man was completely naked. He had a muscled back and a muscled ass and legs, and his lips were right up against the woman's ear and he was talking the way they talk during the sex scenes on the arts channel late at night, only in English.

At first I thought the gasping sound was coming from me. I put my hand over my mouth so no one would hear. But it got louder, popping up behind me and beside me. Thirty kids holding their breath.

"Class?" Mrs. Redimeyer was standing behind the panting couple with her chalky arms out. "Does someone want to tell me what's going on?"

Then I realized that she wasn't talking about the over-eighteen scene that was happening right there in front of her. I could see it. Everyone could see it. But Mrs. Redimeyer couldn't.

In the front row, Andrea Fowler was crying. Tears were running down her cheeks while she looked at Mrs. Redimeyer. Up close to Andrea, as if they were attached to her like a shadow, were a wincing woman in a flowered nightgown and a man looking at his watch while he shoved himself into her. Beside Andrea—where Mrs. Redimeyer had put him to keep an eye on him—Colin Jacks was sitting quietly, for once. In front of Colin a man with a long beard was kneeling against a woman's bare bum while she held her head under a pillow.

I looked over at Norman, who was staring hard at the two people hovering near Astrid Anderson—wearing toques and snowmobile suits with the zippers pulled down—but between me and Norman was another Norman, unzipping his Levis and pulling out a long, thick penis. The other Norman was getting a leg over a gearshift and over a woman lying in the reclined front seat and nodding up and down in a way that made her boobs and her little blonde ponytail bounce. I recognized that bouncing woman. It was a young Mrs. Wilson. It was Norman's mom. Which made the other Norman, Norman's dad. Which meant that what I was seeing was *this* Norman, beginning that Journey to Life.

I would have kept on staring, but Laurel Delveccio was shouting from the other side of the room, "I need to be excused!" and as she streaked through the classroom we all saw a naked Mrs. Delveccio with her droopy breasts straddling a teenage boy that was definitely not the wrinkly old guy we knew as Laurel's dad.

Everywhere I looked, there were people having sex. It was like watching twenty-nine smutty movies playing on twenty-nine different screens. The class was a shimmying, grunting, grinding orgy pit. Okay, watching one couple might have been titillating. Seeing twenty-nine sets of your classmates' parents doing it simultaneously was not. Chairs scraped the floor. Kids rushed the hall.

I looked down at myself, but all I saw was my Ramones T-shirt and my favourite jeans.

That's why it's good to have a friend like Norman. "Norman," I said. "When you look at me, what do you see?"

I made it through the first half of dinner that night by staring at my peas. But all I could think about were those green-chalk eggs. Four hundred thousand of them in a woman's lifetime.

I could hear Lewis fanning his food out on his plate, arranging the presentation of vegetables and grilled tofu in what I imagined was a paisley swirl. "We grow these?" he asked my mother.

"Not the peas," said Tina. "But these are the last of our Brussels sprouts."

I guess I made a face, because Tina said what she always says when she can't think of anything else to say: "Apple, how was school?"

I scraped my knife across the ceramic in a way that I knew would make Tina wince. We were using her favourite set—the one she'd liked too much to sell at the craft show.

I closed my eyes and nodded in her direction. "Fine," I said. I opened my eyes when I bent back over my plate.

"Could you please pass the ginger pickle?" Lewis said.

It was right by my elbow. I could have slid it toward him, but there were casserole dishes between my plate and his. I picked it up and waved the jar toward his end of the table hoping he would take it from me, but when I didn't make contact I had to look up. Ugh. Hurricane lamps full blast. Little kids—my uncles?—sleeping right next to the bed. In all that light I could clearly see the loft in my grandparents' cottage. I tried to focus on the logs in the wall instead of on what was going on under the quilt. I was pretty sure I'd slept under that quilt. I looked back at the peas.

"Apple, did you get something pierced?" That was Tina.

"What?"

"What's that on your nose?"

So I was forced to look at Tina then. Very dark. Missionary position. That's all I'm saying.

"Oh," said Tina. "It's just a pimple."

"Apple, your mother and I are going to go open up my parents' cottage next weekend."

"I hate the cottage."

"Since when?" Tina said.

"That's fine, it was just a trip for the two of us anyway," said Lewis. "We need to get away together."

I was still looking at my plate but I could tell that they were smiling at each other across the table. Then Tina gave a little laugh that got stifled into a cough, which probably meant Lewis had winked at her—or something worse. Then Tina got up and walked over to pick up Lewis's plate. I could hear her kiss his neck.

"I was a thermometer baby!" I yelled before I could think.

All four of my grandparents kept at it, but my parents went very still. They were quiet for longer than they usually are when I say something they don't get.

"What?" Tina finally said.

"You two are fakes," I said. "Always going around kissing and snuggling and acting all in love. But it doesn't mean anything. I was a thermometer baby! Morning temperature. Charts. Calendars. Sex on schedule!"

Tina was sitting down now. She reached out to touch my arm, but I dropped my fork and shoved my hand under the table.

"Norman was conceived in the back seat of a car. Alison's mother got knocked up on a beach in Hawaii. Hawaii!" I said. "I'm the only thermometer baby in my class."

Lewis reached for a piece of bread. "Now, Apple, not the *only* one, surely."

The back of my eyes were starting to sting. "You make me sick!" I said.

As I ran up the stairs I heard Lewis say, "I told you not to tell your sister anything."

Adults think that kids go around thinking about sex all the time, when, I can tell you, lots of us are trying *not* to think about it. I mean, poor Norman. Anything he looks at can give him a hard-on. We can just be sitting there on his couch playing Super Nintendo, the old-school version which is the cool one anyway, and just as Mario is about to free Peach, I can see his pants get tight and his face start to go red and pained like his skin is being stretched to torture proportions, which I guess it probably is. Then I can feel my face getting red too, while we both try to pretend it isn't happening. It's gross, but it's not like he can do anything about it. So I try to make it easy for him. I play harder and stop letting him win.

But the night after the Journey to Life, I was having trouble falling asleep because of all those sex scenes in my head: Ravinder Singh's father chasing his mother around the bedroom while wearing a garter belt, Sophie Johanssen's mother singing in rhythm to her husband's thrusts. Earlier, when I'd climbed onto the bus to pay my fare, I'd had to look away from the driver and his very fat mother and tiny dad, doing it up against the counter of a dirty kitchen, and now that I was lying in bed, I kept seeing it over and over again every time I closed my eyes.

There was a little tap on my door.

"What?" I said.

I felt the bed go down as Tina sat beside me. Then she put her hand on my back and rubbed between my shoulder blades.

"Apple, you're getting older. There're going to be lots of things that you don't need me to do for you any more. But I would hope that you would still ask me questions sometimes. There might still be things I can help with."

I thought about how Tina used to sing "The Circle Game" until I fell asleep. I thought about how she used to put food colouring in my bath so it looked like I was swimming across the ocean. I thought about how good she smelled when I'd climb into her lap after I woke up from my nap, and the slippery fabric of her scarf against my cheek. I thought about how, long after the other kids had stopped crying for mommy, I was still wailing "*Tiii-na*" across the playground every time she dropped me off for kindergarten.

I was quiet for a long time. I was quiet so long that maybe she thought I was asleep.

"Good night, Apple," Tina whispered. She took her hand off my back and the spot where it had been seemed very cold.

Carly was leaning her head against the locker beside mine when I got to school. In front of her, her mom and dad were soaping each other in the shower.

"I fell asleep at five," she said. The circles under her eyes were as dark as her eyeliner.

"What did your parents say? Did they go ape-shit?"

Carly gave me a look that burned. "You think I'd talk to my parents about that?"

I laughed in a way that sounded more like choking and reached into my locker, right to the very back. Farid and his buddies went past. They were snickering, despite the fact that anyone from 8FS could see they were being followed by a whole crowd of their parents, getting it on. But Farid (lots of darkness, silence and a minimum of thrusting) was profiting from the situation. He told Laurel Delveccio it'd cost her fifty dollars a month to keep the 8FS info from spreading to her Christian youth group.

Besides Farid, the only person who seemed happy was Amanda Axley. If Amanda gets 98 percent on a test, it's a bad day, but she just stuffs all her A-plus assignments at the back of her locker. Amanda's dad is the kind who makes jokes about her enormous boobs and asks whether that's why she can't stand up straight enough to make any school teams. Amanda's mom's not so bad. She's not too smart but she's really pretty— except for her hands. She's been working as a janitor on the night shift at the hospital since before she had Amanda and her hands are permanently wrinkled and red, like she just got out of the bath. For fourteen years Amanda's been a freak—a brainiac in a family of rednecks and underachievers—but yesterday after 8FS I said, "You know Dr. Megalo? Tall, good-looking pediatrician, comes in on career day? Back of a supply closet." Now Amanda was beaming and walking with her shoulders pulled back, big boobs and all.

The rest of us from 8FS were shuffling and agitated, staring at the floor a lot. The teachers and the kids from other classes were acting like it was any other day, but for the 8FS kids, there was nowhere safe to look. The halls, the classrooms, the caf—every place was crowded with writhing bodies. And every subject—geography, history, art, math—was suddenly sex ed. Except for 8FS itself. Because when we got to the door, Mrs. Redimeyer (and her bumping, grinding parents) was standing there, blocking the way in.

"Research period," Mrs. Redimeyer said. "Look up 'infant care' in the library. Start with Dr. Spock." But most of us just went for pop and chips until we had to come back in for Science.

After classes finished, I went down the hall to get Norman. Norman's parents don't get home till late and most days after school we go to his place. Usually, he's just standing alone at his locker, waiting for me. But now that everyone had got a good look at Norman's look-alike dad and what was under his zipper, Norman's locker was surrounded by Shaylyn Ramsey and her little posse with the highlights and the shirts that the teachers keep telling them to go home and change. And their parents, of course. I turned around and started walking the other way, but Norman slammed the locker shut and pushed past the girls. He was looking at the floor, but he slowed down when he got to me.

"You see that?" he said.

"Hard to see anything, Norm. You had quite a crowd there."

"You know that hairy librarian at Central whose name tag says 'Roberta'?"

"Yeah."

"That's Shaylyn's dad."

When we were out the door and had turned the corner of the schoolyard, he took my hand and put it in his jacket pocket.

The next day, they gave the babies back. But this time, they got us to pair up, boy–girl, in couples. That was Mrs. Redimeyer's idea. It was an easy way to make the remaining two babies go round the class faster: each couple gets the plastic kid for four days, but the mom and dad take alternating nights. She started at the end of the alphabet.

"Luca Yarrow and Norman Wilson—and whomever you have chosen as your partners. If you are currently a parent," Mrs. Redimeyer said, "you may be excused for the rest of the period."

Colin Jacks started to say it wasn't fair, but I didn't hear the rest of his complaint because Norman and I had already picked our baby up from Mrs. Redimeyer's desk and were in the hall.

"Come on," I said. "I'll show you how to change her diaper."

I spread the baby blanket out on the grass below the 8FS window and laid the baby down on it. I fed her and Norman fed her and then she lay there in the sun, plastic gleaming, eyes closed. I was pretty sure that the kids inside could see us, but the light on the glass made it impossible to see the other way, into 8FS. It was a beautiful spring day, with just a little wind that made the blanket flutter and the tetherball bump against the pole every now and then, the metal reverberating. The baby didn't cry.

Then the bell rang and the kids came out into the yard. We sat and watched them play soccer, or go to the doughnut store, or get picked up by brothers and sisters and mothers and nannies, until the yard was empty again. Then Norman said that since I already had a kid for three days on my own, it was only fair that he take the first night shift.

"Sure," I said, "you'll be great."

I watched him walk to the bus stop. He looked kind of funny, even to me—a skinny, bent-over boy in a jean jacket, with his books under one arm and a doll strapped to his chest. Then I noticed something else. Norman was alone. No parents fucking, thinking or not thinking of the future, thinking or not thinking of Norman and the person he'd become. Just Norman and the plastic baby, standing at the bus shelter, waving.

When I got to my place, instead of calling out to Tina and Lewis I closed the front door really quietly so that it would take a while for them to figure out that I was home. I couldn't hear any of the usual dinner-prep noises—no talking, no dancing, no uncorking of wine. But when I looked into the kitchen, they were there all right. It was just the two of them, no screwing shadow-parents, but Tina had her arms wrapped around Lewis and he was kissing her ear and whispering. I groaned and slapped my hands over my eyes the way I used to do when we watched movies.

"Apple!" Tina's voice was sharp. "What exactly is your problem?"

"You two need to understand the difference between private and public," I said. "Jeez."

"Apple," said Lewis, putting his arms around me and pulling me up against the two of them in a tight hug, "I've been meaning to ask you: how's Norman?"

"Fa-ther," I said, drawing the syllables out long the way I know he hates and sliding out from under their arms, "that's none of your business."

Lewis smiled. "Really?" he said. And then he made me set the table while he danced around the kitchen with Tina.

If this had been a planned lesson, something they dreamed up in the board office downtown, they'd want us to tell them what we'd learned. To put up our hands and say something like "This experience might give Amanda the confidence to apply for medical school." But she might have done that anyway, and besides, who's to say she won't just start hooking up with doctors in supply closets?

It's not like they could pronounce us inoculated against promiscuity or claim that we'd reached some advanced understanding or anything. We all look pretty much the same. This morning by the lockers, Andrea Fowler was still whining, and Colin was back to making smutty comments, and Shaylyn's girl posse were flipping their hair, just the same as before. And maybe someday Laurel Delveccio would come up with the school's correct answer—*sexual intercourse is a positive act between consenting adults*—but today I'm sure she was praying as hard as she ever had, but this time she was praying we could all just forget the whole thing.

But adults love to take credit. Even Mrs. Redimeyer seemed to think she'd done something special last week when the kids of 8FS, staring out into the yard at Norman and me, suddenly stopped rustling and fidgeting. Carly said she turned around and said, "Thank you, class. That's much better," as if she had fixed our problems just by changing the subject, just by writing *Unit 2, Fetal Development* on the board. When really, everyone was just relieved. Relieved that the huffing and the moaning had stopped. Relieved that the classroom had only thirty people in it. Relieved that each of us was on our own again.

No exaggeration: Lewis and Tina are singing a duet. From up here, I can just hear Tina's voice in the background, but Lewis's bass can pierce through walls, so I can tell they're doing "Endless Love" in alternating parts.

It's true that with parents like Tina and Lewis, I never have to worry about them sending me to a convent if they catch some boy feeling me up on the porch. And that's not what I want, really. They're all right, Tina and Lewis, if their fondling weren't up in my face so much. I don't want to blame them for thinking that just because they love each other, they've got everything figured out.

Tonight, hearing them downstairs makes it feel very quiet in my room. But maybe it's just because I'm not listening any more for screaming and crying, because today we gave the baby back. I put her on Mrs. Redimeyer's desk and Norman gave her a little pat and then Randall Ulmer and Laurel picked the baby up and took her away.

This afternoon at Norman's, I felt a little sad. There was no baby to make us jump off the couch to pick it up. We played a few rounds of Nintendo, but I won every time without even trying and Norman said he was sorry he couldn't give me a good enough game. And I said that was okay, at least he always tried.

He was looking at me a lot, like maybe he wished I'd say something. So I did. "Randall and Laurel can give that baby things we never would—like a proper baptism."

I was thinking that he'd laugh, but he didn't. Instead, he leaned over and kissed me. He kissed me for a long time and I kissed him back, until the remotes fell off the couch, and even until I could hear the people in the house next door pulling into the driveway and coming home from work. And I thought how it was fine because his parents wouldn't be home for ages. And because mine wouldn't care anyway. We could have done whatever we wanted to, twice, and no one would know. That was one of the things I was thinking while I felt the lumpy couch cushions under the fleece blanket on my back.

But there's more to it than being caught by your parents. What about getting caught by your kid? What if that condom broke, that jelly didn't kill, if some super-nervy Norman sperm made its way up there to do its butterfly act, what then? I knew I wouldn't want my kid to picture himself beginning there, in the Wilsons' rec room, all that fake wood panelling and smelly carpet, the fleece blanket balled up in the corner of the laundry room afterwards. For our kid, I'd want something better.

I told Norman that.

And then he did that smile behind his hair that makes me wonder if I know anything at all.

PETITIONS TO ST. CHRONIC

—

TWENTY-FOUR STOREYS straight down and what else to call it but *miracle*? Twenty-four storeys and not a scratch on him: that would be a miracle for sure. But twenty-four storeys and a massive internal hemorrhage, broken spine, complete loss of consciousness and drugs to sedate him if he ever does come out of it—that's Gibson.

Carlos tells me not to quibble. Says everyone receives God's gifts—some of us just don't recognize them. But Gibson will believe.

Micheline is planning on making Gibson a better man. She tells me he will look fine in a well-cut suit, silk tie, polished shoes. Micheline calls Gibson "pure potential."

Carlos says that's denying what Gibson is already.

"He doesn't need to ascend. The last shall be first. He is the least of us, and he is loved."

The cleaner mopping the floor past our orange vinyl chairs out by the elevator bank, down the hall from the ICU, says, "Some people shouldn't be allowed to breed. If this guy doesn't die, I'll lose my faith in Darwin."

A nurse in green scrubs comes around the corner, down the long hall and past the sign that says, ICU. VISITORS MUST BE SIGNED IN. She nods to another nurse at the reception desk and presses the down button beside the elevator. Her eyes are all apology. "Only next of kin," she says.

We've heard that for days, but no family is coming for Gibson. It's just Carlos, Micheline and me. Twenty-four storeys, and we three strangers are all he's got.

Each of us saw Gibson on the all-day news. The reporter had hair that was blowing in the mild summer breeze. He tried to hold our attention. Even before we turned the sound up, his face said, *The world is full of peril, but I will lead you through in my pressed linen shirt.*

But the camera wanted to follow Gibson, small like a bug in the corner of the screen. It loved him as we loved him. It was hard to tell what the crowd was chanting, but the volume seemed to rise as Gibson stretched his arms out like a conductor. Then he stepped into the air and fell.

—

The day that Gibson was brought in, a reporter outside Emergency asked Micheline how long she had known him.

"I am not his past," she said. "I am his future." She spelled her name, but the reporter didn't write it down. I asked her to spell it again. "It's French," she said. "One *l*."

By the time Carlos got there, most of Emergency was empty. Just a broken arm and chest pains and a couple of reporters using the pay phones because the nurses wouldn't let them use their cells. But by then the shifts had changed and Micheline and I weren't making any trouble. We could have been waiting there for anyone.

Carlos must have come straight from the garage because he was still in coveralls with a Ford insignia and oil down the front, but he was wearing a thick gold cross and carrying a bible. He burst through the swinging doors, then stood in the middle of the waiting room as if he had suddenly lost his way.

"Where can I find the man who fell?" he called out, and the nurse closed the little glass partition between her and the rest of us.

"Hey, Father Ford!" said the Floor Guy.

"I am not a priest. I am a supplicant."

"Yeah? Well, you're standing in my pile."

Micheline waved her hand in Carlos's direction as if she were wafting away someone else's cigarette smoke. But I lifted up my bag and made a spot for him on the seat beside me.

The doctors give their reports to the media. The media relays them. We arrange our morning meeting place—on the bench outside, where the families of the patients go to smoke—and read the reports. The photographs show Gibson to be dark haired with skin like waxed paper over veins of seaweed sprawl. We hold the papers on our knees as we drink coffee that I have brought from the all-night diner one block away. It is too early for the cafeteria to be open.

We turn the pages back. Carlos says Gibson is pale so that the light can shine through him. Micheline says he needs a little more sun. She will take him to Florida, she says, when he is well enough to stand the drive. To me, he looks as vulnerable as those girls in high school whose hips jutted up against the pocket rivets of their jeans. The ones everyone always tiptoed around: a fracture waiting to happen. The world pressed in closer on those among us who were cushioned by flesh, as if that offered sufficient protection. Despite the skin and the veins, Gibson has hands that look big and capable. They look like hands that could have hung on. But there are things you can't know from looking.

The first time my husband hit me, we were in the bathroom, so it was hard to tell whether the darker bruise was from Cy's hand or from the edge of the sink I hit going down. I felt across the floor to see if I would find blood, but the tiles were dry. When I pulled myself up, I held onto the vanity and stood in front of the mirror as long as I could. The red was spreading under my skin, my cheek, and my forehead was swelling. It looked like it should hurt. I couldn't even remember Cy's fist on me. It was as if something had pushed its way out from the inside like a latent cancer. "This is how I look as a beaten woman," I said. I tried it on like a uniform, and felt it settle on me like something I was always meant to wear.

Micheline says it must have been a woman that crushed Gibson's spirit.

Carlos says, "Why does everyone always think that only women hold such power? There are other things that can destroy a man."

Carlos is worried about what will happen if he is at work when Gibson comes to, when they finally allow him a visitor. "Will you tell him God is love?" he asks me. "Will you tell him for me?"

Micheline says that when he wakes up we will give him the choice of the two of us, confident that he will select her. I could play along, tell her I want a man who is already dismantled, so I don't have to do the job myself or stand by and watch it happen. That I plan to buy us matching T-shirts that will announce our condition, *Damaged*. That when we walk, people will hear what is left of us rattle.

But to each of them I let my smile answer for me. Let them believe what they will. I am not interested in his recovery. You can sew a body up again, but that doesn't make it whole.

Outside Ultrasound no one asks any questions and they have a good TV. While we wait for the press conference to begin, Micheline and I flip through celebrity magazines and she passes on old gossip about washed-up stars. Micheline tells me she has been a child actress, a cartoon voice, a hit songwriter. She makes enough from her songs to never work again, except for licensing the rights to ad agencies for commercials. She tells me I would know these songs if she hummed them, but she doesn't take requests. Now she is more of a scout, she says.

"Take Gibson," she says.

But really, why would you? Nobody would imagine that he could be turned around, become the kind of guy who would buy tickets to Cirque du Soleil, book a holiday on a romantic island, wear a *Kiss the Cook* apron when he barbecues steak with the neighbours. Nobody except Micheline.

Micheline opens her purse and hands me a success

story: a photo of a man with hair greying at the temples. Beside him is a woman with streaked blonde hair pulled into a ponytail, holding a fat-faced baby. An old lover made into a new man, then released: Micheline's gift to the world. "From AA to executive, Silicon Valley," she says. Micheline is the thirteenth step.

Eight hours, twelve hours, split shifts—all around us, the nurses and doctors move through their rotations. For a week now, we three have also split our vigil into days and nights of waiting. We arrange our meeting places, watch for Security, adhere to our schedule. Micheline arrives at 6 a.m., asking if there are any developments. Just before she comes, I go get the morning papers and new coffee for our breakfast overlap. Then Carlos goes to work, returning to relieve Micheline at 8 p.m. We are all together for an hour or so and then Micheline leaves. I pretend to Micheline that I go when she does, but I return with Raisinettes and pretzels from the machine to the place where Carlos and I have decided to wait through the night.

They each think that I sleep when they sleep, I watch when they watch. If they notice that I only wear two shirts and two pairs of pants, if they see that I don't change this old sweater, they never say a thing.

In the back of the hospital chapel, Carlos tells me he wants to talk about where we were when we saw him.

Carlos says he was standing over the engine of a car that wouldn't start. It was his first day on a real job, he tells me, a legal one, the first he'd had in this country, and now the car refused to come to life. He tried all his usual cures: something with wires, with belts. "Just trust me, I can get a car going. It's my talent. But this one was dead," he says. "Think of the heat that day. Think of no air conditioning." The crucifix around his neck dangled in front of his eyes, blocking his view. He says he threw it back over his shoulder so it wouldn't distract him from the job.

While the other guys in the bay turned up the sound on the twenty-four-hour news and gathered under the TV set, Carlos kept working. The sweat was pouring into his eyes. This is a test, he was thinking. He breathed in the smell of old engine. Then the guys started hollering: *The bastard's going to jump!* Just as Gibson hit the ground, the car started. Carlos watched the jump in repeat, impact after impact.

"So, where were you?" Carlos asks.

But my eyes are closing. Carlos balls up his jacket and makes a nest of it in the corner of the pew and I lay my head against the old tweed. Beside me, Carlos smells like roses. When his fingers press the rosary beads the skin is pink and clean, but at the end of every nail, a rim of grease.

When I was in grade nine I had a friend called Angela whose parents were breaking up. Angela sat beside me in science class, in those big double desks with the sinks in the middle. The kids on Angela's street said there had been screaming and crying, there had been accusations of other lovers, there were battles over the children. But Angela only mentioned it once. "Their marriage exploded," she said. She didn't look at me, just doodled around the margins of the science textbook that we shared.

That night, I looked at those ink ellipses spinning out like some ever-changing orbit beside a diagram of the Big Bang, electric blue and orange on a black background. From then on I believed that that was how marriages ended, in a storm of meteors, bright and loud enough the neighbours were bound to hear.

So it was never the heat and the bursting that amazed me with Cy, it was the numbness that followed. The leeside of the hitting was like the dark side of the moon.

It would be quiet for days, weeks, months. The bigger the explosion, the more time it took to repair, but it happened all the same. Fractures, dislocations, bruises—the torn pieces of me just fused together again like a trap door closing over an empty hole. Sometimes Cy would stay home and tend to me, press a washcloth up against the stitches. *Shh, shh*, he'd say, and I'd barely even feel them. But other times, the times he would go away, I could feel the longing for him sharper than any of the splits in my skin. I would leave when it got harder to stay than to go, I told myself. I was waiting for something worse—an injury so severe that it would break us forever, make it impossible to recover. But something in me refused to stay broken. I couldn't escape my ability to heal.

On the tenth day after Gibson's fall, the doctors give a press conference and the elevators to Intensive Care fill up with reporters on their way to the media room. I bring up our takeout lunches the back way—through Emergency to Physio, where they have a television we have not watched before.

A dozen frustrated patients try to catch the nurse's attention, hoping to be called. She keeps her eyes on the desk, except when she lifts them to stare at me.

On the television, a middle-aged man and a woman are mooning at each other across a breakfast table while three teenagers show increasingly obvious signs of revolt, from rolling their eyes to packing cake and beer into their lunch bags. The couple continues to smile and blush, oblivious. The television voice-over lists side effects and encourages us to talk to our doctor.

"One of mine," says Micheline.

The commercial finishes before I realize that she means the song, a tune about perpetual sunshine, its words just beyond familiar.

"It was playing the afternoon I saw Gibson," Micheline says. She was waiting in a hotel bar for her lunch date—another former lover. Once an army private. "Gifted, but directionless."

And now?

"Harvard. Magna cum laude. In town for a conference."

At the hotel, she says, the TV over the bar showed the midday news with the volume off, while a medley of old hits played over the sound system. Just as Micheline heard her young voice played back to her, there was Gibson, standing on the window ledge while Micheline sang about beaches forever. When she saw him jump she threw a twenty on the counter, left a message for her lunch guest and took a cab to the hospital downtown.

The nurse at the desk is staring at me. "You look familiar," she says.

"I was here yesterday," I tell her.

Beside me, Micheline's magazine flutters shut. "This isn't a good place," she says. "Let's go to Same Day Surgery."

She doesn't notice how the nurse watches me as I lift my purse and walk to the elevator.

The media reports the profound effect of Gibson's fall on the people who were there to witness it. A woman cried and fainted. People vomited. Others rushed in before emergency crews arrived to see if they could help.

But where are they now, asks Carlos, if he spoke to them so directly? "The three of us received his call at a distance, and we came. That is what it means to believe," he says.

Carlos tells me about St. Clare of Assisi, the patron saint of television, a noblewoman who heard Francis of Assisi speak and founded the order of Poor Clares, women who lived an ascetic existence, surviving on alms. When she was old and too ill to go to mass, the mass would appear on the wall of her little cell. When he prays for Gibson, Carlos prays to St. Clare, he prays to St. Jude for desperate causes, he prays to the Virgin too.

Micheline is tired of his sermons. She shoves her chair back from the cafeteria table and our cups tremble, coffee spilling over the sides. We watch her push through the doors and out to the hall.

I ask Carlos, Who is the saint for causes almost lost, for causes of the ultimate draw, the endless overtimes, who is the patron saint of those who can't lose themselves no matter how hard they try?

"Blessed are the pure of heart, for they shall see God," Carlos says.

The Floor Guy mops silently around our feet, then pushes his cart into the kitchen. His voice echoes off the stainless steel as the door swings closed: "Blessed are the self-destructive, for they shall save the rest of us the trouble."

—

Micheline meets us in the lobby with a pie she has made herself. "Practice: for Gibson," she says.

The Floor Guy sneers. "He'll never give up the liquid lunch," he says.

"Self-improvement only requires *inner movement*," she says. Then she cuts him the first slice. "You should try it."

Micheline says there are skills every woman should master. She says she can tell I am the kind of woman who knows this. She asks me to think of my greatest talent. I laugh. She doesn't understand that this is my answer. An easy laugh reveals my one true talent: I have the gift of acquiescence.

I am better versed in the things that a woman should not do. *Keep your chin up and your skirt down.* I have remembered the saying, but confused the order. Of all the instructions I have ever been given, it seems I have done the opposite of everything but floss. When the dentist on call saw the teeth in the little dish, he complimented my hygiene. "If it were up to you, these would have been biting into apples until you were one hundred." As if I had nothing to do with it. As if the place I'd put myself in had nothing to do with where I was now. As if this weren't just another of my animal defences I'd surrendered.

The pie is lemon and the pastry flakes away in sheets. Micheline accepts our compliments and tells us she is self-taught. Carlos says the crust reminds him of the layers of stone in the quarry in the town he grew up in.

"Rock Bottom?" asks the Floor Guy, but he holds his plate out for more.

Two weeks. The press conferences are less frequent now. The statements shorter. I have stopped trying to identify the specialists. But Micheline watches, trying to read between the lines, to determine a more accurate prognosis.

Each day over the intercom there are calls for doctors to dash to patients in various states of trauma. We imagine every call to be for Gibson. If we are near the patient elevators, we wait for the doors to open in case we can get a glimpse of him while they rush him to another effort to repair one more tear in his river of ruptured functions.

When a patient goes by on a dais of hospital linen, barricaded by nurses that obscure his face, our voices lower; it might be him.

"If he lives, I will tell him we know it was only a cry for help," says Carlos, collapsing his rosary beads in his hand.

"Just wait till he finds out who answered," says the Floor Guy, and he mops under the television in a place that already looks clean.

—

Micheline says Gibson has been moved to a step-down unit.

"What does that mean?" I ask. "Does that mean he's getting better?"

"It means less security," she says. "Soon they'll have to let us in."

She stakes out a place on the new floor, flipping through the same old issues of the magazines that are stacked in every waiting room.

I walk Carlos to the bus stop and then I go back to the disabled bathroom on the first floor and scrub at my extra pair of underwear with an old toothbrush I have dipped into the Floor Guy's bleach. The smell is all the hospital's comfort, its promise of someone else in charge—so much control, so little attention. It makes me sleepy. These are the things that keep me here: Gibson and, when I am away from him, bleach.

I sit on the high toilet seat and lean my head against the wall to keep me from tumbling off while my eyes are closed.

The last time I was discharged from the hospital, I bleached the sheets three times to get the stain out, running them through on cold in the basement of my building, sitting guard at the washer's glass window. When they came white again, I went to stretch them out over the bed and saw that the blood had seeped deep into the mattress. Before Gibson, at night I would lie over the stain as if it were an inland sea, trying to draw the baby back up into me like water into a cloud.

The nurse in Emergency said, "If you do not press charges, this will happen again and again."

It was when I lost the baby that I knew I would always take him back. But this time Cy stayed away. I spoke to him in our silent apartment. I spoke to him as if he were there: "Come home, Cy. I promise I'll take you back. I will heal and take you back, forever."

And I would have, before Gibson.

I do not know how long I was asleep in the bathroom, but when I come back to the new waiting room, Micheline is not in her chair. I sit for a minute, resting a coffee on each knee, waiting. Wondering where she might have gone. Nearby, there is a bathroom for the disabled, but the door is open and no one is inside. I want to ask where the other bathroom is, but there is no nurse at the station. I go down and around the hall. I find the bathroom, but Micheline is not in it.

The hall is quiet. A doctor passes, but doesn't ask my business. I stand in the new silence and listen. I hear only my own persistent breathing, my own belligerent heart. And an occasional banging.

There is a WET FLOOR sign around the corner. The

Floor Guy moves the mop back and forth, from one wall to the other, raising a damp shine between us. It is a long time before he looks up. Surprised, his face is soft as a chamois.

"Hello. Come to roll away the stone?"

"What happened to Micheline?"

"Packed up and went, I imagine. She must be disappointed. Hardly a return on her investment."

A woman in a silk cardigan walks down the hall, carrying flowers, then turns the corner.

"I don't know what you mean," I say.

The Floor Guy pulls the bucket toward him and leans on the handle of his mop, studying my face. He bends, picks up the sign, and jerks his head so that I will follow.

We turn the way the woman went, and then turn again, passing closed doors with little windows at the top that look into rooms. He stops and pushes one open, unfolding the WET FLOOR sign in front of it. He nudges me forward at the shoulder.

Pink curtains are closed around a bed in the middle of the room. I step forward and push my arms through the opening in the fabric, then pull back as if I am diving into deep water.

The sheet is over Gibson's body, covering even his face. Wires and tubes run out from under the sheet, but the machines he's hooked up to are quiet, their screens dark, the cords disconnected. At a spot half-way up the bed, I lift the sheet to look for something recognizable. His hand is mostly bandaged, the sides of his fingers are purple.

I think of what it was Carlos wanted to say to him, of the songs that Micheline planned to sing in her beck-oning voice.

But it's me who is speaking, telling Gibson our story—his and mine—taking it back to the beginning, to the moment I saw him on television, saw him fall. But wait, that doesn't give us enough time. I stretch it out. I tell him about what came before. The cat food com-mercial, essential nutrients for the senior feline. And then the one for paint that goes straight on over rust, you don't even have to scrub. No. More. Back before that, to the phone ringing, to the voice I thought I'd always be waiting for, back to Cy saying, "Forgive me, darling, forgive me. I'm coming home."

My hand curls around Gibson's fingers. For a mir-acle, he is very cold and still. I warm my palm with my breath and lift his hand to my chest. His arm is splinted. I tell Gibson that after he fell, the TV showed the crowd closing in and the paramedics arriving and that the way the reporter announced he was alive was by saying, "It's a *miracle*. What else could you call it?"

I tell Gibson how I packed my bag and called a cab. How I left the TV on in the apartment so that Cy could fill those empty rooms and make them his own. I knew that when Cy got there, the news would probably have changed to arson or stabbings or blowout sales, but by then I would be free.

I shift my hip onto the bed and wedge myself in beside Gibson, next to the metal bed rail, lay my head on the edge of the pillow and whisper it all again: the phone call, the commercial, Gibson falling, packing my suitcase, calling the cab. But my eyes are closing, and the sequence seems confusing. Is it the cat food commercial and then the one for paint? I am so very tired. The phone rings. I see Gibson. I pack. I see Gibson and I am packing. But now I am packing through the cat food, and the rust remover. I am packing through Gibson's fall and even packing through Cy's phone call. And I can see that I am already leaving. I am leaving. I am leaving before I see Gibson and even before the phone rings, so that when Gibson falls I stretch my arms wide too—to catch him, or hold him, or look with him all the way down.

6:19

—

THERE IS A PLACE ON the track between the main station and the end of the western line where the train that leaves the city at 6:13 passes the train that leaves at 6:02. Both trains leave from the same platform. Both trains, eventually, arrive at the same destination. But one train—the earlier one—makes three extra station stops near the beginning of the journey, allowing those few commuters that live along the tracks in the old suburbs of the city, the places that have ceased to be actual distinct locations and have long since been swallowed up by the sprawl, to disembark. Between the second and third little station stops, the earlier train pulls onto a short spur to allow the later train to pass, hurtling by like a child running past a graveyard.

The seasoned commuter knows about this peculiarity of the ride. And how long, really, should it take to reach this level of understanding? The line runs east in one direction and west in the other. It has no diversions or transfer points. And so what does it say about Nathan Faulk that it has taken him two whole weeks of riding the westbound portion of the Lakeside line without noticing the passing train? What does it say about Nathan in his well-cut suit, his glasses with the invisible frames, his polished shoes, his glowing Smartphone?

That is what Nathan is wondering as the other train streaks past the window in a blur of green and white. To his credit, Nathan thinks, today he did notice that the previous station was somewhere he'd never heard of. "Long Branch! This is Long Branch!" the operator called over the loudspeaker. A woman across the aisle made a disapproving sound high in her nose, then said, "This *used* to be Long Branch," and Nathan—looking out the window at the sign on the platform, blue and apparently recently affixed, or at least well maintained— wondered what had happened to the Long Branch the woman thought she knew. But the question of Long Branch—its origins, its present—left Nathan as soon as the train departed the station.

Then—was it just a few moments ago?—Nathan was travelling as fast as he knew how, to his new home at the second stop from the end of the line. A stop that, Nathan

believed, was very definitely what and where it was supposed to be: a new development in an old industrial area.
Redone and promising something eventually shiny, if one
had an eye for potential. Which his wife, Belinda, did.

Well, didn't she? Nathan felt a vague sense of guilt.
Of course she did. She had a feel for the "good bones"
of houses, for neighbourhoods, opportunities, for things
on the cusp of becoming something better. And Belinda's
ability to make selections—confident, profitable selections—had given Nathan some of his greatest moments
of satisfaction and surety. Properties, cars, vacation
spots—Belinda knew how to recognize the value of
something not-quite discovered and to land the two of
them in the midst of it, like second-wave pioneers, better
equipped than the previous immigrants and ready to
reap the benefits of settlement just before the boom.
Only last night they had been toasting their move and
the eventual return on their investment with a bottle of
Veuve Clicquot Ponsardin.

True, Nathan mostly went along with Belinda. But
if Belinda knew how to pick them, then certainly Nathan
was one of her picks that had turned out a winner. Or so
he liked to think, whenever he wavered on the edge of
misgivings. So he was, in fact, thinking this evening on
the train as he took a break from answering his stockpile
of e-mails, just before he became aware that he was stuck
on the sideline of the track at 6:19.

It was only a tiny crack of doubt. The sort that Belinda would know who to call to patch with putty and a flat knife, but which Nathan would try to look away from until the repair was complete. For an instant, he wondered why this place was so very far from everything that had rooted him: his job, the steady pump of the city's traffic through the windows of offices, shops and apartments. Far from everything—except Belinda. It was then, as he leaned back against the blue upholstery, that he realized the train was slowing.

So when the train eased into a full stop a few moments ago, Nathan felt merely puzzled. He looked around at his fellow passengers, but his seatmates and those standing in the aisles continued to read the papers they'd neglected all day (old news, Nathan had thought—earthquake, cloning, potential autoworkers' strike—stories he'd read before dawn, before stepping into the dark down the wood gangplank over the mud of his new yard). No one seemed distressed by the delay. Across the aisle, four women dressed like mid-level assistants continued to tell a story that proceeded to a punch line that stirred up laughter like a tornado in the space between them, drawing them forward, holding their bellies.

But now that the other train is flashing past, Nathan is experiencing a strange sense of déjà vu, or at least a feeling that he, like a detective in a B movie, has missed a clue obvious to everyone else. There! The other train is headed in the same direction, for the same destination, and it is passing him by. The stop he is now being forced to make—and the two station stops before it—are entirely unnecessary to his journey. The train he has been catching, diligently, at two minutes past the hour, is a train that is less than direct. Which means, Nathan realizes, that on these ten or so commutes home, to his wife, to the increasingly comfortable, increasingly affluent life that she has been constructing for them, Nathan has spent—he calculates—roughly three wasted hours. One hundred and eighty extraneous minutes. Minutes in which he has not been Nathan Faulk, Deputy Communications Director at the provincial government, number eight on an approvals list of eleven (ending with the premier's cabinet office), the man who vets the minister's plans, strategies and speeches before the minister actually performs them. Not the supportive husband who has been suggesting tile for the entryway and leapt (truly leapt!) at another of Belinda's high-stakes bets and moved to the second stop at the end of the westbound line, outside the limits of the city.

In short, Nathan thinks, he has not been who he thought he was at all. And now, as the green blur of the passing train streaks past the stationary Nathan, he looks at his Smartphone. It is 6:19.

He raises his head. The last car of the faster train passes like a curtain drawn back. In its wake, the scene outside Nathan's window seems suspended. The stillness produces vertigo, like getting off a boat onto dry land. Nathan feels as if he will tumble into it. He presses his hand against the double glass of the window to keep from falling.

He can see the edge of the main line, the gravel between the dark ties, which look unstable now, the wood splintering. The grass at the border of the tracks dips slightly into a series of backyards. Three equal plots are framed with identical perimeters of chain-link fence. Two of them are covered over in cement. In one sits a bare, square clothesline. In the other, a blue Datsun is raised on cement blocks. But the yard between them is a quadrangle of green. A vine climbs up and through the wire diamonds. *Virginia creeper*, Nathan thinks. He does not know where the name comes from, but it is there, a fish floating to the reedy surface.

There is a bungalow at the top of the yard, like the bungalows in the yards on either side. Post-war real estate, Nathan knows from listening to Belinda. Whole houses in a kit, half assembled before delivery. To the side of the porch, there is a trash can. At the centre of the yard is a woman, holding a rake.

It's 6:19. It is Monday. Nathan remembers the season: fall. The air is turning crisp. The light outside is dimming and the woman won't be able to accomplish much more in the yard today. But she is almost finished. Small piles are spread around the grass, red circles against the green. At first, the woman seems completely still, as held in place by something as Nathan is by the stopped train. But now he sees that she is pulling the rake around the edges of one of the leaf piles in small strokes. Her moderate motion helps Nathan to steady himself after the rush of the passing train, like bridging notes before the next symphonic movement.

Nathan takes a breath and his nasal passages fill with the smell of hard-earned sweat through a fall jacket. It has a familiar composition and Nathan squirms in his seat. It is his own smell. Nathan feels it emanating from pools of dampness under his arms, along the back of his neck, the hollow in his chest. Do his seatmates smell it? Nathan turns his head slowly, trying to mask his embarrassment, but no one shows any sign of offence. Except for Nathan, for whom smell has become something foreign, even on his own skin. Something to be gotten rid of, to be scrubbed from shirts and covered with the extra deodorant he keeps in his desk drawer. Another scent joins the salty waft of sweat and as Nathan moves his hands up and down his trousers, the odour stirs through the air: sweet, like something just beginning to decay. Nathan lifts his fingers to his face and inhales: leaves.

In the yard, the woman opens her hands and dumps a pile of leaves into the compost bin.

Nathan draws his hands up across the sharp lapel of his suit jacket, presses himself back in his seat. As the train moves forward again, Nathan feels as though his stomach has to catch up with the rest of his body, as though part of him has been left behind. Does the woman really turn to him as he moves away? A shaft of sunlight shears down between them, as the train leaves the spur for the main line. He looks at his Smartphone. 6:19, it says.

Tuesday morning. Nathan finds himself pleasantly early for his usual train into the city and uses the three minutes he harvests getting an excellent parking spot at the end of the lot closest to the station and going down under the tracks and up onto the platform, to pause at the schedule board. He confirms the judiciousness of his route east to the office. The morning train he has been taking makes the best use of his time, depositing him in the central station as quickly as possible. His evening misjudgments can be righted without fuss. Today, he will either take an earlier train or a slightly later one. Both trains are express and will return him to this lot with maximum efficiency.

In the city, he takes the stairs from the platform at the central station, watching his feet step along behind those of the other passengers. Sneakers, tall boots, loafers and lace-ups surround him. Nathan watches the men's dress shoes, more built for movement than the women's high heels, moving in a rhythmic shuffle as the passengers from the various platforms merge into a single corridor. There's a disquieting scuff to many of the men's shoes and

Nathan hopes that his move west won't result in a dis-
regard for his appearance, a dressed-in-the-dark crumple.
Checking his Smartphone as the crowd in the corridor
spills out into the main station, Nathan detours toward
a shoeshine kiosk, where he has his black Italian brogues
buffed to a sheen.

The new shine gives him such a brisk step that he
thinks at any moment the early workers—leaning on
counters, handing out coffee, making change—may
burst into accompanying song. The thought makes him
smile, and the smile makes him stop for a moment, to
hear if the commuters' shuffle stops with him. Now he
sees a flower stand. Rigged over the cashier under the
awning is an uncovered light bulb, glowing in the half-
light of not-quite morning.

Yes, flowers! For Belinda! Nathan leans in toward the
green buckets of yellow and purple blooms and selects a
bunch. He pays, tucks the bouquet under his arm, pushes
through the revolving glass doors into the foyer of the
government buildings and makes his way into the empty
elevator. He swipes his security card, verifying his identity, and strides down the quiet halls to his desk, where he
lays the flowers behind his computer monitor.

The flowers are still there when his assistant, Monica,
arrives at precisely 9:15. "Spring flowers? Wonder where
they flew these in from? How much did you pay for
these? You should have talked to me. I'd have cut you

fresh chrysanthemums from my front yard." From some-where she produces a clear glass vase, with black marbles at the bottom to anchor the flowers in place.

All day, looking up from his colour-coded files (red for approvals, blue for interoffice missives) and e-mails, Nathan enjoys the spikes of the mauve tulips, the frilly yellow daffodils, the winking purple irises. As the day ends, Nathan is staring at the widening petals, when— "Got a minute? Hey! Nathan!"—Jack, his director, briefcase packed and coat on, seeks him out for advice: what to do about the minister's tendency to go off-script and speculate about the government's deeper intentions or possible future plans. And Nathan assures him—as he has other days, and with success—that the minister's speech will be written to mimic the minister's own par-lance, so he will feel comfortable delivering the govern-ment's message and be less likely to elaborate. Then Nathan watches Jack's back—upright and satisfied, it seems to him—disappear around the corner as the director heads to the parking garage.

Nathan turns off his computer screen. He unfolds the paper that encased the flowers this morning and closes an ample hand round their stems to lift them from the water. They're stuck. Nathan shakes his hand back and forth, trying to dislodge the stems from their place in the marbles.

He sits back down and examines the flowers from

his desk chair. Through the clear glass, Nathan's eyes trace the green stalks as they disappear into the black marbles. Now he sees that at the bottom of the vase are thin red filaments, twisting up and around the black spheres like tangled hair. The strands have grown so long they are making their way up the slippery sides. The flowers are taking root.

Nathan might pause to wonder, but he has a train to catch. He pulls now with force, and the flowers, firmly planted just seconds ago, come loose like a door yanking open. They drip onto the paper, which Nathan wraps around them hastily so that he won't miss the earlier westbound express.

The subway platform is crowded with what looks like nursing home residents on a field trip. Nathan pushes through the staggering old people toward the subway doors and receives a rebuking stare from the young woman in charge of the group, who keeps her eyes on Nathan as she sweeps her arm wide to allow the entire battery of seniors to enter. Call it a practical choice: Nathan will wait for the next subway train.

He arrives at the central station too late for the 5:49, the first efficient train home. No matter. Better to find something useful to do while waiting for the 6:13, Nathan thinks, than to sit through the seemingly endless stops on the 6:02. Perhaps he will buy a magazine to go with Belinda's flowers. Nathan is perusing the racks for a decorating glossy when several women stand-ing at the newsstand with him freeze, listening to a crackle of a loudspeaker, then put down their potential purchases and move toward the platforms. Nathan looks up at the departures board. The westbound 6:13 has been cancelled. Nathan can now make out the voice on the loudspeaker. The next train is not for three-quarters of an hour. Which, today, makes the 6:02 the only reason-able possibility.

So, at 6:19, briefcase at his feet, flowers on the empty seat beside him, Nathan is resigned to being sidelined along the track. But still he is surprised to find his car, randomly chosen, lined up exactly as it was the previous day, across from the green lawn.

Today, the woman is on her knees in the grass, the setting sun throwing her shadow back toward the city, as if she is a sundial at the garden's centre. Her auburn hair is hanging in spirals over her face and it moves as she trowels the ground, wiggle and flick, echoing the action of her hands. She shifts her weight to the side, exposing a bare ankle above dirty, laceless running shoes as she leans toward a brown sack on the ground. Nathan presses his face against the glass until he feels himself go with her, so that when she turns back toward him, Nathan is close enough to see her drop a little bulb into the hole.

Her eyes are small and her eyebrows almost in-visible. Her face is a mass of freckles, making her nose and her cheekbones more dark than pale. Her lips are thin and pink.

She wears an old blue sweatshirt with a faded logo and a stain that seems to have come through so many washes it belongs as much as the original dye. The sleeves of the sweatshirt are pushed up and her arms have an honest tan acquired through outdoor work, not planning.

How far does the tan reach? Nathan wonders. October's marks up to the elbows? September's to the upper arms, the summer's richness fading now, but still traceable over her shoulders, across her back? Nathan puts out a finger and strokes the thick, bleached-out hair along her arms. It stands up against the cold and at his touch. He cups his hands under her elbows and lets them graze her sweatshirt and then slide under it, searching for the places the sun has never reached.

Nathan is dizzy with intimacy as he has not been in years. He remembers the tiles with the Dijon accents he and his wife have been considering for the new entrance-way; the lead-glass door that will cost more than carpets for the whole house; the crown moulding along the dining room ceiling. He feels a shiver of unfaithfulness. Not only to Belinda, but to the new house itself, to his entire existence that had, until yesterday, seemed as durable and appropriate as his tailored shirts.

He pulls away. He doesn't want to meet the woman's gaze and so he looks down at his feet. But the shiny

Italian leather is gone; he is wearing dirty grey tennis shoes, eyelets empty. Nathan grabs his chest, and his fingers meet the brush of well-washed thick flannel in a blue plaid. He squeezes his eyes shut and feels himself falling backwards, as the train picks up speed. He waits until the movement is continuous and rapid before he opens his eyes.

His leather shoes are solidly on his feet, his briefcase leaning against them. His shirt is buttoned up to the collar, under his turquoise silk tie. He looks at his Smartphone. 6:19, it says. For a moment he takes comfort in its bright display. He sets it on the seat beside him. Where are the flowers? Nathan leans over the seat and looks in the aisle, and then under his seat and the seats across from him. The flowers are gone.

At home, Nathan steadies himself with the Scotch that Belinda likes to have on hand to serve to guests. It is a variety he impressed her with by ordering it on their first date and their second. The kind she keeps stocked in the art deco liquor cabinet with the blue glass.

After dinner, Nathan spreads Belinda's landscaping magazines across the coffee table and searches online for contractors listed in the magazine's back pages. He considers solid features like water fountains, koi ponds, retaining walls, berms—elements that need excavation and professional installation—until Belinda gathers the magazines in a tidy pile and suggests they retire to the master bedroom. And Nathan, lying over his wife in their sleigh bed under the moon-shaped window, runs his hands over Belinda's pale curves and finds that the ground stays solidly in place. Which allows him to sleep.

Wednesday. Nathan is feeling much better. The ride in was uneventful and this morning he has been going through the work of one of his better writers, who has crafted a conciliatory speech for the minister to deliver at the autoworkers' AGM early this evening. True, on the subway he gave up his seat for a young woman he took to be pregnant but afterwards wondered if she just had a naturally thick form. Although Nathan found his misplaced gallantry somewhat embarrassing, he could hardly call it a seismic occurrence. Unlike yesterday's event on the train. Which would be disturbing if Nathan were to think about it. Which he will not.

The office is as he left it, vase empty of everything but water and the black stones. Nathan returns it to Monica's desk with a sticky-note—*You'll know where this goes.*

And Nathan has a plan for this evening. A plan that will have him stay at his desk a respectable twenty minutes later than usual, reviewing the files for tomorrow and considering the day's news clippings, before leaving in just enough time for the 6:13, after the 6:02 has safely pulled away.

"Nathan? Nathan!"

Nathan rights himself in his chair and sees the director staring at him. "Jack."

The director is sitting at Nathan's clean little table, spread with brochures on the province's productivity created by Nathan's own team.

"You know, I'd feel a lot more comfortable if I knew that speech was getting right into the minister's hands. No possible screw-ups."

Nathan nods to indicate his understanding and his calm.

"You're going past the conference centre on the way to the train. Why don't you just take it right to him?"

Nathan calculates quickly, the way he has always been comfortable doing. He takes into account the time needed to find the autoworkers' event in the massive conference centre, several minutes to exchange pleasantries with the minister, shake hands with a few senior colleagues. If he leaves now, he will arrive at the train station with even fewer minutes to spare before the later train. Yes, it will be all right.

"Nathan?"

It is a particular habit of Jack to look over the frame of his glasses at his underlings. It's a look Nathan has analyzed and determined to be little more than a habit, and not an indication that Nathan is being scrutinized. But now Nathan finds himself standing with one arm partially extended, half reaching for the red folder containing the speech and half drawing the arm back toward him. And Jack, still seated, is looking at him from beneath his glasses, as if Nathan is a car on a hoist and the director is trying to determine the source of a tricky mechanical problem.

"No bother at all, Jack. I'm going that way."

When Nathan arrives at the conference centre, he sees the minister's aide standing outside the main doors, smoking. Which is not the kind of thing either the province's tourism bureau, or Nathan, wants to see.

"Ah! We've been needing that!" The aide claps Nathan's shoulder. "This thing's a bugger. They're all over him. I was going to have to ride him out of here on a forklift if I didn't have that!"

The folder leaves Nathan's hand like a baton, and along with it go the anticipated way-finding and the conversations with government types that were to take up the remainder of the afternoon before the 6:13. The door to the conference centre swings back at Nathan like a bellow, catching the collected dull residue of smoke and depositing it in a warm cloud over him in the fall afternoon, as if Nathan were his own separate weather system.

Even now, Nathan is steady. He will use the short walk to the station to look at the expensive furniture stores that feature the kind of Italian leather sofas that Belinda so admires. He will take the next fifty-three minutes to compare prices, styles, the way the pieces fit together and how they might fill the place in the living room that Belinda has called a dead corner.

But as he slows beside the first faux French window, Nathan feels someone brush his sleeve. A homeless man is standing there facing the same living room set as Nathan. And now, when he asks for some money— "Just a coffee, buddy, just a coffee"—how many times can Nathan refuse?

Three. Once, in front of the ultra-modern couch store, once in front of the William Morris–style dining room sets, once at the entrance to the lighting showroom.

The man is still there when Nathan exits the lighting showroom. Nathan gives him five dollars, which buys Nathan five minutes in the mirror shop. When the man presses his face against the glass ("How about a sandwich, guy? You can afford it!"—coming muffled into the shop, raising the eyebrows of the other customers), Nathan heads straight for the station.

Which means he arrives ten minutes before the 6:02, the slow train, the train he'd intended to avoid.

No matter, Nathan tells himself, looking away from the board that announces the next train. He'll just sit on this bench and wait. He scrolls through his messages like someone with a headache waiting for the aspirin to kick in. And he could have continued to sit here, just like this, until the 6:13, if it weren't for Colin Roy, who has sat down in the seat beside him.

"Colin?"

The man beside him looks at Nathan with a lip motion that readies itself to smile, should it prove to be required.

"Colin Roy? Class of '88?"

"Yes?"

"Lacrosse?"

"I'm sorry . . ." The man is shaking his head.

"Nathan!" Nathan pulls his lips back into a grimace and taps at his front teeth. "It's Nathan Faulk."

"Good God. Nathan. Didn't even recognize you!"

That was a bit of a jolt. He and Col hadn't been the best of friends, it's true, but they had shared three years of university lacrosse, two of them losing seasons and one of them spectacularly successful but more marked, for Nathan anyway, by the many rounds of dental work to replace the two front teeth that Colin had knocked out during an overly rambunctious scrimmage. Certainly you would remember a face you had so radically altered.

But soon they are on to other things. How Colin also lives along the western part of the Lakeside line, how he became a dental surgeon. Colin makes Nathan tilt his head back and show him how the implants have held up all these years. Pronounces them almost undetectable.

So that when Colin stands and says, "There's our train!" how is Nathan not to follow him, up the stairs and onto the platform for the 6:02? Then onto the train? How can he not take the seat by the window that

Colin gallantly gestures to, before sitting down beside Nathan on the aisle?

But only a few minutes into the ride, Colin is lifting his briefcase into his lap and rising to go. "My stop! Great to see you!"

And Nathan, half rising himself, feels like a boy who is being left on the first day of school.

Which is why Nathan is sidelined again, rerouted, put off at the spur in front of the green backyard at exactly 6:19.

Today she is facing the track, waiting. As Nathan walks across the crisp grass toward her, he could reflect on coincidence versus choice, on how his judgment—always an anchor—has left him each evening, like the fog of breath diffusing in autumn air.

But he will only think of this later, reflect and reflect.

Now he is putting a hand, large and manicured, to her face. The woman reaches her own hand, encased in worn gardening gloves, to meet his, drawing it away from her cheek. Then she turns his soft palm upward, and places in it a small bulb. She closes her gloved hand around his naked one and draws him down toward the punctured earth. They are both on their knees. She tips his hand upside down, releasing the bulb into the ground. Nathan stares down into the shallow hole and thinks of the things he is suddenly aware that the bulb requires: a depth of three inches, a cold bed, a dormant period, spring.

He feels his glasses slide down his nose, but as he reaches to push them up—a gesture so instinctive he normally wouldn't notice it—he feels the glasses being lifted from his face. Nathan, nearsighted but nowhere close to blind, can still make out the smile on the face of the woman beside him. It's a smile that Nathan might call triumphant.

He reaches for her hand that holds the glasses, but he is being pulled away and he cannot make contact no matter how desperate his grasp. He kneels on the train floor, face pressed to the window, and watches, blurrily, as the green lawn retreats from view.

His eyesight is bad enough that it will be difficult for him to drive out of the parking lot, over the highway and onto Manor Court, but not so bad that he could not see the readout on his Smartphone, should he wish to check. But he doesn't. He knows what it says.

"Something different about you today, Nathan?" The director looks at Nathan over the tops of his glasses, and not unnervingly from underneath as he did yesterday.

"Contacts."

"Ah."

It's Thursday. There is work to be done. The minister, as Nathan had promised he would, did make the speech word for word as it had been crafted. But in his haste to appease the angry autoworkers, he had delivered his conciliatory message early, before receiving the final go-ahead from cabinet office. Which meant that while the minister was promising renewed investment in the province's auto plants, his government had been in the process of reversing their strategy and deciding to rescind their promised millions. Overnight, the minister had been demoted to the backbench and a new minister appointed. The director and Nathan were now charged with creating a strategy that looked like the premier was following through on the old minister's promises, while relieving the government of all its financial obligations.

The day is built on the adrenalin of correction. Nathan does not stop for lunch. He drinks one coffee instead of three and coasts on the urgency of the task, fed by frantic calls from cabinet office. When the first round of the new communications rollout is approved by Nathan, then by his director, and handed off to the minister's office, the director insists that Nathan knock off early.

Stomach filled with a panini eaten on the way to the station, Nathan feels fine. Robust. Weighty and important and himself. So when Nathan arrives at the station in time to walk directly onto the platform for the 6:02, he thinks, Why not? That nonsense of the past few days is over. Put it down to the busyness of the transition, the moving, the things left in boxes. And if he has been somewhat forgetful, dropped a few things in his general confusion getting used to the new commute, what of it?

Everything is settled now. Tonight, he will take the 6:02 and he will take it by choice. There! He will use his time effectively, answering all the e-mails and calls that have accumulated over the course of the day.

Nathan sits defiantly by the window. He scrolls through his mail and answers it, picking away at the keyboard with his thumbs, through the first two additional, scheduled station stops. And now the train pulls onto the spur at, Nathan has to note, exactly 6:19.

The yard is empty. Green and square and entirely uninhabited. And Nathan feels no relief, only calm. Of course the yard is empty! Why wouldn't it be? Why would a woman stand in that yard, each day at the same time? It had been silly to be unhinged by it all. It was a bump on the sidewalk. A little stumble in an otherwise straightforward hike. That's all. His entire gravitational force wasn't being realigned!

Nathan is pleased to find he can laugh at himself. He looks up with confident good will, a deep intake of breath. He wants to share a look with someone, a "Gosh, pulled over on the track again" look, perhaps a "My, what can you do?", a "Working on the way home again, eh? What a life, what a life" look. Nathan turns from the window, searching for the eyes of one of the other commuters, stopped along with him on the spur as the other train passes.

Sitting in the seat diagonally across from him, her auburn hair covering her face, is the woman. She is wearing a black sweater with sleeves that come halfway up her bronze arms and a skirt bordered in embroidered roses.

Nathan's heart jerks about like a pinball, freed of muscle and sinew and bumping through the territory of his chest. He closes his eyes, turns his head and opens his eyes again on the green yard, the red leaves, the vine snaking up through the chain-link. He ducks his head and looks upward on an angle at the woman. She is still there. Any minute, she will look across the aisle at him.

Nathan lifts his briefcase into his lap and pulls it across his rib cage so hard that he presses the backs of the buttons on his shirt into his skin. He spins himself into the aisle and bangs down the stairs to the train's middle level, then leaps down the three steps to the first floor in front of the door.

"Sir?" says the operator standing at the intercom. "Can I help you?"

"I need to get off!"

"I'm sorry sir, this isn't a station stop. We're just waiting for the other train to pass. Do you need medical attention?"

"No!" Nathan's voice sounds thin and high to his own ears.

"The next station stop is only five minutes away, sir."

Yes! He can get off at the next station. He doesn't have to be stuck on this train, with that woman. He could get off, pull himself together. Sit down somewhere cool and green. Nathan looks out the closed door into the empty garden. He feels himself standing at its centre. Then the artificial green of the passing train breaks through the image like a screen being torn.

Nathan jabs a finger into the rubber weather-stripping between the doors. "I need to be on the other train! That train!" The 6:13 shakes the 6:02, stopped on the track, making it absorb its passing energy.

"Oh, not to worry! We're headed the same way. You'll end up exactly where you were going." The operator puts his hand on Nathan's shoulder and eases him into a seat by the door. "Can I get you some water?"

Nathan closes one hand over the other, feeling for the identifying terrain of rounded fingernails, the sparse hair below his knuckles, the raised relief of his wedding ring. They're all there. And indeed, the train has begun to pull away. Nathan feels the motion lift him forward like a swing, predictable and reassuring, toward home. Any second it will be 6:20. This moment will have passed.

Nathan sees the backyards accelerate to a blur, then become distinct and separate again as the train pulls into the next stop.

The doors open. Cool air rushes into the compartment. The conductor stands back and a dozen or so people walk out onto the platform. Nathan keeps his eyes straight in front of him, his back upright against his seat, looking toward the door, narrowing his vision to a stream of coat pockets and purses. He's almost on his way.

A thin brown hand reaches into his sightline. It is holding a Smartphone and the mailbox open on its screen is Nathan's.

"This is yours, isn't it?" The woman's voice is breathy, with a melodious undertone, a summer breeze moving through wind chimes.

Again, Nathan palms his hands in his lap, exploring their topography. Then, as if jumping into deep water, he lets go and sinks his right hand into his pocket where he keeps his Smartphone. It is empty.

"You dropped it." The woman jiggles the Smartphone in front of him, urging him to take it. The descending tones of the warning bells signal that the doors will be closing.

Nathan grabs the Smartphone with his free hand. He feels the coolness of her rough skin transfer onto his.

"Go," he says. "Go. Don't miss your stop."

The woman hesitates, then pushes through the closing doors. It hardly seems long enough for her to dismount the steps, but the train moves steadily away.

Only when they are travelling at full speed again does Nathan look down at his Smartphone. The screen is frozen. He cannot switch between applications or refresh his mailbox. In the top right corner the readout persists: 6:19.

Friday is not beginning well. The power is out in the new house and Nathan, accustomed to the additional alarm on his Smartphone, sleeps on. He is dreaming of planting bulbs at midnight by miner's light in the October muck of their front yard.

"Nathan! What are you doing? Nathan!" Belinda's voice bites into his dream. "We slept in!"

Which means that Nathan has slept in and not, as usual, as always, awoken Belinda and launched her into her morning routine of scented creams and hair straightening.

Because it is too late for Nathan to get a parking spot, they take Belinda's car to the station. As he drives, Belinda curls her eyelashes while looking in the passenger side mirror. When he checks over his right shoulder before changing lanes, Nathan has a glimpse of the eyelash curler making a cage across his wife's face.

"You know, I've been thinking," he says, "that next year it would be nice to have a little garden out front. Something colourful and maybe one of those things that the flowers climb up."

"What do you mean? A trellis? An arbour?"

"Yeah, well, something like that."

"Oh, Nathan, that's charming." Belinda laughs indulgently, and Nathan has a terrible feeling that later this morning his words will be repeated to colleagues and underlings. "But the front of the house needs stones."

"Stones? You mean like gravel?"

"No. Like rocks, honey. And small trees. Probably two kinds of Japanese maple. And an evergreen for four-season interest."

"All right, we'll put the flower bed in the back."

"Uh-huh. All that work and then we'll be gone long before it looks decent."

Nathan takes the turn into the station parking lot with more caution than necessary. "Where will we be?"

Belinda smiles and pats his thigh. "Just—somewhere else." She flips the mirror shut. "You can pull up right here."

Nathan drives up to the kiss-and-ride and Belinda steps out.

"Remember," she says as they exchange positions, "we have the decorator coming at eight. I'll pick you up right here at seven-thirty."

At the doors to the station he turns back to watch her, vision not quite sharp through an old pair of glasses he had found at the bottom of one of the remaining moving boxes. He sees how her hair swings into a blunt line as she backs out of her place by the curb, navigating around the lineup, cutting into the traffic without a wait. Heading to her office in the city's north end. A place, Nathan realizes, he has never seen and can't even picture.

The latte he buys while he waits for the train spills on his pants in a spot the jacket will not cover. And when he arrives at the office—later than usual but still before the influx of his underlings—his security card is denied and he must wait in the hall until the first of his speech-writers arrives.

"Bitch about Jack, isn't it?" Linda says, sliding her card through the slot. Nathan notes that her lack of niceties, while offensive in personal situations, may be just what makes her a ministry favourite. On-message, that's what Linda is.

"Thanks, Linda," Nathan says, stepping through the open doorway.

"But what can you do? He did jump the gun, giving the minister his speech early. I can see their point. I mean, you don't give a guy like that anything to say until he's well and truly authorized to say it."

So the morning and the early afternoon are about simultaneously juggling rumours of Jack's dismissal, trying to carry out the work Jack left behind and hoping that no one draws the parallel between Nathan's trip to the conference centre and the former minister's gaffe. Nathan stares at the once-familiar approvals form and wonders whether he should leave blank space number 9 on the approvals list or tick it off himself. Nathan scratches at his palms. His assistant, waiting for the folder to be handed back across the desk, reaches over and stops his hand, flipping it over to see the red palm.

"Allergy," she pronounces. "Doing any planting lately?"

"What?"

Monica taps her own callused fingertips against his, and Nathan notes with horror the black lines of dirt under his nails.

"You shouldn't touch bulbs with bare skin. Tulips, crocuses, okay. But not daffodils. And not paperwhites."

Nathan stares.

"Narcissus? Pretty little blossoms, but a bugger on the skin when you plant them. You done with that? Guess it goes straight to the minister, eh? Woo, you just got promoted!"

Really, Nathan would prefer to lie low. To slip out at lunch and find a place that would fix the insistent 6:19 readout on his Smartphone and kick the time forward into evolving minutes and hours and days. But the staff from the new minister's office need someone to go to, and at four o'clock when the new aide to the new minister calls a session to discuss the new strategy, Nathan, hand over latte stain and carrying a notebook and calendar from the supply closet, is the only one to answer the call.

Nathan jiggles his pen under the table while "just a bit of a get-to-know-you" turns into a "brainstorm on strategies to execute a long-term vision" and wonders what Jack would have done under the circumstances. Nathan tries lowering his own glasses on his nose to project a sense of pensive creativity and engaged authority, but all he can see is a blur. What time is it? Nathan leans back in his chair and peers over the shoulder of the minister's parliamentary secretary, who is scrolling through his own messages on his Smartphone.

Almost six!

Nathan shoots out his hand with an exaggerated flourish and reaches into his pocket for his frozen Smartphone. "I must apologize," he says. "I've just received an urgent message from cabinet office."

So tonight, when he has an appointment with the designer, when he must rely on Belinda to ferry him home, Nathan is too late for the 6:02. He is almost too late for the 6:13. He runs up the stairs and onto the platform just as the operator is announcing that the doors will be closing. He jumps onto the train, pulling his briefcase inside, and finds that he has nowhere to move. All the seats, the aisles, the stairway and the space in front of the door are crammed with people. Nathan can feel bodies on all sides of him, but his back is pressed up hard against the door's rubber closure.

The 6:13 does not stop for several stations, till almost the end of the line. Nathan has no hope of getting a seat or even of wiggling his arms free from where they are trapped at his sides. But, pressed up against the doors, held aloft by the other travellers, Nathan feels relief. He is among his fellows. Anchored by their efficiency, their attention to detail over comfort. These are people who are recognized in their lives for their counsel, for their presence. They can't just cut out early or arrive home late. Time is important to them. They are important. And Nathan is once again among them.

The train shudders, but the passengers, held tight against one another, do not fall. It resumes its speed and then lurches again. Nathan feels the vibration of the doors through his back, and senses the train slowing. Then, with a jerk, the train moves to the right and stops.

A groan arises from somewhere in the connected throng and Nathan feels it rumble in his own chest. Another train shoots past.

"Apologies, ladies and gentlemen. We're having a mechanical problem and are awaiting assistance. We thank you for your patience."

Nathan cannot see out. He can see only the faces directly in front of him. Someone coughs and the breath warms Nathan's cheek. Static comes from someone's headphones. In the gathering of people caught before the doorway, someone begins to shake. The spasms vibrate through the pressed bodies so that even Nathan can feel it, out on the edge by the door. The person is thrashing, head going side to side and other bodies move in tandem to avoid it. Someone is shouting, "We need help here!" Is the shouting person the same as the shaking one? Nathan cannot tell. The noise increases and Nathan doesn't know if he is adding to it.

Many minutes pass. Nathan knows that even if his Smartphone were functioning, he would be unable to say how much time has gone by, as it would be impossible to reach down into a pocket or to bring a hand to his face. He wonders if the phone function is still working. Belinda will be waiting at the station. Furious.

The natural light fades. The artificial glow inside the car grows harsh.

Then the doors behind Nathan open abruptly and he falls backward down the step and into the night. Gravel bites into his hip and scrapes his elbow, even through his jacket.

"You okay?" A man in a uniform leans over him.

"Sure," Nathan says.

"That's the way," says the paramedic, and he and his partner swing into the doorway. "Step out please, people. Step out," they call, and the passengers peel out of their cluster, scattering onto the gravel around Nathan.

Nathan pulls himself to a standing position and finds that his ankle is tender. He lifts the weight off it. Shakes it a little to the side.

The light from the train windows and the open door spills out beside the spur. Around Nathan, the people

murmur. "They're taking forever . . ." "Must be serious . . ."
"Can I borrow your phone? I'm out of battery . . ."

The men are coming down the steps now, carrying a figure on a stretcher onto the dark road and over to the ambulance, which, Nathan sees now, is parked at the end of an unused service road, under a burned-out streetlight. Nathan watches the ambulance pull away, throwing its blue beam momentarily across the houses lined up along the track, then filling his view like a sunburst.

Nathan is temporarily blinded. He pulls his glasses up and presses his hands to his eyes. But sketched across his retinas, like a photographic negative, is the outline of three yards, each with a small bungalow in the top. To one side of the image, a white car sits on blocks. At the far side, thin white lines define a bare, square clothesline. The yard in the centre is an open field of glowing white, a fence around the perimeter.

Nathan drops his hands and blinks. He looks at the ground and shakes his head. He searches to his left and right for the reassuring faces of his fellow passengers. But there is no one there.

The train doors are closed. Inside, bodies are jostling and bending, finding a place to fit in the crowded car. He takes a step toward the door he dropped from, but his sore ankle slows him down and he drags his foot through the gravel. When he reaches the step he leans in to knock against the door. He knocks. Knocks again.

Nathan feels a rumble through his leather soles, travelling up through his body, past his tender ankle and into his upper extremities. A train is bearing down the main line. Nathan tucks his neck into his collar and braces himself for the expulsion of air as it passes. But the headlight is veering off now, coming toward the spur, directly for the sidelined train. Any second, the trains will collide. Nathan scrambles backward, as quickly and as far as his ankle will allow, until he feels the ground drop down, into a small ditch.

Nathan hollers a warning, but his voice is drowned out by the coming train. He tenses his body for the crash. But instead he hears the small thud of the cars connecting, like the latch dropping on a garden gate.

The grass in the ditch whispers. Nathan's ankle throbs. He thinks that the distance between the ditch and the train is one that he doesn't care to walk.

The newly added engine pushes the train. Jolts it. Jolts it again. Nathan steps tentatively, testing the weight on his ankle. The pain is less than he had expected. Certainly not too much to bear. But now he feels his pressed shirt collapse against his body like a man sinking into a comfortable couch.

The train chugs forward again. Nathan's limbs grow heavy, as if he has swum a great distance, or has rolled over in bed after a particularly satisfying night of making love.

The train picks up speed. The door Nathan fell from moves away, then another door passes, then another.

Nathan thinks of his briefcase, forgotten on the floor when he fell out of the train. Thinks of it, moving forward without him toward the stop before the end of the track.

The train's last cars are barrelling by, the little squares of light from the windows getting smaller. He should call, Nathan thinks, at least he should call and explain.

He reaches into his pocket. The familiar rectangle and raised keyboard of his Smartphone nestle in his palm. But the screen is dark and shattered. When Nathan pokes at it, the screen crumbles into tiny pieces, like hundreds of shiny seeds.

The train is a pinprick in the darkness. But there, just beyond the ditch, is the fence, vines climbing up through the chain-link.

The screen door is open. The porch light is on.

BECAUSE OF GERALDINE

—

*G*ERALDINE. OUR MOTHER'S lips had formed the name so many times that if I'd been a blind child, I could have read the word in Braille in the lines around her mouth. If my father was nearby, Geraldine was only a whisper, puffed out like the smoke from my mother's menthols, dissipating not long after it met the air. But when we were alone with her, Geraldine took on another form, solid as the jealousies by which she'd been constructed, a person so real she might walk through the door, leave her boots on the mat and take a place at our table.

Don't ask for pie, our mother said. Geraldine was the finest baker, crusts so light and flaky, meringue that hovered like a cloud over sun. Don't even think about a pet. Geraldine was a snake charmer, followed by everything from field mice to forest wolves. And though, as northern children, we might have expected as our birthright a fresh-cut Christmas tree from the forests that surrounded us, we knew our tree would always be artificial—silver from stand to tip—because of those winters when Geraldine had taken my father's hand in her pink mitten and led him to the woods to cut the prettiest evergreen. In our mother's lap, we learned the answer to every question. Venison at Thanksgiving? My father's underwear ironed flat as a pancake? Tulips instead of daffodils? Geraldine, Geraldine, Geraldine.

Gerri Whitehead was the daughter of a logger and a camp cook, who had to get a billet in town if she wanted an education past grade eight. The billet was my father's house, and the school was my father's school, and Geraldine would have been my father's too, if she hadn't taken off his diamond ring and hitched a ride out of town, hadn't quit the North and the whole cold country, to head down south to make it as a singing star.

My father told my mother about Geraldine back in the early days of my parents' courtship. I guess he felt he had to make my mother understand what she was getting: a man who'd years before sent half himself to Nashville, tucked into Geraldine's guitar case like an unfinished song. After those early confessions, my father considered the topic closed, and to us he never spoke a word about Geraldine, or about the town where he'd grown up, and left not long after she'd gone, though we all knew it wasn't far from where we lived now, a distance you could measure with Giddy's baby finger. In our town, he worked the day shift as a foreman at the pulp and paper mill, which to us meant that he wore a shirt that buttoned instead of just the coveralls some fathers wore. Still, day shift and all, our father was a man who was there and not there, and left to our own devices, Lib and Giddy and I, like other female children, might have come up with any number of reasons as to why. But for us there was no need for interpretation. Our mother explained it to us: it was all because of Geraldine.

And whenever the tinny music in the grocery store turned to Country and Western, or someone wore a cowboy costume for Halloween, or even when she was just looking away, with her lips drawn tight across her teeth, we knew that once again she was thinking about what kind of northern girl would head down to America to sing those hurtin' songs, when complaining was only for the soft and the southern, and that where we lived, you just snugged up your gloves and carried on.

That's what our mother did, through those early years of our childhoods, never mentioning the name to our father, keeping a household that functioned with a limited satisfaction of regular meals and church on Sunday and an order and respectability that seemed to meet both my father's and my mother's conditions. And if we saw no signs of outward pleasure between them, we saw no disrespect either, and since that was how it had always been, we must have thought—as children do—that it would stay that way.

At Christmastime, or when Giddy makes the trip up from the city to show off her latest car or man, after Lib puts her babies down, or her bigger kids put the babies down, after Chuck goes down to the basement where he drinks his beer and keeps the score—who's up, who's down—for our marriage, we sisters talk. Maybe we say how we saw Gid in the paper, coming out of court after her client; sometimes we talk about my students; or we wonder why Lib's latest baby sleeps through the night, or doesn't. But when Gid's good wine runs low, and she starts to scroll through her messages on her phone, when Lib rolls her eyes and mutters how some child upstairs is really going to need her soon, then it's time to talk about Geraldine.

We try to figure out how the change began, that summer that Lib was nine and I was eleven and Gid was only six. We each have our variation. Gid figures that our father meant it to happen, the way he left the town paper open that morning to page six, knowing our mother would see it and understand. Lib believes it began as an accident, Dad searching the paper for a good price on lawn fertilizer and finding it in an ad opposite the events listings. Why then, I always say, didn't he just close the paper and put it back on the bench in the hall, where later my mother would turn only to the coupons?

It's thirty years on, but once we begin, there's no stopping it until we come to the end. Just like it did that June morning when our mother read, *Appearing at the Legion Hall, August 21st: that sweet singing sensation, Geraldine.*

"You might as well know now, girls: your father has decided that we won't be going East."

I stood with the dishtowel in mid-air, but my mother shook the wet plate at me, insisting that, whatever our disappointment, there was to be no break in our routine. It was the first Monday in summer, the time when vacation officially began. It was almost eight o'clock at night, but outside on the street we could hear children playing.

Libby stopped sweeping. "What do you mean?"

"I mean, little miss, that your father has said that this year, he doesn't want pink lemonade in crystal glasses, or children who fight in the back seat of the car, or ladies who need to shop every living second. By which he means he doesn't want a vacation. By which he means he isn't going. And so, neither are we."

Every summer we could remember, we took the two weeks at the end of July that the mill shut down and went to visit my mother's parents. My mother would fill the cooler with sandwiches and my father would pack the Impala with suitcases and we would drive three days, stopping at night in motels, watching the rock recede, replaced by asphalt and concrete, until we reached the city and the verandas and the trimmed hedges that meant we'd crossed the border into our mother's childhood from our own.

My grandparents were the kind that tousled hair and presented cheeks for kisses, that waved from the parlour window before our mother took us on a circuit of department stores each morning and every afternoon to experience the exotic chemicals of a municipal pool. Inside, my father would drink his beer from a glass instead of a bottle and marvel at the number of television channels, and, ten days later, we'd reverse ourselves like a magnet of the opposite polarity and go home to show off our worldliness to our friends.

"But what about first-day-of-school outfits, and new bathing suits and good shoes?" Lib said.

"We'll order them from the catalogue, Elizabeth," my mother said.

"It isn't fair," Lib said, and she kicked the doors beneath the counter.

From the corner where she was playing Barbies, I heard Giddy start to cry. Our mother added some more hot water to the wash. The dishes she was stacking in the rack still had soap bubbles on them. She stared at the cupboards in front of her as if the window she had always wanted there had suddenly opened up.

I didn't plan what I said then, I just wanted her to look at me. "Mother?" I said. "Mother, is it because of Geraldine?"

Libby stopped kicking and sat down on the floor. Giddy stopped crying and stood up.

When our mother turned to me, it was with a slow and deliberate sweep, as if she were holding something she was determined not to let fall. The look she gave me made me wish I'd never said it and it made me wish I could have the chance to say it again. I knew even then that it was a look that should pass between two adults, instead of from a mother to a child. It was the look of someone who believes herself understood.

"Could I take Lib and get her out of your hair?"

Lib swears that's how I said it, as if I were the solution to all her problems and not just another one of them. The aisles of the Red & White were full of strangers, loading up on marshmallows and charcoal and ice.

"Fine," Mother said, and Lib looked at me with eyes like SuperBalls, amazed at how easy it had been. But partway down the aisle, she called us back. "Take Giddy with you. I'll meet you outside in twenty minutes."

The parking lot was full of the evidence of summer people: campers and station wagons with roof racks.

"Hurry up," Lib said, as I bent down to lift Giddy onto my back.

The only record store in town was Mysner's Music, run by an old guy with a pipe and big eyebrows. Mother had brought us there only once, the time she bought the soundtrack to *Brigadoon*, while we stood obediently beside her, not even reaching out to finger the yellow centres for 45s.

Lib pulled open the door and out came something orchestral, with trumpets and strings announcing our arrival.

"Stay here," I said to Giddy, setting her in front of the rack of postcards that every store in town put out come summer. She spun it and it squeaked. Mr. Mysner looked up from his paper.

"Hello," I said, giving him my best big-sister wave, and he went back to reading.

There were three sections in the store: a small one up front for 45s, then the LPs, divided into CLASSICAL and OTHER, which were sorted alphabetically. It was just a few summers after Woodstock, but Baez and Dylan, and even the Beatles, were tucked in with the Mormon Tabernacle Choir and Nana Mouskouri.

It was only when we were standing in front of the lettered rows that Lib and I realized we didn't know Geraldine's last name. "You start at Z, I'll start at *A*," I said, so it was me that found her. She was under *G*, for

Geraldine, of course. As if she were the only Geraldine there ever was. As if we should have known. As if she wanted to make it easy for us.

The face that took up the whole cover of *It's Too Late Now*, was different from any I'd ever seen in person or in pictures. She had hair the colour of red granite, but thick and cascading, and her face was a palette—deep blue eyeshadow, thick mascara, flushed cheeks—a style that I would emulate all my teenage years.

Lib pushed up close beside me now. "I knew she'd look like that," she said, and what she meant was, like someone from somewhere else, like she was a star.

"I want to see," Giddy said.

Lib and I shushed her, as if Geraldine were forbidden to everyone, not us alone.

Then Gid reached into the rack and pulled out a second album that we hadn't seen. On the front was Geraldine on stage, guitar on her lap, bathed in a pink spotlight that made her hair a halo.

"Who is it?" Giddy asked.

"That's Geraldine," I said. "That's the lady Daddy loved."

Gid's mouth opened wide.

"Look, baby," Lib said. "If you ever tell anyone you saw this, I will take your Beary Bear, dip him in peanut butter and leave him in the big park for the real bears to eat."

Gid's face started to crumple toward a wail, but her eyes stayed on mine.

"Shut up, Lib," I said. "Just buy it. We have to go." We'd pooled our allowance and Lib's birthday money to get the full $4.95.

"But I want this one," Giddy said, holding up *The Road That's Left Ahead.*

"You don't have any money," Lib said.

"I do. I can get it from Mommy."

"No! No Mommy. This is just a sister thing," I said.

"I'm a sister, and I want this one."

Mr. Mysner had his elbows on the counter now and was staring at us.

Lib shrugged. Really, we had no idea what was on either of them.

"Giddy," I said, getting down on my knees. "Listen very carefully. This is our secret, okay? You must promise never to tell. Got it?"

Giddy pressed the record to her like a hostage. "This one."

"Never. Not anyone."

Gid nodded.

She carried the album to the counter and held it while Lib paid. Which was how *The Road That's Left Ahead* wound up between my shirt and Giddy's tummy on the way back to the grocery store, and behind Lib's back in the car, and how we left *It's Too Late Now* behind.

—

That was the summer we began to notice other things. How the air in July smelled different with the mill closed, breezy and clean, a smell I'd always associated with other places, rest stops on the highway between our town and our grandparents' city, places where no one we knew ever lived. Floating on it were unfamiliar notions. Ideas like happiness and a woman's right to it were arriving along with yogourt makers and university boys who came in camper vans to plant trees and sometimes never went back. One of them had moved into the Dooleys' house and was living there, bare-chested, with the kids and the mom and the dad both, and sometimes there was a flowery smell that Lib and I attributed to lentils and dehydrated fruit. That was the year Douglas Banting sneaked *The Joy of Sex* out of his parents' closet and left it in the woodpile, charging 25 cents to show it to the other boys and showing it for free to any girl who was brave enough to look.

More interesting to us were the changes we sensed in our own house that season. Like how a dirty ring from Gid's bath stayed stuck to the side of the tub for two days. How I began to wake up, not knowing what had disturbed me, to see the house lights on past midnight, past one, past two. How one morning my father left without putting out the garbage, so our mother did it, and just an hour later backed into the can on our way to the library, scattering potato peelings and toilet paper rolls and a whole pot-load of burnt spaghetti into the street.

But bedtime for Giddy still came at eight-thirty and for Lib and me at nine, the sun coming through the patterned curtains that our mother had made on her Singer, the same way she'd made the tablecloths for the dining room, where we ate our meals inside, not from the barbecue, in the yard, the way we heard our neighbours doing through the fence that our father had put up last year. And every day, even in summer, our mother served us hot lunch right at noon: defrosted vegetables, casserole and cooked pudding for dessert. We were still that kind of family.

Most days, after we'd helped her with the dishes, we'd swing open the screen door, cracking the seal on our recognizable selves, and go around the corner to the Langs', to listen to Geraldine and play the game.

Mrs. Lang was the kind of mother who would buy Freshie and let you make it yourselves, without supervising the sugar. Some days, she'd lie in the yard and tan to a dark brown, a bottle of 50 beside the chaise lounge. But most afternoons she'd say, "Kids, there's just nothing here for dinner. I'm going to run in to the store. You'll be fine, won't you, till I get back?" Even before that summer, Lib and Giddy and I had revelled in the freedom of this neglect. So, naturally, we went to the Langs' to play *The Road That's Left Ahead*.

Carrie and Pete Lang had no particular interest in country music, but they loved a conspiracy as much as any children. That first July afternoon, it was Carrie Lang who put the album on the turntable and lowered the needle, but when Geraldine's voice rolled into the living room, pushing before it a wave of sweat and sorrow foreign as a mirage, we all got up and danced to "Blue and You" and "Can't Hardly Believe." Then came the ballads, and while Carrie Lang held up an invisible gown and waltzed like Cinderella, I tried to imagine how all those bad things could have happened to someone as beautiful and lucky and loved as Geraldine.

"Play it again," Lib said, when the record was over. We were lying in the middle of the Langs' rug, very still, as if we could hear her better that way.

"This is boring," Pete Lang said.

"Yeah," Giddy said. "Cath, I want to go out and play."

"Later, okay, Giddy?" I said. Keeping Giddy happy had become a major occupation for me. "Please."

Then Carrie shoved one speaker up under the window and turned the volume up. "Come on," she said. In the backyard, she climbed on the picnic table that said it was property of the provincial park. "I'm Geraldine," she said. "And you're my fans. So, dance!" She held a pine cone to her mouth and when there was no singing, she strummed an imaginary guitar.

Pete and Giddy ran round the yard in circles, cartwheeling and somersaulting, and Lib bounced up and down between the table and the shed. I clapped along, but only when Carrie stopped shaking her hair and pointed at me.

"My turn!" Lib said, but by then the songs were slow again. So Lib stuck her thumb out. "I'm Geraldine on the highway," she said, and Carrie had to be a talent scout that found her there and drove the picnic table all the way to Nashville. And so, over the weeks, with Geraldine's voice in the background, we played out all the stories we knew, until, after a while, we added to them, and changed them, and forgot to play the record at all, until Geraldine's voice was only Carrie's voice, or Lib's voice, or my own.

"We need more songs," I said to Lib, thinking that's what the matter was, the reason for the strange feeling that surged in my stomach each afternoon, a little bit sick and a little bit exhilarated, like the way I'd felt so many afternoons last summer, spinning and spinning then watching how the yard blurred and tilted and finally righted itself. So, when our grandparents sent a package to our mother in the mail, filled with hair ribbons and books and shoes that almost fit and five dollars for each of us, we went back to Mysner's. But the Geraldine record was gone.

—

Though it was my father who'd decreed we stay home, it seemed he was the one who'd gone away. During the two weeks the mill was closed, he kept to his regular schedule, dressing and eating breakfast by seven and leaving the house at eight, with a lunch he'd packed the night before. At dinners, unless we asked a question right to him, he kept his eyes on his hands or his shirt front, like his head was still bowed for grace, until dessert was over and he said, "Thank you, Sarah, for the meal."

Every night when I beat Lib at checkers while Gid was in the bath, he never once leaned over and asked, "Are you sure, Lisbeth, that you want to make that move?"

It was after one of Lib's losses, when she was picking up the checkers she'd thrown before our mother caught her, that I saw Dad in the yard pushing the lawn mower, then stopping to lean against the handle before he started up again. I counted three or four pauses like that, before he left the mower in the centre of the yard and sat down on the bench, looking away from the house and out toward my mother's begonias.

"Dad?" I said, going out to him. "Dad?" The new grass clippings were damp and prickly against my feet. He was rubbing his hand back and forth across his face.

Sweaty and sticking up that way, little patches of skin showed between his tufts of hair. "Dad?" He startled. "It's okay, Dad," I said. "It's me. It's Cath."

I wanted to make it make sense, my father sitting in the yard like that, doing nothing, just staring into space. I wanted him to have a purpose. "Would you like—?" I searched for a prop that would make it all right. A beer? The paper? But what I wanted to know was if I was welcome. If he wanted my company. I thought about how to say that.

"No," he said. "But thank you."

"Where's Daddy?" Lib said.

It was an early August evening, the mill had started up again and Lib and Gid and I were at the table, napkins unfolded on our laps. They were paper, not cloth like at my grandmother's table, and we had juice instead of wine, but we understood the sanctity of these things. Our places at the table never altered, our hands were washed without our being asked, no fork was picked up till my mother was seated. Above all, there was timing. My mother's shifts at home had the time-clock regularity of my father's at the mill. At six o'clock, we were to begin supper.

"Where's Daddy?" Lib said again. My mother didn't answer.

She didn't answer at quarter after six, either, when

Giddy said, "I'm hungry." She just sat, hands folded in her lap, staring at the mantel clock.

I could smell the roast beef, sitting out of the oven on the stovetop. The minute hand moved toward half past. At six-thirty, I would speak, I decided. But who would I speak for? I could defend my father, I thought, at twenty minutes after. Find a way to make some gentle excuse on his behalf. It would be an exaggeration, if not an outright lie, because I could think of no reason, really, he could be late. The mill had never kept him overtime without enough warning for him to call and say so. But it would be okay, I figured, because my excuse would be forgotten when Dad walked in the door and gave his own, perfectly plausible, reason.

I could defend my mother, I decided by twenty-five minutes past. She looked more tired than she had when Giddy was a baby with colic. I didn't know what could be making her that way, but I wanted it to stop. I'd tried to keep my sisters' fighting to a minimum and was doing extra chores around the house, like bringing in the laundry from the yard and folding it into baskets, trying to erase the purple ditches under her eyes. She needed that help, I could tell. Last week, she'd left the sheets on the line for three days, and then it stormed and they had to stay out another two days to dry again.

My father should have been at the table on time. We all should have been at the table. And we were. My sisters and I were. And we were hungry. I should say so, I decided, as the hand approached the halfway point. I should say that we should go ahead and eat.

The front door opened. We three girls turned and saw our dad walk into the dining room and pull out his chair. Our mother kept her eyes down, as if she were examining a stain spreading across her lap. But when he sat, she sprang out of her chair as if thrown out by his weight.

"Where have you been?" she shouted. Her arms and neck seemed cartoonishly out of proportion, like she could reach across the tablecloth all the way over to the salt and pepper shakers at the centre.

"Thinking," Dad said, not like an excuse or an apology, just like it was that simple.

"Thinking?" My mother yelled it back at him. "It's a little late for that, Hugh. It's a little late for that!"

My father folded his napkin beside his plate and got up from the table without meeting my mother's eyes. He walked away from us, one shoulder lower than the other, as if he were pushing a door that wouldn't open.

Our mother followed him, arms dangling on either side of her apron. And Giddy and Lib and I went too, her anger a vacuum we couldn't resist.

"Fine! Go!" she said to his back, which was retreating down the hall. "You're not listening anyway. What would it take to get you to listen, Hugh? What could I say to you? Or perhaps you'd like to hear me sing it!"

And then, that's what she did.

"Now's a little late for chasing second chances
It's a little late for turning back, when you left my hope
*   behind*
It's a little late for talking with our lovers' voices
So, my love, you best keep walking on
It's too late now . . .

"What do you think, Hugh? You think I have a career ahead of me? Maybe I should leave tonight!"

But it was my father who scooped the car keys off the hall table. None of us followed him to the door, but we heard the car back out of the driveway, the muffler bumping against the curb.

My mother pulled a cigarette from her apron pocket and lit it and breathed in deeply. Then she turned and walked up the stairs, her former good posture restored. Halfway up, she looked back at the three of us—Lib and me standing side by side and staring, Giddy pressed up behind us, her face poking through but her eyes squeezed shut—and then she turned and kept climbing, as if there was nothing to say that would make sense, or maybe as if she thought she didn't need to explain to us at all.

Lib and Giddy and I stayed like that, pressed together, for a long time. And maybe because I didn't have the fortitude to figure out what it all meant, I thought about how my mother was a passable singer for "Abide With Me" and "The Old Rugged Cross" and "Rock-a-Bye

Baby," but that she squawked like Lib blowing air against a blade of grass when she was doing Geraldine.

The next morning, my father was back at the breakfast table at seven-thirty, eating porridge with us before his shift. "Whoa, Cathy," he said to me. "Easy on the sugar."

Lib laughed and kicked me under the table. But I wasn't fooled. If we could act like nothing had happened now, what did it mean about the other days? Days that had looked just like this?

New things were being introduced to us, but my child's experience told me they were being dangled in front of us just so that something else—something much better, something we were already holding—could be taken away. My mother began to talk about "opportunities," decent schools and ballet classes. Things our mother had had, growing up. Things it would really be a shame to miss. Things, apparently, you could only get in the city. I looked at my legs scabbed from mosquito bites and Lib's "outside pants" with the knee worn through. Gid went to the slipperiest part of the floor and did a little turn. "That's right," our mother said. "You'll love it."

At the Langs', we caked Gid's face in makeup, calculating that it would be less horrifying if our mother saw unscrubbable traces of lipstick on the baby than on the big girls. Giddy would sit completely still while we brushed her hair and put on Mrs. Lang's rouge, but lost interest the minute we were through, surrendering the starring role to someone else.

Over the afternoons of early August, Lib developed the storylines for her part: the hard life Geraldine was leaving behind, the logging camp with mean men and bad food. Her scripts now required more stops at roadside bars to prove her talent. "And you say, 'Gerri Whitehead is not the name for a star.' Say it, Cathy."

Only my scene ever stayed the same. I was Geraldine at the lake, accepting a proposal from the man I loved, the backdrop familiar not just to Gerri Whitehead, but to me. The clear water, the dropping hawks, the smell of cedar.

Because Pete was the only boy, it fell to him to give the line "Will you marry me, Geraldine?" and put the plastic ring on my finger. His efforts varied, depending on his mood. Once, he'd buried the ring under the picnic table so he could discover it like treasure. And another time he wrecked the whole thing by saying he'd love to marry me, but he was off to Nashville to become a singing cowboy.

And then one day, after Geraldine said "Yes, oh yes," he brought his face up close to mine, eyes closed. There was Cracker Jack on his breath and a dirty line between his nose and his top lip.

I shoved him back by the shoulders. "What are you doing, Petey?"

"Kissing," Pete said. "That's what getting-married people do."

It wasn't just the idea of letting Pete Lang's lips meet mine that unnerved me—the next summer I would kiss Carl Tanner not once, but five times—it was the sudden realization that he was right. It was impossible and inevitable, all at once. The closest I had ever seen my father come to my mother was when he offered her his arm if the church parking lot was icy. But at the lake that day, and maybe on other occasions, our father had kissed Geraldine. Had my mother ever kissed a man on the edge of a lake? I wondered. I'd never thought about it before. Our mother wasn't in our game at all.

It was the second half of August. The leaves on the maple in the yard had already crisped and curled. When our bedroom lights went out at nine, no light came in through the curtains.

While Giddy and Lib slept, I'd hear our mother talking on the phone to her family. I listened for clues to my parents' sadness, but it was all details: train tickets and deadlines for school enrolments. During the day, I'd look at the things that surrounded me, trying to make myself experience how I'd feel when I was missing them. But I couldn't. Maybe I wouldn't miss them at all, I thought. Maybe, when you left something, that's how it stayed. Just: left. Maybe only those things that were left behind felt sad. Maybe our father would feel it too. And I tried to imagine what it would be like to be his second biggest regret.

Years later, when there were no more Geraldine records, when it was hard to find anyone who'd even kept the old ones, I realized that there must have been some trouble in her life to make her drive up north to play a Legion Hall, a Tuesday night in August. But those were questions for an adult mind. Adults like my mother, who stared at the entrance, saw that there was still no lineup half an hour before the show, and wondered why we were stopped at the door.

"No minors," said the man taking tickets.

Our mother looked over her shoulder, but the cab had already pulled away. By then, the family car was out of the driveway so often that sometimes the chalk drawings could stay for a day or two without being smeared by tires.

"They'll be perfectly behaved. I'll insist on it," mother said, as if the problem was our lack of manners and not the liquor licence.

The man laughed and flipped open an ink pad. "Oh, go ahead, lady," he said, stamping a red star on each of our hands. "By the time the Mounties get here, they'll *be* eighteen."

It was hard to make out mother up ahead in the dark,

so I reached for Lib's hand. There were still a lot of open tables against the wall, even close to the front. Our mother picked one halfway back from the stool and the microphone stand. On the wall beside us were medals and pictures of old men with Remembrance Day wreaths. In front of us, a woman nuzzled her boyfriend's neck.

"I can't see," said Giddy.

"There's nothing to see yet," Mother said, but she put her on her lap.

Mother was wearing the blue dress that she wore when one of us had a birthday. Something made me reach out to touch her hair, piled on top of her head in a bun. It was sprayed and didn't move.

"Don't fidget, Cathy," she said, and her face, too, seemed fixed solid.

Other people were coming in, but we could only see their silhouettes because now the lights were on at the front and most of the people crowded up in the dark near the bar. The man at the table behind us saw Lib watching him.

"Hello there, gorgeous," he said. "I don't believe I've seen you here before."

Mother turned and the man slid back on his chair and into the shadows.

And then Geraldine sat down at the mike. She was small. So small that the bigger girls in my grade six class could have worn her lacy shirt and long skirt, though inside them she had a woman's breasts and hips, the neckline just low enough to show a crush of cleavage as she leaned over her guitar and strummed. There was no pink light, there was no band, but when Geraldine took hold of the mike and said, "Could I have a little more guitar in the monitor, please?" Lib and I looked at each other and grinned.

We didn't know the first few songs. Maybe, I thought, they were from *It's Too Late Now*. Around us, silhouetted heads bobbed in time. The woman and man in front of us got up to dance, and for some time I watched them with as much fascination as I did Geraldine. I'd never seen people dance like that before, looking into each other's eyes, except when I was very young and went to my mother's cousin's wedding. *You were mine*, Geraldine sang, *Oh, all that time that you were mine*. People clapped and the guy behind us whistled.

"Thank you, Sugar," Geraldine said, and I heard my mother sniff.

At the end of every song, I turned away from Geraldine to sneak a look at my mother. She didn't clap. She kept her arms around Giddy, who was almost asleep.

But when Geraldine began to sing the songs that Lib and I had danced to in the Langs' yard, I forgot that I was sitting next to my mother. I closed my eyes and mouthed the words. I opened my eyes again. Geraldine was smiling out into the dark. I wondered what she could see, who she might be smiling at, and then I closed my eyes again. *You promised me,* Geraldine sang, and I forgot myself and joined her, seeing first the talent scout and the picnic table and the lake that I had imagined looking out on, beyond the Langs' basketball net, and then the real lake and the trees, and the Red & White, and Mysner's, and our yard and all the things that had been ours and wouldn't be any more.

Something thumped against my leg. I opened my eyes but kept singing while I scowled at Lib, until I saw that she was looking over my head at Mother. I turned and my mother's eyes locked on mine. I closed my mouth and clamped my lips shut. At the same moment, Geraldine stopped singing, as if her voice had actually been coming out of me.

"Thank you," she said, while my lips were still pressed together. "You're all so very sweet. It's been pure pleasure to spend this night with you. God bless." She got off her stool and then leaned back to the mike. "There are records here for sale."

Our mother stood and Gid woke up, cranky and with the impression of our mother's collar across her cheek.

"Can we get a record, Mother?" Lib said. "Just for a souvenir?"

"No, you may not," our mother said. "We'll leave that to your father."

That's when we saw him. He was standing with his back to us, behind the whistling man who'd talked to Lib. Just an arm's length away from us, standing in line, waiting for his turn with Geraldine.

Our mother didn't seem at all surprised. Maybe she had seen him all along, had watched him out of the corner of her eye. Or maybe she understood that he wouldn't miss this night, and that our meeting up with him here was inevitable. Or maybe she just sensed him out there in the dark, his longing particular and familiar. But to me, looking at his face that night as he stood in line, my father seemed as much a stranger as any of the other men in the room. And so I wasn't surprised that he didn't notice me and Lib when we came to stand behind him.

To one side of our father's good shirt, we saw Geraldine smile broadly at the whistling man and sign his record. She nodded once or twice, gave a small laugh, and then she reached up to pat him gently on the shoulder. And though he looked slightly embarrassed, he moved on, letting the next person—our father—step up close to her.

"Hugh!" Geraldine said, and she hugged him, her embrace closing around his rib cage and making him lean down to receive it, to let her head press against his cheek, his chin over her shoulder, so we couldn't see his face. "You look so well, Sugar!" And my father's arms stayed around her until she said, "And these must be your beautiful girls."

"Hello," Geraldine said, extending her hand to my mother, "I'm Gerri Whitehead."

"Sarah," my mother said.

And then Geraldine let go of our mother's hand and crouched down, leaving my parents staring at each other across the empty space.

"Aren't you big," she said to Giddy. "You're near as big as me. Here, try these," she said, pulling off her green cowboy boots and losing another inch of height. She picked Gid up under the armpits and stood her in the boots. "See, they almost fit." Gid shuffled around us in a circle.

"Don't you have the loveliest hair?" Geraldine said to Lib. It was true, I saw. She did. In another year or two everyone would say so.

And then she looked just at me. "I saw you, singing," she said, so quietly that even I had to listen hard to hear her. "You're an awfully little girl to know such sad, sad songs.

"Girls, I have something for you," she said then, and she took a record out of the box beside her and signed it to me and Giddy and Lib, but when she stood back up, she handed it to our dad. "Thank you for bringing your family to meet me," she said. And then she touched him on the shoulder, just the way she'd touched the man in front of him, to tell him it was time to move on.

And so our family crossed the empty floor together, walked out the door and into the parking lot.

"Hugh," my mother said. "Will you drive us home?"

"In," my mother said when we pulled into the driveway. "Pyjamas and teeth." And she walked into the house and straight to the kitchen.

I could hear her rubber gloves snap and the water filling the sink. Our father stood at the door, holding the keys in one hand and the door handle in the other.

It seemed like Lib and Giddy and I stood between them for ages, turning first down the hallway toward our mother, then over to our father, as if we were witnessing a life that we wouldn't see, quite like that, ever again. Then our father looked at us, not with empty eyes that forgot who we were but as if he wished he could, and we scrambled up the stairs.

We listened for the front door to close and the car to pull away. But instead, we heard his footsteps, slow and heavy, and then the soft *click* of the double doors to the living room, closing.

Lib and Giddy and I knelt down to look through the wrought iron banister.

Geraldine was singing "Otherwise."

It was a song about regret and longing, about what

people might have been if they had made different choices. It wasn't a song we'd heard before, and though we would come to know it well, we'd never hear it quite the same way again, because over it, we could hear my father sobbing.

And then our mother walked down the hall. She stood for a minute, her fingers resting on the handle, then she pushed the door open and stepped inside. The crying went on and on and on. It seemed that it would never end, but when it did, we couldn't say exactly how it happened, or just when the music stopped, or how long Geraldine had been silent. Because what we heard was our mother's voice, durable and tuneless. A steady, reliable hum.

Over the years, I must have played that record dozens of times, and Lib and Giddy did too. We played the record, and we stayed in town. Our mother's hair grew long and she wore it down and straight, even when she worked at the library. Our parents played bridge with the Langs on Saturdays. Sometimes when there were no babysitters available, they even let us put ourselves to bed.

Our mother never mentioned Geraldine again.

We each have our variation as to why. Gid says it's because our mother realized she'd got what she wanted, and that Geraldine was the one whose life was missing something, hawking her crate of records up and down the highway. No competition, Gid always says.

Lib says that our mother saw something good in Dad that night, a romantic side of him she could claim for her own. They went on dates after that, remember? I think there were dates, she always says.

But I remember something else, something from years later. I remember the first time I moved back home, after I married Chuck. My eyes were so swollen from crying that I could barely see the streets I had to travel to get there, and it was past midnight when I came in. My mother answered the door with a whisper, put a sandwich on the kitchen table in front of me, and then she lit a cigarette. We sat like that for a long time. And then she said, "Everyone has a little hurt inside them, Cathy, that no one can take away."

Gid takes off her spiky heels and tucks her stocking feet up under her. Lib goes up to check on the kids, and when she comes back down she tells us everything is fine. And Lib and Giddy and I, we know that we've said everything we're able to.

Some things are like that, I think. There isn't much, but it bears repeating, so you wring it out, again and again, get everything from it that you can. After that, all that's left are those things that you can't say.

Which is when I put on that album we got more than thirty years ago.

"Sing it," I say. "Sing it, Geraldine."

PRECIOUS

—

KRISTI-ANNE MARTIN WAS the second child of
Gordon and Muriel Martin, a daughter born
seven years almost to the day from the hard
birth that brought her brother Alex into the world. From
the beginning, Kristi-Anne was everything that Alex
wasn't. Kristi-Anne sparkled. Alex was merely greasy.
Kristi-Anne cooed and chimed. Alex rasped like a file
against a metal post. Kristi-Anne's teeth poked through
without the need for gripe water and arranged themselves like seed pearls along the hem of a christening
gown. Alex's teeth fell inward and his face followed, like
a swimmer gasping for air. It seemed that Alex's bones
were never far from the surface. But Kristi-Anne had no
angles. Her entire being seemed to curl: hair into ringlets, lashes upwards. She was a bow and glossy wrapping,

a present her mother could not believe that she had received. And from the moment she first laid eyes on the child, Muriel Martin devoted herself to ensuring that Kristi-Anne would never be snatched away.

This meeting between mother and daughter occurred several hours after Kristi-Anne's birth, in the near sterility of the maternity ward, where Muriel had been installed to sleep off the effects of a particularly potent dose of scopolamine. Waking from that twilight sleep, Muriel had a sense that something significant and unexpected had passed in the time she'd been almost unconscious, something beyond that predictable miracle of pushing new life into the world. There was, at once, a delightful feeling of retreating heaviness, as if someone had lifted a thick blanket off the bed on a warm spring day, and also a terrible dread that something important had been forgotten. But what could that something be?

No sooner had Muriel formed the question than the door to the ward opened, admitting a bassinet, followed by a nurse with lines between her eyebrows that seemed set there by the same iron that had pressed the creases into her uniform. But the old face softened and seemed to glow as she hovered over the bassinet, before she lifted the pink-blanketed bundle into Muriel's arms.

Muriel, too, looked down, and what she saw filled her unpractised soul with awe. Kristi-Anne's skin was already luminous and her infant's hair fluffed up in a

Precious

halo-like crown. She didn't cry, instead emitting a kit-
ten-like sneeze, her little nostrils flaring to reveal passages as pretty as the inside of an apple.

Was the child a reward for something Muriel had
done? She drew aside her hospital gown and fitted the
baby's rosebud lips around her nipple. She had a sense
of connection unlike any she had ever known. No,
Muriel decided, when she lowered the satisfied baby
back into the bassinet at her bedside, this was an investment in her better self, the mother she could be. A loan
against future earnings. And she resolved to make herself a worthy prospect.

When the nurse returned, she was pushing a stainless steel cart bearing a dinner tray. The nurse set the
tray across Muriel's lap, then clutched the side of the
bassinet where Kristi-Anne was sleeping. Muriel
grabbed the other side.

"Dinnertime for Mother is bedtime for Baby."

"No," Muriel said. The word had slipped out of
her with less consciousness than the baby had and her
sudden insurrection caused her pulse to race. She pushed
the tray to the edge of the mattress. "No," she said.

A horrific thought had come upon her: the possibility of child swapping. Ignorant nurses placing Baby
Carlotta in Baby Emily's crib and Mrs. Carlotta and
Mrs. Emily not being any the wiser for years and years,
just wondering why Carlotta was so red-headed and

Emily had a swarthy tone. Or worse, some childless woman—or woman blessed with less of a child (and what child would ever be equal to this one?)—tucking the silent baby into her coat when the night staff were distracted with shift changes and cigarette breaks.

"She's mine," Muriel said, the unbelievability of it echoing in her ears, "and she stays with me." Power rippled through her, like an answer to every bit of wonder the day had yielded, even to the dread she'd felt upon waking. Surely, this was it, she thought—embracing the perfect simplicity of her interpretation and turning away from all other conclusions—that awful feeling had been a warning to not let her guard down, to never again let this child from her sight.

She bent over the side of the bed and lifted the baby awkwardly from the bassinet, a residual dizziness putting her momentarily off balance. "Careful," she scolded herself. She brought her lips close to the baby's delicate ear and whispered again, "Careful, Kristi-Anne," composing her maternal credo, her daughter's lullaby.

From the levelling accommodations of the maternity ward, some infants went to houses with views and housekeepers and the smell of Murphy Oil Soap in the halls, but Kristi-Anne's father's car turned toward the opposite side of town, an area of broken sidewalks, treeless boulevards and lawns the size and colour of Scrabble tiles. It was an unpromising forecast, but Kristi-Anne's infant eyes were not yet capable of the long view, and anyway she kept them closed tight against her mother's car coat, sleeping through the entire ride, even when the car lurched in and out of a pothole. Neither did her ears pick up the little sigh her mother made in her father's direction, which sounded surprisingly like a rebuke.

Driving into the pothole had not been Kristi-Anne's father's fault. Gordon Martin had only been trying to get a look over the top of the blanket at the child who was now a week old, but whom he had never seen, men being barred from the women's floor of the hospital. And though he'd waited many a morning and many a lunch break at the nursery window, Baby Martin had never once appeared for viewing. Even now he was denied a peek, the unexpected intensity of his wife's sigh forcing his eyes back to the road until he pulled up at the curb in front of the house on Weaver Street and pushed open the driver's side door.

By the time he reached the sidewalk, Muriel had already stepped out and across the boulevard and Gordon was left to follow his wife and infant daughter past the curious children with cold fingers playing hopscotch on the sidewalk, up the stairs to the porch that badly needed paint and in through the front door of the house they'd lived in for the past eight years. Gordon trailed Muriel through the living room and, seeing how she did not stop even for old Mrs. Couteau, the babysitter, seeing how she passed by even Alex, their son, who stood up from tracing his battered train in circles around the rag rug to salute her, Gordon too stepped around the ugly little boy and followed Muriel to the kitchen, where she settled herself on a vinyl chair by the radiator and bowed her head to peer into the blankets in her arms.

Gordon felt a jab of air beside him as Alex joined him in the doorway.

"This is Kristi-Anne," Muriel said. "She'll be living with us now."

Where the blankets parted, Gordon caught a glimpse of a perfect cheek before it was beckoned back to his wife's closed breast. Alex stepped forward, but Gordon put a hand onto his son's ridged shoulder, and when the boy turned his out-of-alignment eyes up to his father, Gordon shook his head gently and looked pointedly at the floor, the way you might signal a child not to ask for a second piece of cake.

Muriel did not say, *This is your brother Alex, Kristi-Anne.* Not on this day, and not on any other. Nor did Gordon explain to his bundled daughter that Alex, too, or at least the idea of him, had once held the promise of something wonderful and that this promise had led to an unsettling gift. In the days before Alex's birth, Gordon had decreed to everyone that his first-born son would be christened Alexander. It was the name of

Gordon's great-great-grandfather, the name at the base of the statue in the public square in the better part of town, the name of the man who had launched the family in this new country and had once owned not just the land that their own, rented house stood on, but the land on which their neighbours' houses stood, and the factory, and the churches and all the town. By the time their son had ripped his way into the world, it had seemed too late to alter their decision, and the name had stuck, a constant reminder of the difference between their expectations and Alex's reality.

Certainly the Alex that looked on Kristi-Anne that day did not seem very great. Kristi-Anne opened one china-blue eye and rolled it across his uneven face before it went back again behind her damask eyelid.

If Alex registered his sister's dismissal, it did not surprise him. As a child whose life outside the house fluctuated between being avoided and being taunted, he had learned to make the most of his opportunities to be insubstantial in others' landscapes. If he understood that Kristi-Anne's arrival meant that even here, in his own home, he would now be camouflaged and forgotten, he didn't protest. For Alex had all but forgotten himself at that moment, so focused was he on Kristi-Anne.

She was a pretty baby. He could see that right away, his crooked perspective taking away like puzzle pieces the disparate parts of her that peeped out from her coverings and reassembling them in his mind into a full and visually accurate composite. But what else was she?

He would have liked very much to hold her, to get a sense of her heft. But of course he could not; his mother never set her down—not then and not in the many weeks that followed.

Muriel and Kristi-Anne moved around the house as if they were as tightly joined as when the baby was in his mother's womb. Alex trailed along, wondering how he alone could fail to see the child's magnificence. It was as if something were hidden only from him. Or as if everyone else were looking at something that wasn't there at all.

Careful. Careful, Kristi-Anne.

Listening from outside, you'd never have known there was a baby in the Martin house that winter. Kristi-Anne rarely opened her mouth, except to take in a milky nipple. It was a strange thing, but also fortunate, as the air in the house had a particulate quality. A fine dust settled on the surfaces of that house on Weaver Street, causing her mother to *tch* as she drew cloth after cloth along the sideboard and the table, shaking her head at her husband's sudden zeal for electrical enhancement.

Gordon Martin had previously been content to leave his tools on the floor of whatever job he was working, to come home and plunk himself in front of the radio with a strong cup of Darjeeling. But now he brought home his belt and tool kit, and, as his wife collected the dinner dishes, Gordon set about drilling and sawing, shaking the old family portraits of the founding Martins, phishing lines up through the lath and plaster, and bending them to new and complicated circuitries. The fixtures were an odd assortment that he gathered from various job sites—warehouses, storefronts and the demos of the town's formerly elegant businesses and public buildings—so that an industrial pendant lamp was strung across from a brass sconce adorned with fleurs-de-lis.

All this Alex watched with interest, collecting the bits of blue and red and copper wire his father dropped. Occasionally, his father would hand him a hammer and, upon taking it back again, ruffle Alex's unruly hair. It was almost enough to light Alex's heart. He was at an age when a description of current and voltage would have gone beyond welcome entertainments to reveal themselves as significant connections, for Alex, like all boys, wanted proof that there was something shared between himself and his father. But instead, Gordon just stared into the walls, as if whatever was pressed between them filled him with a vast and secret joy.

And it did. For Gordon, joy pulsed through mortar, across the floorboards and up and over the roof of the little house on Weaver Street, as if a switch had been flicked. All through the flat, accumulating facts of his existence—the prophecy of despair suggested by the twisted child that should have been a source of pride, as the first-born son in an old, though fallen, dynasty; the trickling disappointment of his wife, which ran like an underground stream through their union—Gordon Martin had never given up hope. And on the day that his daughter came home from the hospital, he felt he had been rewarded.

Oh, she was beautiful, startling so, a painting of a child by an Old Master. And she was good, as quiet and as sweet-smelling as a baby of art not flesh. But Kristi-Anne was not the miracle Gordon trembled before. The miracle was in his wife, Muriel. For as she held the baby in her lap in the corner of the kitchen, settled the child against her breast in the worn chair by the radio, shrugged her to her shoulder over the bath, Gordon could see that his wife had been transformed.

Never mind, any more, that it was winter in a house that had small windows, facing north. Or that the rooms were grey, the walls dingy, the paper peeling along the seams, and that bits of calcified kettle lining floated on the tea. Wherever Muriel went with the babe, he felt her new power. That Muriel, so formerly obedient and silent, rarely looked up from the infant didn't faze him. This way, Gordon could look on her without having to meet her eyes, an experience that had, for many years now, left both of them uncomfortable and seeking the anonymity of people who share a space without acknowledging their intimacy. That Muriel had changed her former acquiescence for assertive lobbying on the child's behalf did not bother him. That soon he would be relegated to sleeping on the chesterfield instead of in his own bed did not dismay him. He looked on his small and generally dowdy housewife with something akin to the awe the larger community would soon heap on Kristi-Anne. And also with something more: an ardent, but courtly, love. To Gordon, she was magnificent. The urge to touch this new flush was almost overpowering, but he resisted with the caution taught by years of live wires.

"Is there anything you need, m'dear?" he'd ask, and Muriel would look up at him, distracted, as if searching for his name, and identify instead whatever task she was planning to undertake for Kristi-Anne.

Oh, how he loved her. She would have whatever he could give her. And what he had was light.

No one thought to take a baby out in winter, especially a baby such as Kristi-Anne. But even as the weather warmed, the Martin family stayed inside. Muriel took to ordering her groceries to the door, as if she were a lady from the old Martin house that was torn down to build the factory, gathering the bags from the porch only when the delivery boy had taken the cheque for the previous week's order from the mailbox and hoisted himself back into his truck.

At work, when Gordon Martin was asked about the new arrival, he always gave a favourable report, but he never brought the fellows round to see the child, and the locals began to speculate that the second offspring might be afflicted in the same way as the first. Only Gordon and Alex came to church now, and the congregation gave them a wide berth on the pew.

After several weeks of this hibernation, the curiosity of the neighbourhood women became too great. And so they came to call. They came to witness, and chronicle, the marvel of Kristi-Anne.

Muriel Martin had never been one for entertaining, being equipped with neither the expected social skills nor the teacups. She had only four—a partial set saved from the old house before the wrecking ball—but they were beautiful. Before the birth of Kristi-Anne, she had counted them her greatest treasures. The exterior of each cup was a different rich, deep colour, and all were rimmed in gold. The interiors were white, but each had its own flower: lilies of the valley, violets, snapdragons and bluebells.

Alex had never seen Muriel use these cups, but once a month she would take them from the back of the shelf and submerge them in soapy water. She took such time and care that it seemed she wasn't only washing them of the grease and bugs that accumulated in the cupboard's corners, but repainting the designs themselves. But now that the ladies came, Alex saw her set the cups on the table in the living room, watched at a distance as his mother lifted the blue or pink or green or purple cup to her mouth with obvious pride, answering, between delicate sips, the ladies' questions—How had she felt in her pregnancy? How was Gordon doing at work?—until they enticed her to move Kristi-Anne from her shoulder to her lap, where they could get a look at her.

The day of Mrs. Knox's visit was instantly notable, because four ladies arrived at once. Alex moved unnoticed along the baseboards, wondering how his mother would supply this crowd. Would she drink her tea from one of the rougher ceramic cups they used for everyday, or drink no tea at all? Alex opened the closet door and rolled inside, closing the door behind him. It was dark but he could smell the spring air trapped in the fabric of the ladies' coats.

"I'm so glad you were home, Muriel," said a high and squeaky voice. "I said to her that she really must see her." That was Mrs. Myrna Cotton. When she'd come last week, there had been butter tarts. The pastry had been delicious, but the filling was cooked to an eggy paste.

"It was kind of you to come," said Alex's mother. He heard her shoes as she passed around some sandwiches.

"It really is a blessing. A blessing on the whole community. I was saying so to my Robert last night." Mrs. Gladys Rumford. "I couldn't pass up the opportunity to look in on you again. To see how your stunning girl is doing."

"We're very well, thank you, Glad. I think she's about ready to smile."

"But of course, they change so much from day to day. You really can't know what they'll do." Penny Gordimer, from next door, whose baby boy, Simon, wailed for hours every night, shaking the thin panes of glass and the pebbled siding that separated the houses. "She might seem entirely different in a month or two."

It was quiet until a teacup was set into a saucer.

"I don't know how it's possible, Muriel, but she's more beautiful than she was on Tuesday," said Mrs. Rumford.

Someone cleared her throat.

"God bless her," said Mrs. Gordimer. "God bless her to her piggy toes."

"More tea, Penny?" Alex's mother said. "I see you're already finished your cup. I'll boil some more water."

"That would be lovely, Mrs. Martin."

Alex sat up in the closet, his back stiff against the peeling wall. He had never heard Mrs. Knox's voice outside of Sunday School.

"Oh, Muriel," said Mrs. Cotton. "That's so much work. Don't you want to put that baby down?"

"Thank you, Myrna, but I manage just fine."

From the side of the closet that abutted the kitchen, Alex heard the *click* of the gas and his mother moving dishes.

"It has to be said," said Mrs. Gordimer. "She bears no resemblance to either of them."

"But the milkman isn't pale and blond either," said Mrs. Cotton.

"Myrna!" said Mrs. Rumford.

"Would anyone care for another slice of Mrs. Knox's pie?" Alex's mother called to the women in the other room.

"Perhaps I would," said Mrs. Gordimer. "I shouldn't, but I might. Shall I bring my plate?"

"No, no. I'll just be another minute."

"Besides," said Mrs. Rumford, "the boy doesn't look like either of them, either."

"Yes," Mrs. Cotton said. "He hardly looks like anyone at all."

Alex reached for the cord for the closet light, but his hand swung into emptiness in the spot where he thought the cord should be, and as he moved his fingers through the space it seemed like not just the cord but his hand itself had gone missing.

"Here's the tea"—Alex heard his mother set the teapot onto a trivet—"and, I'll be right back"—her steps were brisk past the closet, onto the linoleum and back past the closet again—"with the pie! Thank you, Mrs. Knox. The raisins are delicious."

"It was nothing," the Mrs. Knox voice said again.

Alex's hand found a hairy coat poking out at an odd angle. The light cord was wrapped around one of the buttons. He pulled it and took stock of his wire pieces.

Outside the closet it was quiet and he thought of the ladies chewing. He hoped there'd be enough pie left for dinner.

"I don't know if you've heard, Muriel"—Mrs. Rumford's voice was quieter now, and Alex had to strain to hear it come up from under the thick, wood door— "but Mrs. Knox has a knack for—not to be irreverent, but, shall we say—predictions? I'm delighted to say it was she who first suggested to my own, dear mother, may she rest in peace, that my Robert and I would be joined together. And I was only seven when she said it! And she saw right away Billy Cooper's calling to the ministry. Picked him out of Sunday School class and made sure he learned his books and verses early."

"Really, Mrs. Rumford, you flatter me. It's merely that I hope the best for people. Granting it is in the good Lord's hands."

"But Constance Lowry's accident on the horse—" said Mrs. Rumford.

"I prayed for her recovery," said Mrs. Knox.

"And the McEachrans' three sets of twins," said Mrs. Cotton.

"That one," said Mrs. Knox, "I can't explain." Her laugh was the sound of an entire congregation looking up the same hymn. "But I wouldn't be so bold as to guess at the Lord's reasons."

"Anyway, I was thinking that it would be a benefit for you to know—oh, not know, exactly, but perhaps a bit of fun—for her to see your lovely Kristi-Anne and think a little on her future."

"I'm honoured to have you in my home, Mrs. Knox."

"Oh my dear, the honour is mine," said Mrs. Knox. "Such a pretty baby. And so good. Angelic, shall we say?"

"Thank you"—Alex had to lay his head against the floor to hear his mother properly. She said it again— "Thank you."

"So," said Mrs. Gordimer, "if she could only hold her?"

"I beg your pardon?" said Alex's mother, though Alex had heard Mrs. Gordimer just fine.

"My little party tricks are no good at a distance, I'm afraid. I require contact."

There was a silence long enough for Alex to scoop all the wire bits into his hand. Then he heard the old chair squeak as Muriel rose out of it. Alex pulled the light cord again, preparing to open the door. He wanted to see the baby come to rest in someone else's arms. But there was a gasp and a cry and the sound of something thin and delicate hitting the floor.

"Oh, oh," said a shrill voice that Alex thought was Mrs. Cotton, but when he opened the door he saw Mrs. Gordimer holding only her saucer. His mother was standing over her. Everyone was looking at the shattered pink and gold pieces.

"Dear me," said Alex's mother. "I hope I didn't ruin your lovely dress."

"Well no, somehow I managed to stay quite dry," said Mrs. Gordimer, who was nervously lifting her saucer up and down as if she couldn't quite believe how light it had become.

"But your lovely cup," said Mrs. Rumford.

"It's entirely my fault," said Alex's mother, but she didn't bend to mop the spill. "I don't know how I could be so clumsy. Maybe you were right, Myrna. Maybe it's all just a bit too much for me."

"We've kept you too long," said Mrs. Knox. "You have the rest of your family to tend to," and she looked right at Alex.

Muriel hoisted a sleeping Kristi-Anne higher up her shoulder and walked to the closet, where she retrieved the coats and passed them to the ladies. Mrs. Rumford, Mrs. Cotton and Mrs. Gordimer stepped toward the door.

Mrs. Knox stayed behind. She put out her hand and touched Alex's cheek, the one on which the eye rested low. She nodded to him in a way that made him feel that he'd been bidden farewell before a long journey. Then she followed the other women out onto the porch and out of his sight.

Careful. Oh careful, Kristi-Anne.

In the hot summer days of her babyhood, while other infants lay in their carriages on the porches and in the small front yards of the houses on Weaver Street,

Kristi-Anne stayed inside, lying in her cradle between the sink and stove, surrounded by the additional shimmering heat waves from the gas stove and the glare of the new lights that beamed down from every corner.

Muriel did not worry about the effect of the heat on an infant. Outside in the deceptively cooler air there were percolating dangers that Muriel entrusted no one but herself to keep from Kristi-Anne. Those days of trundling the cradle and wringing the diapers through the washer in the tiny kitchen provided Muriel with ample time to conjure a list of threats that hung over Kristi-Anne's existence out there in the wider world, and, as the days grew even hotter, these threats seemed to move from her mind into the atmosphere around her like the vapors over the washtub. The world was full of predators, twisted men who'd love to touch themselves to her daughter's tiny lips, jealous children who might run her into the woods and leave her stranded in the elements. Better, she thought—repeatedly putting her foot down on the cradle runner, so that the baby always swung back toward her—to stay in the house. And so they did, through the entire first year of Kristi-Anne's life.

Alex's memories of that year were largely gathered through windows, watching, from the inside, the street in the front or the laneway in behind, until dusk, when the curtains were drawn and the lights were turned on.

He did not mind watching. In the schoolyard, he was never invited to play anyway, and found it safest to find an inconspicuous spot near the fence so that he didn't become the object of others' games.

All his seven years, he had spent his free hours at home. It wasn't that it was a welcoming place, but it had been a refuge. His math tests had been considered, his fingernails checked, and his mother made him bland desserts of johnnycake and bread pudding. And in that home, with his mother, Alex had felt love. True, it had been a weaker sort than that displayed by other mothers, as if he were trying to draw it from a tea bag that had lost its potency, leeched out by previous uses. Still, it had been love, of a sort.

But now Alex attracted no love at all. While his mother nursed the baby, the family menu trickled into brothy soups and stale bread. Alex's marks on computation ground down to a D, and no one seemed to care. His nails developed a rim of grime until, despairing of ever being told to clean them, he did it himself. Rarely did his mother even speak of him, except when his father asked after his behaviour, and his mother asserted that he was "No bother," to which his father's single wink was the high point in his day.

Alex knew that he deserved this lukewarm compliment, for he never interfered with his mother and the baby. It wasn't possible to get anywhere near Kristi-Anne;

she was always in her mother's arms or lying right beside her.

But Kristi-Anne grew, pulling herself up in the kitchen cradle and threatening to topple out, and eventually Muriel had Gordon set up a playpen in the living room, in the place where the coffee table had stood. Kristi-Anne's playpen thus became the house's centre-piece, especially when Gordon hung an elaborate crystal chandelier directly above it. The house was a small one, and it was only a few steps for Muriel to go back and forth between the wash bin and the dishes to shake a rattle over the playpen's edge. The arrangement was not ideal, but it kept Muriel's mind more or less at ease. And Kristi-Anne seemed unlikely to complain.

Since her arrival, Alex had been watching Kristi-Anne as if she were a rare, shy bird. Using his long-developed skill of blending into the surroundings, in this case the yellowed upholstery, the mottled wallpaper, he had studied her from a vantage point where his presence would not cause alarm. But now that she was out in the living room, there was a necessary increase in the intervals when his mother did not hover at his sister's side. And Kristi-Anne's position on the floor offered him the opportunity to try to look her in the eye.

Over a succession of early spring afternoons, after he came home from school, Alex approached ever closer to Kristi-Anne, testing both his mother's powers of observation and Kristi-Anne's willingness to let him near. And then, one day, as he played nearby, cutting, bending and shaping his collected bits of wire, he saw her drop the rattle she was gumming. It fell to the playpen mattress with one scuttling bounce. But Kristi-Anne did not look for it. Instead, she stared at Alex.

Alex held her gaze, afraid to blink. He put down the scissors and the wire boat he was building and waved. She flapped her little arms. He popped his hand over his mouth in a warrior's cry, but silent. He looked up at his mother, thinking that she might have heard the accompanying *woop woop* that he had only imagined. But he heard her turn on the stove. *Click, click, click*—a stopwatch, counting down.

It was frustrating, looking at Kristi-Anne like this. The wooden bars in the sides of the playpen sliced across the baby's face, providing equal bits of tantalizing revelation (her skin really was a rosy pink) and obfuscation, as large parts of her stayed behind the painted posts even as he shifted his head to try to get a sense of what he was missing.

And then there was the hair. At birth, she'd already been graced with a fuzz of blonde curls and those curls had grown at a surprising speed, so that now she had a mass of golden ringlets that fell almost to her shoulders. Her mother, enamoured with yet more evidence of her daughter's unrivalled beauty, refused to pull it back with anything but her own hand, which meant that, as Kristi-Anne and her brother contemplated each other—nearer still now, because Alex could hear bacon sizzling—they were kept from each other by a curtain of blonde filaments, seen from either side.

Everyone assumed that Alex's vision was as twisted as his features, when in fact he saw very well. But how could Kristi-Anne see, he wondered, stuck behind that hairy curtain? It worried him. Alex pushed his hand up and over his own face, ruffling back the short bit of bang that stuck out over his forehead. But the baby put her hand to her mouth again instead and bounced it there. Maybe, Alex thought, he'd been wrong. Maybe she couldn't see him at all. But then she pulled herself up on the bars and reached for him, her delicate fingers finding the hollow beneath one eye, and Alex and his sister touched for the first time. He had just enough time to note that her skin was as soft as he'd imagined, before she pulled away.

"Hello, mama's little darling." Muriel poked her head through the kitchen doorway. Alex made himself flat against the floor like a lion in the grass. "Won't be long, mockingbird. I'll be out in a minute."

Alex heard the pan rattle again and sat up. There wasn't much time. He pulled himself towards the play-pen on his forearms, dragging his belly across the floor, and when he had pressed his body alongside the bars, he waved the little boat out in front of Kristi-Anne. She gurgled and reached for it. "Shh," Alex said, and smiled. He waved the boat again, this time a little farther away. She had to lean right up against the bars now, if she wanted it, and she did, the blue and red and copper dancing in his hands, just beyond her reach. Then she pushed her head into the bars and reached one hand through. Alex let her take the toy, grabbed the patch of hair that fell over her eyes, and snipped it off in one cut, right at the hairline. He had only an instant to look into her astonished eyes before his mother began to scream.

Muriel reached for Alex, knocking the scissors out of his hands and raising a hand to strike him. Alex pushed his bony shoulders up and scrunched his neck down, as if he were wishing that life had provided him with some natural protection like a turtle's shell. But it wasn't anything external that kept him from his first blow at his mother's hand, the first she would ever have made. It was his mother herself who saved him.

She had no idea why she did it. Later, in the kitchen and in the glow beaming down over her night table, she would hold herself to account. How could she have failed so utterly? It was a dangerous flaw, this weakness. Alex should have received a slap and twenty more. But she did not do it. She could not. And, what was worse, for a moment she had an impulse to bring her arm down to her son's contorted body in an embrace more forceful than any slap could have been. She had barely been able to resist. Remembering it, Muriel felt a crush behind her heart, like something malignant growing undiagnosed. It was all right, she told herself, she'd recovered. Not more than a second or two had passed before she leaned into the crib to lift out Kristi-Anne, the wire boat falling out of her grip and onto the floor.

The five days in his room until supper, the requirement to stay completely away from the baby and the newly suspicious gaze of his mother hardly made a difference to Alex's routine. But he was aware that it was he who had provided Kristi-Anne with the gift of the outdoors that spring, his mother saying that if she needed to be on guard in her own home she might as well put on her armour and go out into the neighbourhood. And so she walked with Kristi-Anne to the mailbox, then onto the street and, eventually, around the block, pushing the perambulator with the canopy pulled up, testing the new distance of her outstretched arms, while Alex followed behind them, being relegated always—on those walks, in the yard, at the table, in the church pew where the whole family sat again—to the place that was farthest from Kristi-Anne, so that she remained a distant ornament, ornate and colourful, its value never determined.

With only the doting tea party ladies to report on her astounding beauty and her angelic temperament, the citizenry of the world—or what Kristi-Anne would come to know of it—had spent over a year in expectation. The noticeable spike of foot traffic on Weaver Street had spurred residents to successfully petition for sidewalk repair, and even the workmen in their orange jumpsuits had been seen to dawdle in front of the Martin house as evening fell and the many lights came on. But the curtains had always been quickly drawn, shutting out the view, along with the peepers, and focusing the incredible light down on the house's inhabitants.

And then, suddenly, there she was, curls spilling out from under a crocheted cap (hiding her haphazard haircut while the wisps at the front grew into bangs), smiling and cooing without the usual baby wonder but as if she had expected this place to grow up overnight and that all of it was put there for her pleasure. The neighbours, the milkman, old Dr. Tansley, the lady sprinkled with flour at the bakery—Kristi-Anne waved to them all, making them adoring spectators to her parade.

This was not how they seemed to Muriel, for whom every human being was equally likely to take on a major and malevolent role. So though it was with definite pride that she pushed Kristi-Anne's carriage, then held Kristi-Anne's hand as she toddled, then hovered close to Kristi-Anne as she walked smartly beside her, Muriel took far less pleasure than she might have in the auxiliary benefits of being Kristi-Anne's mother. There just wasn't the time. When it came to Kristi-Anne, Muriel was ever alert.

"Good day, Mrs. Martin. A fine, fine day." Why did Mrs. Larry Cosset have to lean in so very close to the pram? "But I don't believe the sun could be any brighter than your daughter's smile! Hello, Kristi-Anne." There was something about those fingers, permanently bent by arthritis, that looked like she was already in mid-clutch, like a hawk coming down on a vole. Muriel rolled the pram up and back, as if to quiet a fussy child, trying to stay out of the old woman's reach. Kristi-Anne just beamed.

"Mommy, look, look. It's Kristi-Anne!" That little Lindsay girl, whose face was perpetually crusted in lollipop smear.

"Hello, Muriel," Mrs. Lindsay said. "Say hello to Mrs. Martin, Rose."

Rose did not say hi. "Can Kristi-Anne play?" Rose said, reaching in close to the toddler.

Muriel pulled Kristi-Anne imperceptibly nearer. Rose's tacky skin might stick right to Kristi-Anne and draw her away—onto the slide, and onto the swing and into the woods.

"How do those feel?" Mr. Scott said, fitting Kristi-Anne's four-year-old feet into a new pair of Mary Janes. "Why don't you take a walk around? That's it, just go on a little cruise."

And Muriel would watch Kristi-Anne make her orbit of the store, feeling the openness of the door to the street, the door to the stockroom, as if they exerted a gravitational pull. By the time Kristi-Anne was halfway round, Muriel stood to meet her.

"We'll take them," she said, and picked up her daughter like the girl herself were the item she'd purchased.

"How are you today, Kristi-Anne?" people asked, to which the child's reply was always polite, always positive, always delivered in a crisp, enunciated manner, as though she were a student of the finest elocution teacher. "Oh, I'm very well." Or, "Absolutely splendid." Or, "Thank you, I'm perfectly, perfectly fine."

"And how are you, Alex?"

When Alex first followed his mother and sister on their rounds in that spring when he was eight, he had worried how he would answer that question. But no one in the centre of town asked him anything that year, and Alex realized that it was likely no one ever would, and so he turned his energies to listening and looking, examining the place and the people that seemed to belong so easily to it.

Before Kristi-Anne, Alex had hardly visited the shops or the square, and certainly he'd never lingered there. His formerly shy mother had done her shopping in blitzes, moving in and out of the stores as quickly as possible, her eyes so downcast that the family was often fed on whatever had been displayed on the shelf closest to the floor. On all but the most sudden of trips, Alex had been left behind with his father, who spent his

Saturdays at home with the paper spread open on his lap, rarely turning the pages.

The town centre that Alex discovered wasn't tinged with peril, as in his mother's imagination, nor glinting with possibility, as his sister found it. For Alex, it was a place of storefronts and exteriors, of conversations overheard from afar, for he maintained the distance that his mother had determined for him: close enough that he was in her sights, but not so close that she would worry about him touching Kristi-Anne. If you had been reaching for a tomato at the grocer's or entering the hardware store to select a length of twine, you might have been forgiven for thinking that it seemed like the boy was lurking there, judging the place, and plotting where he might stake himself within it.

If Alex's father had come across the boy, leaned up against the library cornerstone while his mother and sister climbed the steps to look at the collection, he might have recognized something of himself in Alex's measured surveillance. For Gordon, too, had spent years looking at the town as if he were a spectator rather than a resident. It was a detachment he had learned from his own father, and since it was the only inheritance Gordon had received, it seemed impossible to refuse.

Unlike Gordon or young Alex, Gordon's father Alfred was accomplished at giving his suffering volume. And there was so very much of it. Alfred was haunted by memories of polished banisters, tormented by recollections of dinner parties with appetizers and dessert, spoiled forever by visions of tailed footmen placing slivers of ice with silver tongs into his parents' golden spirits. While Alfred's sickly wife produced, in quick succession, two sickly daughters who lived only minutes, and then Gordon himself, whose arrival into this world offered her a passport from it, Alfred measured out his own drink (without ice) in fingers, then in tumblers.

And what could Alfred do but drink, when his hands were made for rifling stocks and bonds, not the building and tearing apart that was the work of more primitive men? This was the dilemma he posed to young Gordon, as they walked the town together, Alfred pointing with his ebony cane to the abandoned mill, the old distillery—all the monuments and assets that would never be Gordon's. "Turkeys, my boy!" Gordon's father would say, seeing through the new bowling alley to the mansion garden that had served the family and its extended household. "Peaches. French beans. Eggs of every colour." And Gordon would nod as if the rows of tomatoes and rosemary were rising up between the lanes.

This way of finding his bearings by what had been lost had dogged Gordon, though silently, into his adulthood. In the early days of his marriage, it had led to the exorbitant purchase of a car (owned first by a descendant of one of his great-great-grandfather's employees, who'd managed to hold onto his much smaller fortune and pass it to his descendants), which caused additional strain on the household budget, but helped drown out the persistent voice of his dead father while Gordon moved the few blocks from various job sites to home.

But after Kristi-Anne's arrival, Gordon left the car at home, his triumphant outlook further heightened by the daily exercise. Now, he moved along the town's grid unencumbered, and each night, returning to the uneven footing of Weaver Street, he thought again how it didn't matter—perhaps had never mattered—these things that had been lost. Here was his daughter, standing directly in the staged lighting of the kitchen; his son, finding the more diffused pockets or alerting Gordon to a still-shadowed corner; and his wife, sharing the glow of the twinkling Christmas lights or the bridge lamp, as if she herself were the spark that lit them. How could he mourn that life he had been denied, when this—all this—was his?

It was a potent antidote, more than adequate when passing any landmark or address that had previously made him melancholy. Except for one: the village square. There, where the marble bust of Gordon's great-great-grandfather Alexander looked out on all he had once owned, Gordon could not help but feel his ancestor's censure, his dismay at having left it all to a succession of unequal stewards. And it was because Gordon avoided the little park, and the man's far-reaching gaze, that Gordon never saw his son—as he waited there for his mother and sister to finish exchanging pleasantries with the other mothers and children or to return from some nearby errand—run his hand over the marble face, or lean in close to scrape a bit of moss away from the dead man's cataract-coloured eyes.

To understand how completely Kristi-Anne accepted her station in life, consider this: even as she grew and encountered the broader citizenry of the town, she never questioned her guarded existence. And though in most cases overly doting mothers are pilloried, or at least mocked behind their backs, Muriel Martin's behaviour with her daughter was largely accepted as appropriate. What woman, the other mothers asked themselves, would not do the same had they a child so precious?

Which is not to say that it was all reverence. Certainly, there was a streak of jealousy that accompanied the curiosity. But who would seek to depose her? One look and it was obvious that no other Little Miss stood a chance. Fair it wasn't, but it was true: there could only be one Kristi-Anne in town. And many of them believed most fervently that there could only be one of her, anywhere.

Besides, each had a vested interest in her protection. Mrs. Cotton and Mrs. Rumford's little girls played with Kristi-Anne in the floodlit bedroom she shared with her mother, and their proximity to Kristi-Anne conferred a certain status on those miniature ladies-in-waiting. The banker's wife and the wife of the school principal groomed their sons as possible suitors for a grown-up Kristi-Anne, who might distribute among their grandchildren her petal cheeks, her doll-like eyes, her thin and graceful fingers. Others, like the old man at the hardware store, felt blessed by even her presence, and there were many who believed that one day Kristi-Anne would lift them all from obscurity, discovered like Lana Turner at the lunch counter, gracing their town with a sign HOME OF KRISTI-ANNE MARTIN and a new way to find them on the flat or folded map.

All this solicitude did nothing to soothe Kristi-Anne's mother, who was suspicious of each individual expression of concern. Doubtless, some of it was sincere, but what of the one wolf in sheep's clothing who made her look away for a minute too long?

Still, Muriel Martin was a practical woman. A time was coming when Kristi-Anne's hand would be out of hers, when she could no longer make a physical barrier between herself and her treasure, when Kristi-Anne would need something more. So, before Kristi-Anne started school, Muriel Martin began to provide her an education.

The Pied Piper, *Little Red Riding Hood*, *Sleeping Beauty*, *Snow White*, the books were stacked on the table at their shared bedside, and each night Muriel turned on the gooseneck reading light and read to her daughter with the inflection of a revivalist preacher. Muriel Martin pointed out each cautionary message: the wolf behind the tree, the danger of the lilting flute, the sharpness of the spindle, the poison in the apple. Never dreaming that, despite her emphasis, her daughter remembered better the carriages, the towers, the castles. What Alex took away Muriel never imagined, for as usual she failed to see him, sitting up against the hallway wall, listening at the open door.

And so, when she started school, Muriel Martin sent her six-year-old daughter with a pencil box like her brother's, but also with a caution, folded and at the ready like a monogrammed handkerchief: Careful. Careful, Kristi-Anne.

Each weekday morning, Muriel walked her daughter to school while carrying her own satchel, full of needles and wool and thread. In cool weather, Muriel sat in the front windows of the library across the street, or the vestibule of the post office, taking breaks with the regularity of a secret drinker, to walk into the schoolyard and peer through the school's lower windows onto Kristi-Anne's classroom.

In the warmer weather, Muriel sat out by the swings, or perched at the axis of the teeter-totter, wool emerging in a wavy string from her canvas bag, her needles moving while she stared straight ahead at the school wall. The boys in Kristi-Anne's class—who were already beginning to turn from rambunctious little things into the marauding, sarcastic mob that they would become by the older grades—formed taunts and rude observations in their tow-headed brains, but when they turned to look at Kristi-Anne, their sour words would drain away and she, catching their eyes, would acknowledge them with a nod befitting a tolerant monarch. Even the older boys kept their spiked insults away from Kristi-Anne, letting her pass through their games of dodge ball unmolested, and saving all their catalogued jeering for Alex.

"I heard your mother's building a moat to your place, Alex Martin."

"Yeah, so you can live under the bridge. Like all the other trolls!"

Alex was unfazed by the insults, understanding with the wisdom of the ugly and excluded that the town's children—and others, too, he supposed, were he elsewhere, were he ever to be elsewhere—did not need the ammunition provided by his mother's eccentric behaviour and his sister's contrasting beauty to turn their sights on him. Their arsenal was full already with his Picasso-painted face and his twisted frame.

It was probably coincidence—an alchemy of pubescent hormones and prevailing social forces (they were thirteen, after all, a terrible, turning age)—that made the worst of the boys, boys like Terry Moffatt, the principal's son, and Peter Lindsay, and their select crew of strong and obedient followers, ratchet their abuse from words to blows that year. Oh, Alex had always suffered kicks under the desks, when the class was supposed to be colouring the giant map of conquest, and the predictable shoving at the water fountain, bumping Alex up against the porcelain and sending a ringing through his teeth. But now, the boys expanded the boundary of their assault beyond the halls and the schoolyard. They started to follow him home.

It was just three blocks, with a couple of turns, and you might have thought that the openness of the streets would protect Alex, would make the boys temper their persecution, fearful of the censure of witnesses. But they made little attempt to disguise the nature of their attentions to the boy, shoving him to the sidewalk and cuffing his pronounced brow on the very pieces of concrete from which Kristi-Anne and her mother had waved to neighbours just minutes before. Only when they reached Weaver Street would the gang disperse, leaving Alex to walk by himself past the last few lawns, arriving at his own house with a slightly more obvious limp, scraped and bruised, a rip in his shirt pocket or the knees to his dungarees torn open.

If Muriel minded the extra work removing stains or patching her son's clothes, she did not say. She didn't scold her son on his rough play and his carelessness with the clothes that they could ill afford to replace, nor did she speak to him, or ask his father to speak to him, about the extra purple tinge below his eyes.

It seemed there was no help coming for Alex, but then, Alex would not have expected it. And so, each afternoon, he learned to suffer the abuse in those three blocks, its predictability making it almost manageable. And then, he decided to take a different route.

Why he did it, Alex himself could not have said, but one afternoon he turned right instead of left, and headed for the thin corridor of forest that remained at the town's centre. The forest had been rich and plentiful when Alex's great-great-grandfather settled the land five generations before, and so he had systematically set about to purge it of its bounty. Now, it was a border between the relative prosperity of one side of town and the forgotten outskirts on the other, slated perpetually for redevelopment, for an expansion that never seemed to come.

Within a few minutes of entering the paths beneath the trees, Alex was lulled by the sound of birds, and the trickle of the little brook, into thinking he'd found a refuge.

"Into the woods, Alex. That's right. This is where all the monsters go."

Alex had only a second to perceive the ambush before he hit the ground. It was softer than the concrete, but the kicks and punches erased the sensation of leaves and twigs beneath him. And then there was a little lull in the beating, and Alex prised open his swelling eyes just in time to see Terry reel back his arm before he delivered a punch worthy of a full-grown man against Alex's lower eye.

But it wasn't Alex who cried out. It was Terry.

"My hand!"

Through his other eye, Alex saw Terry's hand hanging at the end of his sleeve at an odd angle. The fingers were twisted and overlapping. Two of the knuckles were markedly lower than the others.

It was silent except for Terry's low moaning. When another boy spoke, it was in a whisper. "Your hand looks just like his face," Peter Lindsay breathed.

Terry grabbed his forearm and ran. The other boys backed away slowly, then whipped around to follow him.

Muriel saw the blood pooling on her clean floor before she noticed the source. She swept the rag from the sink and tried to staunch Alex's wound, but the blood seeped around the cloth and onto her wrist as she steered Alex to the bathroom and sat him on the toilet lid. She pushed harder against the gash and she felt her son's skin give at the pressure. A current of pain moved up Muriel's arm, as if the injury were her own. A gasp escaped her. Then another. She felt as if something large and dangerous were forcing the air from her chest. She should go for the doctor. She should send for her husband. But she couldn't let go of her son.

Alex swayed, light-headed not only from the pain and departing adrenalin, but from the shock of his mother's touch. And then he slumped into her arms.

"Mother?" Kristi-Anne stood at the threshold of the bathroom. She emitted a delicate sniff. "What is that?"

Was she talking about the blood? Muriel wondered. Or the tooth that had fallen from her brother's mouth onto the bare floor?

"What's happening?" Kristi-Anne's voice was louder now, the frequency pitched perfectly for Muriel's ear.

She pulled her arm out from under her son. His head nodded forward, then jerked back as he righted himself, once again.

Muriel blocked the doorway and prayed it wasn't too late.

"Don't look," she said to Kristi-Anne. "Don't look."

Kristi-Anne's life had shown her none of the fairy-tale world her mother threatened. She was not made to work like Cinderella—though her home had the drafty feel one took away from the pictures of Cinderella sweeping the hearth—and though her parents could barely afford to keep either of their children, there was never any chance that they would lead them to the woods and leave them there, picking their way back along disappearing bread crumbs. But Kristi-Anne did not know these stories, her mother having borrowed only those that provided a clear and easily communicated message about the safety of home and the perils of everywhere else. Neither had she taken out—she'd never even considered it—"Rapunzel," the story of the golden-haired girl locked in the tower.

Kristi-Anne's world, day by day, week by week, was the street, the block, the shops, the school, and church. And not one of these places was to be explored alone. Even at the church, long after she was old enough to pull up her own frilly panties, her mother held the top of the stall doors in the bathroom, when the lock wasn't even broken.

But it was church that Kristi-Anne loved best of all. At church, the admirers did not have to be sought out and visited, but came packaged together, forming a dense crowd of worship and belief—all of it for Kristi-Anne. Before they were seated for the service and afterward in the foyer and at coffee in the basement, her mother held one of Kristi-Anne's hands while a steady flow of worshippers squeezed the other, or knelt and looked into her eyes, or laid a reverent hand upon her head. Kristi-Anne smiled, nodded and accepted each offering.

Minister Cooper was himself a devoted fan of Kristi-Anne from that time her mother had agreed to hold Kristi-Anne over the baptismal font so that he could consecrate her to God. But that had been his only prolonged contact with her, as her mother limited each interaction, afraid of turning any individual into too much of an intimate. Perhaps it was his unrequited admiration for the girl that made him abandon his sermons about false idols, focusing instead on the blessedness of children and the visitations of angels.

Mrs. Knox, who ran the Sunday School, had no such limits. She was an old-school Christian, favouring the weeping sores of Job, and Jesus turning out the money-changers. Mrs. Knox's God had mystery and muscle. Despite her sticklike bearing and her dry voice, this made Mrs. Knox quite a favourite with many of the children, who felt that they were being told a story that the other grown-ups had kept from them. But they would have attended Sunday School whether they liked it or not. That was the nature of Sunday School: children were to go there during the Sunday service—though they were allowed to join the congregation for the final hymns and the benediction—until they were deemed old enough to sit in the pews without squirming or kicking the kneeler.

But each week, while Alex took the stairs down to Mrs. Knox's basement room—where he found a spot near the back, as he always did, despite the lady's unfathomable urgings that he come sit near her at the front—Kristi-Anne sat the entire service in the pew between her mother and her father. She folded her gloved hands in her lap, stood at the appropriate parts of the service and kept her eyes focused ahead until it was time to sing, when she joined in with a clear and tuneful voice. Who could complain? No one. Which was why Mrs. Knox had never done so. Still, she watched the girl throughout the coffee that followed. Did she see how Kristi-Anne's eyes were only ever trained on her next visitor? Did she note how quickly her interest changed when each person had passed, scanning the room for the next who would come and offer their praise? Mrs. Knox never said anything of the sort, but Kristi-Anne noted—as did her mother, with a kind of relief, for the woman had always frightened her, her fire and brimstone Sunday School teachings being offered now to three generations of parishioners—that Mrs. Knox always spoke only to her parents, offering Kristi-Anne no more than a nod as the conversation finished.

Then, one Sunday near Christmas, Mrs. Knox's nod turned into a stoop, and Kristi-Anne saw that she was holding something out to her.

"Since I never see you in Sunday School, Kristi-Anne, I brought you a little treat that I shared with each of my pupils today." The thing in her hand was brown and square and glossy. "It's a humbug, Kristi-Anne." It did, in fact, look a little like a bug, maybe the centre of a small spider with the legs pulled off. "It was my mother's tradition to give these out to children at Christmastime. I've kept it up myself. I pass one out to each of my students. Well, those of them who are old enough not to choke. You wouldn't choke, would you, Kristi-Anne?"

"No," said Kristi-Anne. It was a rare word for Kristi-Anne, and it felt strange fitting her lips around it. The thing at the end of the outstretched fingers, whose nails were short and clean and filed but ridged and a little yellow, did not look that appealing.

"Perhaps," said Kristi-Anne's mother, "we could save it for after lunch." She squeezed Kristi-Anne's hand just a little.

"Certainly, you may do that. Or you don't have to take it at all, do you?" Mrs. Knox said.

"No," said Kristi-Anne again, feeling this time not just the foreignness of the word, but also another strange, new feeling as she watched children her own age climb under the table of coffee. Kristi-Anne was not used to the idea that others might be given things that she was not. Perhaps the gift was not a pleasant one, but it was a gift nonetheless. "Thank you. I would like it please. Yes," said Kristi-Anne. And with that, the legless humbug was suddenly in her mouth. Surprised, Kristi-Anne sucked in hard and very nearly lodged the candy in the back of her throat after all.

Mrs. Knox turned away more quickly than it seemed a woman of her age should be able to do and Kristi-Anne's mother crouched beside her and offered her cottoned palm for Kristi-Anne to spit into. But by then, the essence of the candy had been released. It was sweet and tingly, the opposite of everything that its name suggested.

"What have I told you, Kristi-Anne?" her mother hissed. She squeezed Kristi-Anne's hand most tightly.

"Yes, Mother, I remember it all," Kristi-Anne said, speaking around the candy's edges.

If Kristi-Anne had only returned her mother's squeeze then, Muriel Martin would have felt much better. But Kristi-Anne did not.

For the first seven years of Alex's life, birthdays in the little house on Weaver Street had gone by nearly unnoticed. And in the years after Kristi-Anne's birth, for Alex they continued much the same. But each February, two days after Alex had turned a year older, Kristi-Anne's arrival would be marked with cake and singing.

Undoubtedly, it was both Muriel and Gordon's favourite day of the year, and every year it seemed their pleasure in it increased. Gordon rushed home to witness his wife lighting the candles and carrying the cake to where his daughter sat, waiting. He could see how Muriel delighted in her offering, even suffering the presence of a half-dozen other little girls for her daughter's happiness. But the year that there was pale yellow cake and sugar dyed to match, Gordon noticed that the room seemed to darken suddenly when Kristi-Anne blew out the candles. Maybe it was because there were so many of them: seven, spaced evenly across the frosting. It was a fleeting perception, and it wafted almost instantly away, along with the little whiff of smoke above the blackened wicks.

Of course Kristi-Anne enjoyed her birthday. Even Alex appreciated the thin slice of cake that his father retrieved for him from the nearly empty plate, and that he ate away from the party of little girls, looking out the living room window at the sun going down. But for Kristi-Anne, each day was a cascade of attention, and the modest party her parents could manage might well be topped on any other day by a neighbour bearing a random gift or the introduction of a new acquaintance, who would instantly become another fervent admirer.

Kristi-Anne didn't think particularly about her birthday, because she rarely thought about her beginnings. Of course if she had, she would have assumed they were spectacular, in keeping with every other aspect of herself. The truth—that she was an accident resulting from the infrequent but predictable coming together of a fumbling workman and his tepid, disappointed wife; that her beauty was a random chromosomal collision, a genetic blip in a family that otherwise ran from plain to decidedly unattractive; and that her continued blossoming was merely the result of expectation and habit set up by the surprise of her appearance—would have been as impossible to understand. But as she grew from leaning in to her mother's skirts, Kristi-Anne did begin to question the likelihood of her situation. This didn't manifest itself in self-examination or questioning whether she deserved or could continue to carry the golden mantle she'd been wearing since she'd appeared like a vision in her hospital bassinet. Instead, she began to question her parents.

Because Kristi-Anne knew that all of it—the school and the church and the street, the intensely bright house with its dreary furnishings and the patches that would never be fully repaired, and even Kristi-Anne's stifling, controlled routine—was temporary. A world with a broader palette awaited her. Everything that now held her back, and in, was only a preparation, a tightly fitting cocoon that soon would crack and release her, and when it did, she would fly away without looking back at the brittle carapace that once contained her life. And so, night after night—after the bath and the fairy tales and the kisses and turning the many lights out—Kristi-Anne would spread her hair across the pillow, arrange her arms across her chest and wait for her real family to come and take her away.

Oh, she was fond of her mother—the dishy smell of her, the soft flannelette she always wore to bed (not for herself, but so that Kristi-Anne's cheek would not be grazed by buttons or rough cotton), her way of putting in the toast just as Kristi-Anne stepped onto the lino-leum, so that it would not be soggy when she arrived at the table—but these were not things that Kristi-Anne anticipated missing. Instead, at the age of seven, she had already begun to see her mother in the manner of a much older child, one of eighteen or nineteen, who no longer chafes against her parents' restrictions but looks on their stewardship with a nostalgic gratitude, giving it all a backward nod while moving on to independence and new ventures. Her father, a man who could not be looked upon without squinting, he was so frequently installing or fixing a new light or a brighter bulb, meant even less. And her brother—his split-eyed gaze on her or on the wall, who could ever tell—meant nothing, she thought, at all. She looked at him so rarely.

No one looked at Alex if they could help it. The wound had healed into a rough scar on Alex's forehead as if he'd called forth an additional eyebrow, and as he grew, his body had lengthened, the growth turning back on him like a badly trimmed tree. He was as grotesque to the world as she was beautiful, but to Kristi-Anne, who lived every moment of her life with Alex at its margins, he was nearly invisible. She didn't, as someone else might, follow his lonesome progress along the street, or through the woods. Didn't consider that he looked like someone tilting into a headwind, except that his chin jutted out, though his body stooped down. And she certainly didn't notice how his particular affliction made it look as if he were peering out over reading glasses while consulting a map in his hand, intent—in spite of everything—on getting somewhere.

"Careful. Careful, Kristi-Anne"—the words would follow her for the rest of her life, when no one else followed her at all, and she would gather, weigh, rend and put back together that day. The scrape of leather soles—her own and those of Misty Rumford and Simon Gordimer, who was allowed to play even though he was a boy because he was weak and never pushed—sliding forward across the hopscotch grid in front of her house, the children's feet scuffing the lines and obscuring the places it was safe to stand. And out beyond this territory, her mother knitting in the porch chair, nodding along to Mrs. Gordimer's gossip.

Kristi-Anne would have occasion to speculate, again and again, to go over the distance between the porch and the hopscotch, the children and the street, and how long someone might think it would take a mother to run, in a housedress and even those low pumps, all the way to the sidewalk, to gather up her beautiful girl and beat a retreat to the safety of the house. To think about how it couldn't be done. How, in the time it took to reach out to snatch her from the street, it couldn't be done.

No one was paying attention to Alex that day, but it's impossible not to recall how he was poking a stick into the storm drain, just a few feet away from the game, when the bird shit—right in the middle of the "3"—and Simon Gordimer bent to judge if he had landed safely home and Misty Rumford said he hadn't, and Kristi-Anne said it didn't matter, she had won anyway, and they all agreed, when the blue car drove up to the curb, opened its door, then slammed it and pulled away.

And in that moment, and in all the subsequent moments when she turns it over and over in her mind—how Alex's face was framed in the car's back window, looking out over a plaid blanket, looking out at Kristi-Anne, looking out at the street he was leaving behind—Kristi-Anne knew that she had been passed over. That Alex was not a pale and mistaken substitute, not a consolation for the child the captors would have preferred, had her mother not been dangerously close. That Alex was not a sacrifice offered by the street so that she and the other, better loved, children could live on undisturbed. No.

Alex was chosen.

There was nothing left for Kristi-Anne to do but wonder why. To try to detect what had made him so special, those fourteen years he'd lived with them on Weaver Street, the family that looked so little like him, sheltering him until that time when he should be recognized and sent for. To slip into the shadow he left behind, and wrap it around her to see if she could get it just right—his stoop, his stringy hair, his unwashed scent, how his feet never left the ground as he walked, not stepping or leaping or jumping, just shuffling as if to show her he had nowhere that he was expected. Oh, there was an entire catalogue of Alex to try on in an attempt to possess whatever he had possessed that made him the one who was wanted.

And even before her mother—Alex's mother—
followed her daughter's gaze as she watched the car
move with alien slowness down the street to the intersection, then one more stop sign and turn at the corner
with the lights toward either the highway or the country
roads beyond it; before her mother understood and
dropped her knitting, the ball of wool bouncing down
Mrs. Gordimer's steps and rolling into the gutter; before
Muriel Martin pulled down the Christmas lights and
tried to hang herself by their cord under the cellar stairs,
and before her husband Gordon lifted her down, took
her in his arms and became a sentry to her babbling
existence; Kristi-Anne saw how Alex's face wavered in
the glass, saw how it looked—had always looked, Kristi-
Anne realized right then—like some other face, caught
mid-ripple in a pool, that might right itself when the
surface had stilled. And she saw how he took one last
look at the dandelions in bloom, the telephone poles,
the houses, the children, the neighbourhood, as if he
were absorbing them, as if he were falling heir to these
pieces of the world, as he would to all of it, cities and
countries and castles, in a way that would forever be
denied her. And then, how he turned away.

DIGGING FOR THOMAS

—

"SASKIA—" THE HARDWARE store owner looks at me over his glasses.

I do not let him finish his sentence. "Why so surprised, Mr. Farrell?" I push the seed packets across the counter. "Aren't we all interested in Victory?"

He counts the change without a nod.

The seeds shake inside the brown paper bag as I hand them to Robby, who reaches one hand up to take them, but keeps the other arm wrapped around my leg.

April is still too cold to plant, but when the first warm days arrive, the kind that follow one upon the other, we will be ready. As ready as everyone else.

Since November, my husband's things have been disappearing. His pipe, his grandfather's pocket watch, the stamp he saved from the coronation, crisp in waxed paper. I noticed these things first. Next was his shaving brush and then the picture he kept of us, with the ridge down the middle, like a wishbone—he on one side of the fold, Robby and me on the other. Now, it has become a ritual: on the sixteenth of each month I open the box to see what else is gone.

Twice, I have moved the box to a new hiding place. Once, I filled it again, scraping the house for other traces of him—a half-finished package of tobacco, old gloves, one with a hole in the finger, some binoculars someone gave him once and that he never used. They disappear only in increments, but all of it seems to be of value. Last month, even his socks. I pretend not to notice. I take long walks out into the country and leave the door unlocked. Let them take what they can.

The farmer across the road is turning his field. It takes me much of the morning to find the shovel in the shed. By late afternoon, I have only managed to rip up half the back lawn. Robby pushes his metal car in the soil. It is stuck and has to be rescued by a tin horse tied to the window with a piece of string. By evening, it is cold again and Robby sits in the kitchen while I heat the leftovers for dinner.

The next day there is a layer of frost against the upturned earth. Robby stays inside, but I put on my mittens and keep at it, while Robby watches through the window. At ten, the sun comes out. It cannot stay away forever.

Thomas caught the train like the rest of them, and all of us waved. He wrote of ways to measure wind speed and fly by the stars. Of shiny buttons and good English tea. In front of the post office, we wives compared our imagined trinkets—things our men would send back if they could.

Other towns began appearing in the papers, with numbers of dead and wounded. Plain Canadian names twinned with exotic places—Winnipeg and Hong Kong, Chatham and Dieppe, Saskatoon and Sicily. How grateful we were to see our names only in familiar script, on the fronts of letters, not in the hard cast of typeface on telegrams. And then, how proud. Some people said it was candles lit at church, or a particular pitch of prayer that better reached the generals. Others scoffed. Why bother with superstitions? How could we not be confident? Our boys were better. They had simply refused to fall.

We have seeds for carrots and lettuces, for beans that will run up along the fence, for squash that will pretend to be an ornament only, flowers hiding the fat pulpy gourds. I split the sprouting potatoes and tell Robby that they will make themselves again, whole live potatoes from these shrivelled things that have been too long in the cellar.

He puts his fingers close to the blade and I push the knife farther up the counter where he can't graze it. Two summers ago, he would sneak the fruits and vegetables from their baskets in the cellar and feed them to the Percherons that belong to the farmer across the road. Thomas and I smiled and pretended we didn't notice the missing apples, carrots and pears. Pretended that we didn't see our son climb through the lowest fence poles and walk right up to the horses' hooves the size of spades, hold out his hand to their teeth. We were so sure of our bounty.

Shot down, said the telegram in August. *Confirmed dead*, said the letter from the government in September. In October, condolences from the King: *an honour to his countrymen.*

But no countryman, no neighbour, came to console me. They left casseroles at the door, but didn't knock. At the service, they wouldn't meet my eyes. How quickly they exchanged their mourning clothes for their usual suits and smart dresses, their everyday hats. In the stores, the chatter and carousing grew louder when I approached, as if by turning toward the bins of flour and oats, the buckets of lard, they could ward off my disaster. "No, I never did hear that one before, son." "A purple wedding dress, can you believe it?" "Well she's sixteen and absolutely beautiful, reason enough for a party." Laughter was their armour.

I sewed a new and dour wardrobe. Wore black like the omen I was.

The packages promise easy gratification with beans and summer squash. Carrots will arrive by mid-July. "When it's time again for school," I tell Robby, "we'll be eating our potatoes."

I work the hoe an inch below the surface, completing a narrow trench that Robby marks out with stake and string. He's strong enough, but his boy's interests turn to the earliest bugs crawling by the edge of the house. I lead him back, determined that we share this plot and whatever it reaps.

"They'll only grow if you plant them right." I spill the seeds into my hand so Robby can pick out one or two. I help steady his finger as he pokes it into the earth.

"It's cold," he says.

I press my own index finger in to check. "It takes longer for the sun to get down there," I say.

I twist my wedding ring to let the dirt out from underneath. I'll make us pies from the pumpkins. My ring will tighten up again.

—

Last fall, after the telegram came, Robby turned six and started school. He didn't linger after the bell to play kick the can or to knock out flies, but each night he laid out his clothes without being asked, and smoothed his hair with tonic in the mirror.

I rose every morning just for the comfort of chopping eggs for his sandwich, buffing his shoes. I cinched tighter the belt on my coat, planned my visits to the centre of town strategically—went out to the shops only so I'd have flour for his bread, to the post office to pick up and pay the bills, just so that every night the lamp would light, and I could read to him from *Peter and Wendy*.

They no longer crossed the street when I approached, just clustered closer to shop fronts and benches while I walked the edge of the sidewalk, nearer to the road. When I think of it now, the distance they gave me then seems almost reverent. As if mine was a sacrifice that meant that they'd be spared.

Now that the garden is planted, Robby spends his days in the yard. Sometimes I hang laundry from the line or sit on the bench and watch him push his cars in slow circles around the roots of the maple or turn his handkerchiefs into parachutes, strung from the old tree's branches. But when I go inside, his play must turn rambunctious, because when he comes in he is the picture of any rough and tumble child—dirt up to his elbows, ground into his knees.

I try to catch him at it, to witness this bit of boyhood abandon. I peer out over the ironing board while I press the sheets, open his bedroom window and shake out the mat. But I see only my quiet son, arranging his toy soldiers around the garden's perimeter.

In November, Dolores Brett's husband was wounded. At the post office, I heard her father say, ". . . a hospital near Ortona," heard ". . . one leg for sure, maybe two." Three weeks later, I saw her, while queuing for chickens at the butcher, our arms so near we were almost touching. Even through her wool coat I could feel her warmth, pulling me in like an embrace. This is what we could offer each other, I thought: eyes that won't look away, bodies untroubled by the faint smell the lonely give off when we see no reason to wash.

"Dolores?" I said.

When she turned, I saw that her eyes were red rimmed and it seemed they wouldn't focus. She didn't know who I was. I put my hand on her shoulder and squeezed it gently. With that touch, recognition coursed through her. She clenched her jaw and pulled her body back, squared her shoulders—then she burst into tears and stumbled out of the shop. I followed her to the doorway, calling after her, but she ran beyond the hardware and around the corner.

I stepped backward into the shop and let the door close. The bell echoed as if the shop had emptied. But the customers had only fallen out of the queue, and now they were standing, several deep, between me and the counter. Even the butcher in his stained apron stood with them. A solid front.

There was only one way for me to go. I turned and cast myself into the street.

In the middle of the night, I open my eyes and listen to the still house. I put on my dressing gown and slip my bare feet into my shoes, go downstairs and check the doors. The front door is locked, and the door to the backyard is still bolted. I slide the bolt and step out. The air is cool enough to stunt any lingering thoughts of sleep.

A full moon hits the fences and the yard, all of it shining but colourless. I can't tell the red of Robby's bicycle from the black of the open earth. Things that were small this morning throw tall shadows—the hoe I left plunged in the dirt by the lettuce corner, the stocky wheelbarrow, the clothesline pole—as if the things themselves are plants, grown like Peter Pan's tree overnight. Even a thin, dark version of me, bigger than it is possible for a person to be.

On school mornings, Robby had to be roused from bed. One day, I saw a bruise along his back. Another, a scrape against his cheek. He brought home a satchel full of writing exercises, all undone. I flipped through the wide lines to see what he was missing, but mentioned nothing. One November morning, I let him lie on in bed past eight, past nine, both of us aware that he was not ill, not sleeping.

When we had to go to town, I scanned pocket tops for a glint of a particular silver watch chain. I followed men for paces, until I could rule out the curve of their pipes. Otherwise, we spent our days at games inside or going up the country lanes for hours, neither of us talking. Walking away was easier than coming home, even in the deepest snow. The door gave too easily. Pretended we were welcome.

It rains. Robby sets up dominoes and I must applaud as they tip into one another, climb over the books on the desk and down the other side, finally landing in a pile right at my feet, where they knock over the horse and the four tin soldiers, push the car into my slipper.

By bedtime, the rain falls harder, drumming the roof, closing us in. It's reassuring, I tell myself. It says that we are safe here. The roof is whole, the windows closed, the cellar impermeable.

It's good for the garden. It is spring, after all.

One dead, one injured, was how they counted our defeat. But I knew that others, too, were lost. I could see it in their wives' eyes: how they had stopped believing in husbands that would sit at their places at tables, settle with papers on couches, lie on their sides of beds. As if the spaces the men had occupied had sealed shut, behind doors with rusted hinges. But I would not let Thomas march away so easily.

I would make him a garden. I too would dig for Victory.

It rains and rains. The eavestroughs spew water, choking on leaves that should have been cleaned out last fall. I can't see more than a foot beyond the window. I can't see the garden, with its fragile shoots just beginning to push through. I am as anxious as a sailor's wife in a storm.

Finally, I pull on galoshes, tie on a bonnet. But I'm wet to the skin before I've walked two paces. When my boot sticks, I look behind and there is my boy. There's no point now in telling him to go inside. He's already soaked through.

We reach the edge of the garden together. The rain is scything down, digging out soil and throwing it beyond the bed into the sodden grass. Tiny sprouts are pouring up and over the banks made by the lawn. All my aspirations wash away.

A foot inside the garden's border, I see something silver. I squat and plunge my hand into the murk. It's Thomas's grandfather's pocket watch. My other hand finds a soggy clump speckled with something that looks like duckweed—his socks, covered in carrot seeds. Midway through the bed bobs a shaving brush with sodden bristles. I cannot bear to reach for the photograph I see at my feet, face down, in a dead-man's float.

I shake and Robby throws his arms around me. His tears are hot in the cold rain. "It's okay," I say. "I'm just very wet and very cold."

He peels his little face off my leg and turns his back to me. He roots for a moment in the mud. He hands me a package of tobacco, wrapped in string, and I realize how long our separate hopes have been growing, staked together.

"Shh," I say, "shh. It will be all right, little man. We will be all right."

I will save these things and lay them out to dry. When the rain has stopped we will gather more: his binoculars and pipe, perhaps the glove, the stamp—anything the earth will give us. What is too much for this season, we will put up for another.

RISE: A REQUIEM
(with parts for voice and wing)

—

Record of the Frontenac County Court House in the matter of the Queen versus Carlisle. Sworn testimony of Enoch Carlisle, former Reverend of St. Andrew's Presbyterian Church, Clergy Street, Kingston, taken this 18th day of February 1889.

THE FIRST THING you need to know is that I wasn't there. Not there to wear the dirt into my own useless hands. Not there to ease the struggling heart inside a young man's chest. Not there for the beauty of the bodies, lifted. Oh, there was joy. Rapture even. But I was not part of it.

Still, you will try me. Do what you will. I make no claim of innocence! A greater court than yours has already taken my account. If I have been found guilty, so have you all.

You ask me to tell. I am not reluctant. I have given my testimony at every occasion. I told it to that man there, taking notes. I told it to those gentlemen outside this courthouse. I dare say I will be telling it for the rest of my life: one that stretches on now without hope. I did indeed tell it to some gentlewomen. But I thank you, gentlemen, for barring ladies from this room. Screams and fainting will do nothing for us now.

On, on to it, you say.

First, there were the pigeons. The birds were already a miracle. Something rare. When I was a boy, I remember the skies blackening with their bodies, pressed tight against one another, the air so full of sound that I could only speak to my mother inside, while sitting on her lap with my mouth against her ear. Surely you remember them too?

On those spring days, my father would leave in the morning and return with a dozen of them strung along a pole. And on the first night, that squab would taste rich and sweet, its meat dark as some other bird's organ. But by the third day the meat would ball in my mouth, swell in my throat, and my father would whip me after dinner while the pigeons screamed until nightfall.

But it had been years since I had seen them in these numbers. The sky was not dark with them, as back then, but dotted, with seeping blue and white behind their formation. There were hundreds, not thousands, but still more than in the nearly thirty years since I had come to Kingston.

I was in the steeple when Sebastien saw me. "Something wrong with the bell, Father?" he called.

When I finally noticed him he was standing across the street from the grey stone of the church, with its fence around the yard, the rectory, the cemetery in between. But the birds were calling too, and I was not attuned to answer such a greeting. I had no wife, no children. No one called me Father.

"Father, can I assist? Is there a problem with the bell?"

"No, no. Only birdwatching," I shouted down.

I was a little chagrined to be caught at this, midway through a Thursday morning. My Sunday sermon was unfinished. But this young man did not know that. He saw only a man of the cloth hanging out the steeple opening on a loud and sunny day.

But it wasn't just the noise that came between us. His accent too made him difficult to understand. Accents rasp at the edges of the voices of many of my parishioners. But mostly Scottish. This was French, and thick.

He seemed eager to go on his way, but now that I had been caught in my observations I wanted someone to share them with. Before the birds had arrived overhead, my study had been too quiet and my sermon languished, despite the fact that I had instructed Mrs. Greenleyside to tell all visitors that I was not to be disturbed. I did not wish to return to its confines so I signalled him to wait. At the time, I thought he did so because of my position, because of my standing in the community. Now I wonder if he had been waiting for me all along.

I came down through the stone steps inside the steeple, down into the choir loft and along to the front of the church where I opened the thick oak door. There were carriages passing at the intersection and boys in the streets were pointing up at the flock. I shooed away the few who were throwing pebbles from in front of the church, but I doubt they heard my admonitions over the sounds of the birds.

Sebastien waited at the bottom of the steps. He was a young man, and his dress was black and formal. He wore the clothes of a gentleman, or perhaps of several gentlemen, for it appeared from the thinness of the cloth that it had hung on many sets of shoulders. I beckoned him to join me inside where we could hear one another without shouting.

"Do you know birds, sir?" I asked him when the thick door closed behind us.

"Bells," he said. "For three generations, my family are makers of bells."

I was too bent on sharing my knowledge to inquire about his history or how a young man with such an astounding French accent came to be standing on Clergy Street in Scotch and Irish Kingston.

"Well, passenger pigeons. I haven't seen them in numbers like this since I was a boy. One of God's miracles."

Sebastien snorted. A most ungentlemanly laugh, but it startled me so much that I felt obliged to echo it.

"Pigeons are the closest cousins of the dove. No doubt they shared a berth on Noah's voyage. Who is to say that really it wasn't a pigeon that returned with the olive branch? Fascinating creatures. Release the pigeon and they know their way home—from anywhere. Been carrying messages across battlefields since the Old Testament."

"These are not those kinds of pigeons." His English was good.

"Ah! You are correct! These are *Ectopistes migratorius*. Passenger pigeons."

"Passenger? From '*passages*'?"

"Yes, indeed! Famous for their great migrations, their great '*passages*.' Audubon writes of them."

He seemed a willing student. "Would you like tea? Mrs. Greenleyside would make it. I need only to ask."

"No, Father," he said, and his eyes turned serious. These were his first weeks of medical school, he said, and there was so much he needed to study. Already he felt himself falling behind.

"Surely you are not alone in that," I said, remembering my clerical studies and the long nights memorizing verses.

Sebastien shrugged. "The others play cricket," he said.

"And you?" I asked. "What were you doing out if there is so much learning waiting for you?"

His answer was so quiet that I had to bend in to hear it.

"Researching, Father," he said.

I laughed then, as I pushed the oak door open. "Dear boy, you are still a few blocks from the library."

Sebastien stepped out of the cool enclosure and into the fall sun as though he were reluctant to be released. But he almost stumbled at the stair. There was a little body there, not quite a carcass, it had so recently fallen. I bent and picked it up.

"Hello, too-weary traveller." I felt for a heartbeat, but it had stopped. The body was still warm, even hot. The fawn-coloured feathers on the wing, built for catching air currents, ruffled, giving way to a crimson breast that was reflected in its still-open eye, a shining orange, like a dried apricot.

"Father, let me take it," Sebastien said. He held out his hands, uncreased but surprisingly dirty at the nails. "I would like to look more closely at this miracle."

I would have buried it, in the garden at the edge of the churchyard. I swear I had no thought of dinner. Still, I was reluctant. But he looked so gentle: a poor student in a hostile town. So I let the little body roll into his open hands.

—

You ask for the facts, without embellishments. You ask for the truth. But this, gentlemen, is the truth. A man came calling to my church, naming me Father. I let him in, or I believed I did.

"Be not forgetful to entertain strangers: for thereby some have entertained angels unawares." Surely each of you has heard it, at sermons in your own parishes. Luke McGovern, I know you have heard it in mine.

It was more than a week before I saw him again. The pigeons had made their way across the top of my church at the foot of the town for two days and then had gone, leaving enough silence for me to have no excuse but to write a rather uninspired sermon drawing on Matthew's birds of the air, "they neither sow nor reap."

I cannot call myself an ornithologist. Cardinals, grackles, herons have all passed my notice with merely a glance. Only the pigeons captured my imagination and respect. Was it their spectacular colour? One might say: what of the robin's breast? I would not trade the passenger pigeon's true scarlet for the robin's orange vest. Or the robin's common black eye for the passenger pigeon's, bright as a tavern window on a dark night. But it was more than beauty. What man with a compass could find not only a lake where he had camped for a single night in other seasons, but also the very fence post he chose to sit on, a year, or three, before? Pigeons know their way home better than any man, or any creature known to him, and they will ferry their brothers to and from it, home and out again, like something passing between worlds. Their fearlessness also drew me. When one preys upon them, they do not scatter, take flight with their fellows and never return, marking this a place of danger. Instead, they sit still and look upon you as if to say that there are things worse than death, and there will be a time when you will know them.

I was thinking this as I was cutting back the hedge that had grown scraggly in that dry, dry summer. Mr. Greenleyside had not come that morning, I don't remember why now. Ah, there. Why didn't you come, John? No matter.

I looked up from my pruning, something I am not proficient at, and saw Sebastien walking the rows of graves between the rectory and the church.

"Hello, young doctor!" I called to him. He was still at a distance, but I could tell it was he by his too-early stoop—whether forged over books or bells I did not know—his thin frame and thinner coat. He froze, but when I raised my hand he walked toward me as though he were following a beacon.

We were in what I think of as the new part of the churchyard, where the more recent stones are laid. It is not new in the ways of the big cemetery out at Cataraqui. We've become quaint and outdated, burying our dead so near our living when most of the other parishes send their deceased to the outskirts. But it has been a matter of pride in my parish, one that I may also have engaged in, to think that our dead were in our embrace at the same time as they were drawn to the bosom of the Lord.

We met up near the freshly dug grave of Mrs. Wilkins's baby. "It's a quieter day than when last we met. How are your studies, Sebastien?"

When he looked up to answer, I was startled by the change in him. He had dark circles under his eyes and he did not return my smile. I found it difficult to imagine the roaring snort that had come from him on our first encounter.

"Father, will you take my confession?"

I told him I was not that kind of man of God, that Presbyterians trusted a man to settle his accounts with the Lord without human intervention. "God already knows your heart, Sebastien."

I have seen men and women attend the funerals of their most beloved, I have seen men off to the gallows, but rarely have I seen a face so stricken as was Sebastien Montague's when I told him that I could offer no absolution.

"I cannot intercede with the Lord, Sebastien, but I can still listen as a friend," I said.

He shook his head.

"Perhaps another time," I said. He forced a smile at the edge of his nearly purple lips. He had not shaved and there were shadows on his jaw and chin.

"Is there not a priest at St. Mary's? Perhaps that is more what you're looking for?" I did not like to leave him agonizing and silent.

"What happens to us, when we go into the ground, Father?"

"Please: Reverend Carlisle will do."

"The Bible says we return to the earth. But what stages do we make to do so? Worms eat us, Father. But our nails continue to grow. Did you know that?"

I said that I had never heard it, but I was a man of God and not of science. In those matters, I would defer to him.

"When Miss Flora Connery collapsed on her way to class, I was walking in a group behind her. I saw her lying in the sidewalk. They took off her gloves and hat to give her some air."

It startled me to hear our worlds had crossed. I had attended at her funeral two weeks ago, as Miss Connery's family had been members of my parish since they arrived from Toronto. I myself had held her over the baptismal font. She was quiet even then, a weak but pretty baby. When they laid her in the ground a row over, I could not forget the watery eyes above the christening gown.

"She had the most beautiful fingernails, Father. Smoothed to a circle along the edge and a little moon at the bottom of each of them. Short, just reaching the tip of the skin. Now her nails will grow long as a harlot's."

His overly familiar words shocked me and made me

wonder if perhaps he had held some secret love for her that now would never be reciprocated or denied. And because I have always found it easier to speak of losses over love, things of the spirit over more corporeal matters, I sought to address what I thought was troubling him most: his nearness now to illness and to death.

"Doctors and ministers come in handy only when there is suffering. We are always the last resorts." I looked up, but his face was on the newly turned earth at the baby's grave.

"Today, I must say a funeral for six members of the same family who died in a fire on William Street. The Barclays. They belonged to this parish. Belonged, in that they are Protestants, Presbyterians, and their parents worshipped with the men and women of this church when first they came to this country. I saw them in the church but rarely met them. You know why? They did not need me, young Sebastien, until today. Today, I will look into their faces, though they will not see mine." I laid my hand on his thin coat. "Do not worry, Doctor, you will become more comfortable making the acquaintance of the dying and the dead."

They say only God can make a miracle. But he cannot do it alone. You think this is blasphemy? God can make a miracle but He requires us to recognize it. When we dismiss the first flower in the garden, is it that He has not performed His majesty, or that the audience was sleeping? What if Saul on the road to Damascus had got back on his horse, kept his name and continued on his journey? To see miracles, we must live with eyes open. Though it hardly matters now.

That following night, I was not conscious of how long the knocking had been going on, for when I heard it, it was loud, but also rhythmic, as though it had built from a much smaller sound. It took me a moment to light the lantern and to cover myself. I thought first of a fire or some other crisis, but there was no shouting, no light in the sky. The night was very dark, so dark that when I first pulled the door to the rectory open, I did not recognize Sebastien.

"I have been sent," he said.

My first thought, I admit it now, was irritation. I had been dreaming of my father's table and the nights the squab tasted finest, before it became a chore to swallow. My mother and father had been looking at me in the light of the fire and they both had love in their eyes. The love was all the more poignant because I knew, in my mature understanding, my lacing of memory upon experience, that it was fleeting, and soon my father's face would cloud with disappointment that his son could reject something that had been provided at his own hand, and with such bounty. Already in the dream I was curled up against the cold that was coming, aware that morning would steal it away, make me put my feet down on the hard floor of the present and walk across it into another day. Sebastien had pulled me from the last of my comfort.

But when he put his head against the door frame, knocking his hat to the floor, I saw that his face was rapturous, as if he were the one who had just woken from a beautiful dream, or as if it continued still. And in my wonder at the transformation, I forgot my anger.

In my limited understanding, I imagined that he might have come to tell me he was in love. That some young beauty had overlooked his accent and his thread-bare circumstances.

"Come in, come in," I said. I bent and picked up his cap and sat him in a chair before the fire that I attempted to stoke.

The glow lit him first from below, illuminating the muddy boots that Mrs. Greenleyside would have to clean up behind in the morning, then moving up the dark trouser leg and onto his coat, both of which were mud splattered. When it reached his face I saw that my initial inability to recognize him was not only because of the moonless night. His face was smeared with cork.

"Father, I want to speak to you about the bird."

In my heart I had suspected he had eaten it, the beautiful thing. I understood this to be a likelihood when a poor student is offered a free meal, even one that has so recently had its heart beating, so I could not fault him for that. I would have buried it given the chance, but would I not then have gone in to eat Mrs. Greenleyside's chicken dinner?

I put his hat on his knee and patted it there. "It's all right, Sebastien. Perhaps we may think of that bird as an offering, something presented to you in your time of need. I am sure there cannot have been much meat on it, a single migrating pigeon."

"No, Father. There was not much meat." But at this confession he did not show any shame. "There was muscle and sinew, and the most marvellous joints where the wing met the body. She wasn't stiff yet; she still moved with suppleness. It seemed that if I took my hand off her, she'd lift off to join her flock."

Whether unconsciously or for emphasis, he cupped his hands before him as he spoke. "Even with her sliced-open belly, still she might have taken wing."

I tried to keep a grimace from my lips, but his eager description made my stomach turn.

"Don't think me a monster, Father. I needed her. I needed her for practice."

"Practice for what? The stewpot?"

"Practice for the corpses, sir."

Dissection. I had heard rumours of this in the medical schools. Young men sinking sharp instruments into bodies gone cold, those wretches who had no family to claim them from hospitals and poorhouses, no minister to shepherd them through death and on to the afterlife. But it was hard to reconcile this gentle boy with those groups of knife wielders.

Men of the cloth, and men of science, often see things that other men do not. I have sat by the bedsides of ailing men, heard their final breaths and smelled the stink on them that followed their souls' departure. I have felt lonely there, left behind with the abandoned bodies. I thought perhaps this troubled him, the thought of a mere shell, empty of its life. But he continued with an enthusiasm that stabbed at me as if it were forced there by his very blade.

"When I cut into her, I wondered how the knife would feel. I had to press to get through the feathers, but the skin gave easily, as if it were surrendering."

"Sebastien, it is not necessary to tell—"

"But it was the wing that perplexed me most. I grabbed its little tip, its longest feather, and pulled it out from her side, stretched it as far as it would go, up beyond her head. Each feather like a lady's fan, one upon the other, as if stitched there by God himself. That was what I thought: our heavenly Father sitting late nights like a tailor, so careful to match the thread so it remained invisible. Brown feathers became light as deerskin and then turned the colour of the cream at the top of the milk pail, then into white. I flipped her over onto her red belly, and held her wing wide to the side of her.

"The joint at the shoulder looked like a woman's. It was a woman's back I was looking at, attached to the feathered wing!"

I thought the young man, Christian though he was, was confusing his immature fears. I have understood that young unmarried men are often tempted to think of the natural beauties of women and then to feel regret at their sinful thoughts, but remain as powerless to dispel those thoughts as if a real woman stood before them. And so, shaken though I was, I asked him, "Sebastien, have you ever seen a real woman with bare shoulders?"

Another young gentleman would have blushed at such a question, stammered his way to an answer, unsure which was more damning, the "no" of the innocent or the "yes" of the experienced. But Sebastien seized upon my question as if he had been waiting for it.

"Not until we cut into Miss Flora Connery."

I felt myself falling, but I remained firmly in my chair. The practice of the cloth, the stoic face, the detached look that allows a man in my position to attend at bedsides and gravesides and prison cells, officiate over crying babies, hear marriage vows for those who should never be joined, did not fail me even then. But my voice must have shaken.

"Sebastien, you are mistaken. Miss Connery is with the Lord and her body is in the ground. I watched her father shake a handful of earth across her coffin."

"I did not want to do it, Father. I had to. All of us

have to take our turn—it doesn't matter who is before us, man, woman or infant. For me, it was Miss Connery."

I rose and stepped behind my chair, gripped it like a pulpit. "You are ill. Miss Connery is from a loving family, a reputable parish. She is not some castoff from the charity wards of the hospital. The destitute and the abandoned have no protection against such injury. I do not know the name of the poor woman you have desecrated, but I will pray for her soul, and yours as well."

"You believe those unwanted bodies are enough?" His voice was quiet, an adult explaining an obvious truth to a child. "There are never enough."

The fire dimmed and surged, and for a moment the things of the room disappeared, and the light seemed to burn right into me. How far did my responsibility extend? I had held Mrs. Connery's hand at her daughter's bedside. I had stood next to Mr. Greenleyside while he put the girl in the ground. I believed I had escorted her as far as I could between this world and the next. My hands clutched at the fabric at my wrists and hips, searching for the constancy of the stiff cut of my reverend's frock coat, its precise cuffs and pockets. But I found none, and when the flame flickered and steadied, I saw I was only a man standing in my living room, wearing my dressing gown.

"I did not want to be a doctor," Sebastien said. "But when I went to the priest he said, 'The good son does as his father wishes.' Then he laughed. 'But I do not think you have much to fear. Remi-the-bell-maker's son will never be a doctor.' When my father heard, he said, 'You will go where they do not know you.' But under what disguise? They know me by my voice, by a purse so empty I cannot pay for books and instruments. When they told me I could pay my way in bodies, I wrote to my father. 'Do what you must,' he said. 'God will worry about the soul.'"

"Sebastien, I can hear no more."

"Please—you have to. Because when I cut into Miss Connery's white skin, I saw something there, Father."

"You will address me as Reverend Carlisle!"

"It was as if, even as her skin was darkening, her human limbs stiffening, she was still growing."

"Sebastien. That is decay. Rot! The things left behind when the spirit is taken."

"No! I looked around the theatre to see if anyone else could see it. But they only chided me to get back to the cutting. 'Look at him! The Frenchman's turning green! That why they call you Frogs, I guess.' 'Careful, Montague. If you pass out, we might just start dissecting you.' And so I pressed the knife in again—and they were still there."

It was then I began to abandon my duty. I wanted this young man out of my rooms, removed from such close proximity to my church, to my congregation, to my soul.

"You need to go to the priest, Sebastien," I said. "He will set you right with your God. It is not something I can do."

"Feathers. It was as if the girl were wearing a feather collar over her bare shoulders. They are changing, Father. The corpses are growing wings."

I had been confronted before by young men who misinterpreted their morality. I had seen the bruised faces of wives of men who took their role as master of the household too far. I had ministered to men at the prison before their execution. Sebastien's eyes burned orange as the bird's had, that morning in the sunshine. And I could not name what I saw there. Was it madness, or the hard ember of evil?

"I will speak to the medical school."

"I will not be a student much longer."

"I will speak to a priest."

"I am not here for absolution."

"Then, why tell me these things?"

"Because they are wonderful! Oh, at first I was afraid. I feared the bodies on the slab, the empty weight of them when I held them lifeless against my chest. And then the shock of it: the old skin blue and puckered where the new feathers are breaking through. How to explain it? Who to explain it to?

"But then last night, I walked and wondered for many miles. I looked into the faces of classmates, neighbours and strangers. And what I saw horrified me more than the dead have ever done. In every passing face I saw the skin turn purple, as though the blood had pooled there. The eyes sank in and fell inside the skulls, as if each taunting look were coming from a body in advanced decay. And then I understood: it is the living who are decomposing, while the dead are becoming beautiful and new! They are ready, Father. And I am ready too."

There was a shout from outside. I had forgotten that the world could intrude, so locked I felt in this small orange room. I was startled, then relieved. Something else, someone else! I would be released. Sebastien took up his hat and stood. I heard the noise again as he walked out through the hall and opened the door himself. And I bid myself to follow.

"Since I have come here, I have been stolen from and taunted. Not a single man, woman or child has offered me even a kind glance. Except for you. You have not gone unnoticed. I will not forget."

Beyond the door were the voices of men and the sound of a cart, rolling on the street past the churchyard. Sebastien ran in the direction of the sound and his figure was lost to me.

I would not sleep that night, what little there was left of it. I looked out to the churchyard thinking of how others believed this place a sanctuary, trusted their souls and eventually their bodies to my care. I was afraid to stay in by the glowing fire, to recall his face. It was as if I feared that something he had tracked in with him had remained in the small room to haunt me. I was even more afraid to step outside the door of the rectory. Once outside, I knew I would have to verify my suspicions, and I did not want to believe.

But this was not an exploration I wanted Mr. Greenleyside to undertake. I was not even certain I could ask him to do such a thing without calling for a violation that I myself would have to condemn.

I lit a lantern and went out into the last of the autumn night. I walked past the graves of the families of our parish, those that had survived into their elder years, wizened and persistent, and those who had succumbed, young and sometimes not even baptized, been taken back to God. Who was the more fortunate? Those who had lived or those who had seen this earth and retreated from it instantly, sparing themselves decades of harshness and hunger? Certainly, I'd always called them chosen, to their mothers and fathers presenting me the wrapped bundles before we laid them in the earth.

It was far too dark to read the inscriptions, in those places where prosperity had allowed them, on the headstones. Still, I knew many: *Catherine, beloved wife of Josiah, gone to His care this 4th day of January in the year of our Lord 1881 . . . Matthew, second son of Ewan . . .* the entire list of Michael Christopher Grants, one for every year from 1872 to 1885, a testament to near-boundless hope. And I found again, even on this desperate mission, that my sorrow lay not with the old and the infirm, and not even with those poor souls who had barely had a body to inhabit, so short was their time. It was with those who had laid them here. The widower with twenty years to endure before his own calling, the mothers and fathers who gave the little bodies to my arms. All left behind.

The ground was resistant under my boots along those established pathways, but as I neared the newer graves, the grass gave way to mud and I felt my feet slipping forward as if I were being drawn closer even as I wanted to step back, as if I were sliding downhill on the churchyard's level ground. I tried to hold my concerns at bay by reminding myself that of course the ground was softer here. Hadn't mourners just tended to this place? Hadn't Mr. Greenleyside stood here for hours, his own boots planted firmly on the turf while he dug at the cooling ground?

Soon, it would be too cold for burials. These were the last of the autumn interments. Those that were ailing or had some fate awaiting them in three weeks or four would spend the winter stacked and stored.

But I could feel the give of the ground in a way that belied the season. It might have been May for its softness. It was as if a whole procession had tramped this little piece of ground, or as if some warmth, some fire, were coming from within. I stopped beside the Barclay grave with its six inhabitants laid side by side. I set the lantern down and watched it settle into the earth.

I cannot commend more highly the work of Mr. Greenleyside. It is always tidy. He could have been a woman stitching at the squares of a quilt, his lines are so steady, could have made the finest marks on architectural blueprints, his angles are so fine. True, oft times others assist him. Some springs there are so many bodies that Mr. Greenleyside must command whole crews to stand beside him, as though they were building the foundation for a spectacular edifice, something that would exist long beyond their labour. But always he supervises their work. Nothing slipshod, nothing out of place.

But the edges of the graves no longer bore Mr. Greenleyside's straight marks. The earth was piled recklessly, as if only a gesture toward filling the space. More of it was scattered between the rows, and on it were the boot prints of several men, their feet various sizes, all crowding in and stepping on the places others had stepped before.

You would think that would be evidence enough for me, wouldn't you, gentlemen? You would wish it. Would have had me instantly go to the authorities, report the young man, my young friend, so that Sebastien too could sit here, could be condemned before you all. For it would be he, wouldn't it, who would have filled this hard chair? Not the others, with their better names, who accompanied him, who pulled the dirt back from the earth while he made his confession by my fireside. And it is here that you first begin to question my account, suspect my motives, wonder what man of God would keep such secrets. But I remembered the light in Sebastien's eyes, and it seemed that the reflection of the fire lingered there, even as he turned away from the hearth, even as he stepped back onto the little threshold and turned out into the night. And so I sank the shovel into the twice-disturbed earth and began to dig, looking for the proof in finding nothing.

And though I dug swiftly, then covered the ground again, I am not a man used to physical labour. My progress was slow and continued even as the light began to grow. I believe some of you saw me there that morning, on your way to your work. And it hardly seemed that you had jumped to conclusions when later you decided what you had seen.

Later that morning I wandered, not knowing my purpose, until I found myself at the university, asking for the young man with the French accent, the bell-maker's son. Outside Summerhill with its circular folly, upright young men laughed at the mention of his name and soon I was directed away from the newer grand edifices, past the College and the churches where other men of God tended to problems that before last night had appeared to me to be the full extent of life's conundrums and nothing God would not lead us through.

Up Division Street, beyond St. Mary's, where men and women of Sebastien's faith apparently were lying undisturbed, the poor and the wealthy, side by side in restful sleep. The day was warmer than it should have been for the season, and the walk had been long when finally I turned onto a street where the houses leaned up against one another for support. I inquired of the landlady, but she said she had not seen him or heard his footsteps on the stair since the day before.

"Sometimes he does not come back for days," she said, her accent thick and Irish. "What do I care, so long as he pays?"

I told her that I would return. But by afternoon there was the blessing for Mrs. McWilliams who wondered why there had been no news from her sister's family in England, and ministering to Mr. Craig regarding the moral education of his six sons. By the time Mrs. Greenleyside was clearing away the dinner dishes, I decided only sleep would settle me, but when at last I sat at the edge of my bed I knew that I could not sleep. Several times I rose and went to the window, thinking I had heard a stirring at the door, but it was quiet. When I heard the bells strike four, I gave up and dressed and walked back out to the cemetery.

I knelt down beside the Barclay graves, their temporary resting places, and tried to pray for them as if they were still held in the safety of my parish. I tried not to think of where they lay, what hard surface was now their bed. I tried to banish the images of their bodies, parts disconnected from one another, in some configuration never meant by God, as if He were merely a watchmaker whose beings could be dismantled and His secrets discovered like the handiwork of some ordinary craftsman.

It was there that Sebastien found me, his voice rising out of the darkness like something that already rested in my ear.

"The passengers are nesting east of the city. In the field of a farmer called Colquhoun."

I pronounced it correctly for him then, certain he had read this name in the *Whig* rather than heard it said. Perhaps, most likely, the business of farmers was not the sort of thing that medical students spoke about. Perhaps no one spoke to him at all.

"Impossible," I said. "It's October. The birds fly south now, hundreds of miles every day. Those birds we saw have crossed into America."

"I have seen them," he said.

And what was I to do with that? I wanted to insist he was wrong. Perhaps he had seen some other birds.

"Come, I'll show you," he said.

I thought I forgot myself for a moment then. Thought I forgot my bond with my parishioners, my duties to the souls in my care. I thought then that when I accepted, trusting him to ferry us out past the city borders, I was more a child than a man of God. But I know now that it was my last step toward salvation before I turned away.

What is the difference between faith and instinct? Where do both reside? Is faith a resident of our hearts? But faith is not the same as love. And if instinct lives in the brain, there it must wrestle with logic. What made me stand and follow Sebastien, a man I barely knew? What made me walk to the corner of Clergy and Princess, pull myself onto the dirty cart that had so late ferried the soulless bodies of my congregation, and drive with him through the nearly black streets? I felt as powerless to resist him as if it were he and not the ragged horse that pulled us past the closed shop fronts, the tailors' windows, the post office and out into an area of empty lots that soon became more country than town, then up some concession and along a road that revealed itself as the light made sticks of the treeless branches alongside. He turned into a wagon rut that ran over a ditch and then we were in a cornfield, lately harvested.

"There," he said, though he needn't have. Along the field's perimeter were trees, ash and beech and some maple, and every one of them was tossing as if it were a hurricane, instead of a still, fall dawn. The trees began to wail and creak, and as the light came up behind them, the bare branches looked like they had regrown their autumn leaves, in shades of brown and red. If I had not seen them and heard them, I would have smelled them. Dung had accumulated in heaps as big as boulders under every perch.

"Someone will shoot them," Sebastien said.

"That is the way with things that are both beautiful and food," I said.

"Do you not care, Father?"

I thought of my responsibilities, my duties, and how I had always believed that I had executed them—not with perfection, but with a good heart and the aid of God. I had never felt comfortable with the easy condemnation of my fellows. I had tried my best to comfort equally the mothers of the murderer and the hangman, assuring them both that an eye for an eye was God's will, but so too forgiveness.

But Sebastien's words rapped at my conscience like a summons I had long ignored. It was true that I had never been the first to thrown the stone. But neither had I walked into the circle's centre to put my arm around the fallen woman. Grabbed the hands of those who gripped the stones, and forced them to drop their weapons to the ground.

The idea that my response had been lacking chilled me and I must have shivered against Sebastien's own thin coat as we sat in the cart, as if I were the man less prepared for the chill of the season and the strangeness of the world.

"What is it, Father?" Sebastien asked.

"Why are they here?" I asked. I did not expect an answer.

"They're only waiting, Father," he said, his voice strong and calm as any man who had achieved standing and the respect of all who know him.

"For what?" I asked.

He smiled then. "They're waiting for the last of the passengers. They're waiting for you."

What is the difference between a madman and a prophet? What separates those who dare to follow from those that would choose the same paths they walked yesterday, the day before?

"Tomorrow this field will be empty." Sebastien rested the reins against his knees and opened his arms to take in the screeching masses. "There will be no more chances, no more migrations. Do not be afraid, Father. The journey is long, but they know the way."

What made me do what I did? What made me clench my hands into fists, and then heave myself with all my strength against his chest? What made me shove my shoulder up under his chin and thrust my elbow into his ribs just as his arms came forward as if to embrace me? Was it indignation? Ignorance? Or merely fear?

It had been many years since my hand had been used against another and the force with which he toppled startled me. I found myself standing, the momentum of the shove having lifted me from the wagon seat, and I watched him fall. But as he tumbled backward, a darkness opened between us, as if the distance I stared into were not the few feet from the seat of the cart to the dried-out stalks of corn below but the distance seen from a mountaintop. And then he stopped and hovered there, as if suspended somewhere partway down a dark well.

My remorse lagged only an instant. I fell to my belly and reached out to him, but he was beyond my grasp. But I know, I know that even then it was not too late. I could have jumped down from the wagon, followed him into that narrow cavern. I could have made myself a sacrifice, an offering to assuage my violence. But I did not. Instead I screamed and screamed his name until it sounded as if the word was echoing inside me.

It was the birds' screeching filling my ears, reaching down inside my throat and lodging there. The pigeons were rising from the trees and circling the cornfield, each circuit drawing in more of their flock. And then I saw Sebastien's black coat lift at the shoulders, turn cream and then brown. He spread his wings like a tarp over the wagon, and when he rose I saw the scarlet of his open heart and in his eye the sudden spark of an innocent betrayed.

You say I cannot substantiate my claims. That you need more than the ravings of an old reverend, found weeping under his pillow, rags stuffed in his ears. Something to counter the grave robbers' wagon, pulled up alongside the churchyard, in the very place you saw the old fellow digging some nights before. But how will you explain the brief and sudden shadow over the medical school and then the hour of darkness over that church on Clergy Street when everywhere else the sun had risen? How will you account for the four hundred graves opened and emptied in a single night? And what will you use to do it?

Reason?

You think a single man, or even two or four, could accomplish this, one of them digging with hands whose only calluses were earned holding the hands of the dying and cradling babies?

You may hunt on for Sebastien. Or you may confine me to the very cells where once I ministered. You may look for proof. Or you may act on faith alone. It matters not, to any of us. We are all beyond judgment. There will be no trumpet call. No horsemen. The rivers will not flow backward or run with blood. The apocalypse is over. It came and went with only the beating of ordinary wings.

This afternoon, you will walk out and look at the sunlight off the lake and pull your collars against the wind.

You will go back to offices and pubs or home to supper. You will fight with your neighbour, lay with your wife. And whatever verdict you hand me you will count yourself lucky. For today at least, you will think your life not so very bad.

But think on this, gentlemen: this is all there is.

SLEEPING FUNNY

—

A T THE PARTY, Clea's daughter Minnie got a goldfish instead of a loot bag. On the way home in the car, Minnie held the plastic bag in her lap. Out of the corner of her eye, Clea watched the fish bob like a shimmering piece of guilt.

Clea went into Carter's Critters to buy it a bowl. The man behind the counter wore a happy-face T-shirt. It was faded and too small for his muscled chest, as if it were a boyhood conviction he refused to discard.

"An invitation to a birthday party should not be a life commitment," Clea said.

Carter said, "It's easy. Just add water," and then he packed up the food they were supposed to feed it, twice a day, in exactly the right quantity.

Back at her dad's, Clea put the fishbowl in the centre of the kitchen table, rinsed the stones, washed and filled the bowl, then tipped the bag and let the fish swim, unprotected, into new water. Before bed, she counted the food into Minnie's hand and watched her shake the pieces in. The flakes clumped on the surface, then floated out like an oil slick.

When Clea came down, groggy and off balance, Monday morning, Minnie was brushed and dressed and eating her cereal. The fish was lying motionless at the top of the water. One clouded eye stared up at Clea.

"This goldfish was not the right pet for us," Minnie said. She tapped the fishbowl with her spoon. "This goldfish did not know how to adapt."

Clea looked across the bare surface of the kitchen table, the one place she'd managed to clear completely, to the furniture and picture frames piled up in the corners, the quilts and rugs on the radiators, the magazines precariously close to the stove. Even to Clea, it was an incomprehensible and daunting landscape. Who knew how it looked from inside the fishbowl, looming distorted and enlarged behind the clean blue pebbles and the plastic plant?

After the March Break, when Clea's father had moved to Intensive Care and it was clear that they could not go back to Vancouver, not yet, Clea enrolled Minnie in the school down the road, the one that Clea had gone to. In the years that Clea had been away, a two-storey wire fence had risen around it, like Sleeping Beauty's castle, the inner-city version.

When Clea walked Minnie up the front steps, birth certificate in hand, they stepped over a condom encased in ice.

"Is that what I think it is?" Minnie said.

"It's all right," Clea said. "This is only temporary."

The next day, Clea's father took a turn for the worse. Clea and Minnie sat a vigil beside his bed, not sure if he knew that they were there, or that he was. He died that night.

Driving her father's car past the schoolyard on the way to the funeral home, Clea thought she heard the word *bitch* strike at the window and cling like a wet snowball. Relief fought to the surface over grief: Minnie would never go there. Clea would clean the house, and they'd be gone.

But every quilt that Clea removed revealed another pile of debris. There was mildew behind the shower, mould on the basement ceiling. The floors that her mother had kept washed and polished were lifting where the radiators had leaked. There were twisted things on the lawn, springs and frames that looked like skeletons from which the flesh had rotted away.

While Clea cleaned indoors, Minnie made pictures with a wet rag on the nicotine-coated walls, or watched out the window as a man pushed a shopping cart up the sidewalk, so close to the house that you could see the stains on his jacket, because now the road was four lanes instead of two, because now the trees were gone.

Clea woke in the night and couldn't go back to sleep, or slept and felt she hadn't. In the morning, the rooms seemed as dirty and disorganized as they had the morning before. One day, bent low to a baseboard, Clea took a breath and felt the dampness seep into her like a sponge. Reeking of Lysol, she drove up the mountain to the new part of town and enrolled Minnie in a bright and sprawling school set on land so flat it looked like the building had been dropped right onto the planner's drawing. Minnie gave their address to the principal.

"It's temporary," Clea said.

And then Minnie was invited to Stacey Hellman's birthday party.

The card said *1209 Tamarack*, but it could have been 1209 Tarmac, there was so much asphalt on the long street, so much interlocking brick in the driveways. Trees ran up and down the boulevards, but they were stunted, their roots unequal to the underground systems of new sewers and floodlighting. Clea parked her dad's car in front of three storeys of beige stucco, with urns stuffed with hyacinths and snowdrops that had clearly been forced.

The door opened with the sucking sound of good weather stripping and a muted alarm announced the sudden influx of outside air. The woman at the door was blonde and toned and wearing a sweater set that matched the house's neutral interior.

"Hello, Mrs. Hellman," Minnie said. "Thank you for inviting me to Stacey's party."

Clea reached out to drape her arm over Minnie's shoulders, but Minnie had already stepped over the threshold and into the foyer. It had always been like this, Minnie seemingly equipped for the next experience, Clea fluttering in the background, articulating too late the reasons for caution.

"Well, what do you know?" said Stacey Hellman's mother. "Minnie *Osler*. *Clea* Osler. And never mind that, just look at her! I should have known."

Clea heard an interior door being opened and the foyer filled with the off-stage babble of little girls. One of them was sliding across the marble.

"You're here!" the girl said, and Minnie nodded.

"Stacey," Mrs. Hellman said, "Minnie's mother and I went to school together too."

And of course, now that Clea looked, Stacey Hellman's mother was Melanie Geary. Or she had been, once. Melanie Geary, pretty, but not pretty enough. Melanie Geary, smart, but not smart enough. Melanie Geary, a friend, but not friend enough for Clea—willowy Clea, intelligent Clea, promising Clea, Clea with the better house, the better parents, the better prospects—to defend her at the end of high school when the other kids and even some of the teachers whispered that she'd been knocked up in the back of Greg Hellman's building supply truck. Or for Clea to leave university and come back across the country for the wedding the next fall—or even to send her regrets.

But really, this woman was not Melanie Geary. This woman was Stacey Hellman's mother. They had matching blonde hair (dyed, of course) and matching blue eyes (were those coloured contacts?). They cocked their heads like birds, listening to something that played at a frequency that no one else could hear, their identical earrings trembling beneath identical earlobes. It seemed as if the process of heredity had been altered, as if, in birthing Stacey Hellman, Melanie Geary had received an entirely different set of genes, a reconfigured DNA.

Stacey Hellman's mother shooed the girls out of the foyer and Stacey retreated with Minnie, her little muscled arm slung around Minnie's neck.

"Clea," Stacey Hellman's mother said, "now that you're here, you'll have to stay. Come in, come in."

They walked through the kitchen and past a countertop that divided the cooking space from a living room with a vaulted ceiling. On the island, a dozen perfect bubbles were tucked, like silicone implants, into a cardboard tray. Each one was tied with ribbon above a nucleus of gold.

"Cute, aren't they?" Stacey Hellman's mother said. "Something a little different, not just the same old loot bags." The goldfish were as still as pieces of fruit in moulded jelly.

The living room had plush white carpet—Scotchgarded, not to worry. Stacey Hellman's mother passed Clea a coffee. "Architecture, right?"

"Engineering," Clea said.

"And how is it?"

A fantasy blueprint. It wasn't that she hadn't been good at it. She had. The formulas came easily, the plans were a delight to draw. It was the application that had baffled her.

"I work for a manufacturer now," Clea said. "In the office." Clea heard the white noise of the cubicle, the way it muted everything, filled her ears like water, focusing her world down to a phone, a screen and a framed print of Minnie that she hadn't changed since Minnie had begun to walk. No late nights, Clea would say, no weekends, Clea would say, it was easier when it was just the two of them, Clea would say when Stacey Hellman's mother asked.

A herd of ponytailed eleven-year-olds barrelled through the living room, shrieking. Minnie was among them, her hair loose, her thrift-store sweater unbuttoned, but her mouth open in the same contrived horror. At the tail end was a slightly older boy, his hands cupped in front of him.

"Graham, no crickets until the girls leave!" Stacey Hellman's mother called after him. "They're for the tarantula," she said to Clea. "God, it's a menagerie around here. Boas and newts and cockatoos and—what else am I forgetting?" The crowd came back the other way, screaming more loudly, but running more slowly, letting the boy catch up. "Oh yes: four children."

Greg owned the building supply store—more of a chain, really—and their eldest was sixteen (which the math meant was the baby conceived among the two-by-fours) and, oh yes, please, Maria, it would be great to have another pot of coffee on, they'd never be able to do it without her because spring was the biggest real estate season and she was out almost every night. "I'll give you my card. No sense delaying the inevitable."

"I don't know," Clea said. The couch was a buff leather, slippery and ready to eject her. She stood and crossed the room to the kitchen island and added more milk to her coffee, even though it was already cold.

Stacey Hellman's mother was right behind her. "Clean it out and someone will snap that place up as a rental property. That area has a big demand for rooming houses. Or, even better, with that gas station across the road now, you might be able to get it zoned commercial. That's good money."

Clea imagined the man with the grocery cart wheeling it up the steps and into the front hall. Where would he park it, in among all her father's debris? She reached out and ran her finger along the bags of goldfish. The ribbons had little cards attached, each with a girl's name: *Samantha, Jessica, Gabrielle*. Minnie's goldfish wriggled, a small and insufficient protest to coming home with Clea, to leaving all this behind.

"What if I had some work done? Just a bit. Replaced the porch? Had it painted?" Clea said. "Maybe someone would see how beautiful it could be."

Stacey Hellman's mother smiled. It was a new smile, made by braces in early adulthood, straight and falsely suggestive of a natural predisposition to success. "Oh Clea," she said, placing her manicured hand near Clea's, close but not close enough that they touched. "Around here, no one has a memory that long."

On the way home from the party, Clea made a left three blocks before her usual turn.

Minnie looked up at her. "What's the plan?"

"Scenic route," Clea said, and Minnie held the fish up so it could see out the window.

Clea hadn't been on these streets for years. Not on this trip, and probably not the last time she was home, when she came for her mother's funeral.

She'd just finished her third-year exams and was

about to roll into a summer job with a firm that often hired its summer students. And then her mother died, a microscopic explosion in the brain—an instant, and relatively tidy, end that seemed to fit her mother's sense of grace. The garden was in full bloom. The house smelled of wood polish and spring air. There were guest towels that Clea and her father laid out for visitors after the funeral. Robin's egg blue and with a pink embroidered flower. Stacks of them. As if her mother had prepared for this eventuality in linen, the way other people did with wills.

"Stop sign," Minnie said.

Clea hit the brake. The belt pulled Minnie against the seat. The fish sloshed in the bag.

"That's new," Clea said.

But she couldn't be sure. It was a child's map she was following.

When they were kids, these streets between Clea's house and the Gearys' rented duplex had been easily navigable. On the official plans archived at city hall, Clea and Melanie's neighbourhood was the same, but no one would have confused Clea's environment for Melanie's—no one except Melanie and Clea.

Encountering each other over the wooden stove in Mrs. McBride's kindergarten class, Clea and Melanie had happily shared their pretend carrots and potatoes. They had held hands in the playground. They had picked each other as partners for projects that involved glue and glitter and old magazines.

What grade were they in, Clea wondered, making the only available turn, the time she looked at the B– they'd received and realized that it was probably because Melanie's printing sloped to the left? Or the time Clea had been invited to a party, the girl—her name escaped Clea now—tucking a pink envelope into Clea's school bag and saying, "Don't tell you-know-who"? Or when Clea noticed that Melanie's pants were wide at the bottom when all of the other girls' pant legs pulled tightly in? Old enough to walk themselves home after school, because the blocks between the houses seemed suddenly longer, the smell at Melanie's of frozen food heated after her mother came from work seemed foreign and cloying, not like the rich smell of Clea's house where her mother had been roasting something in wine all afternoon. And the TV that played on through dinner and into the night at Melanie's turned from innocent background babble into something that was acceptable only in certain company, and wouldn't be welcome at places like Clea's, where voices didn't exceed a certain level, or overlap, and stopped in polite deference when her mother played the piano.

The further Clea stepped away from Melanie Geary the clearer the distinction became and, it seemed, the clearer Clea herself became: an example of ideal girlhood—a decent family, the appropriate wardrobe, pleasant high school boyfriends and a whole raft of friends who called on her, except on those rare occasions when those friends just weren't available. Then Clea could always call on Melanie, convincing herself that she was showing Melanie a kindness. And the next day, when Clea walked past Melanie in the halls, no one else would know.

"I have to go to the bathroom," Minnie said.

"I'll only be another minute." Clea slowed and angled the car toward the curb to the place she remembered as the Gearys' address. But of course there was no duplex there, just an empty lot that might once have held a duplex. Or maybe the duplex had been on some other street. Perhaps she'd passed the house already and hadn't recognized it.

"Let's go home," Minnie said.

"Sure," said Clea, turning to look for a landmark.

"That way," Minnie said, holding her arm out straight, the bag dangling at the end. The fish wobbled like the needle on a compass, and Clea drove where it pointed.

"I was happy with just the two of us," Clea said when she went to replace the goldfish.

Carter looked at her like she was lying, but he was too polite to say so. Clea glanced over at the reptile area.

A girl with a shaved head and thick glasses was watching a chameleon slowly change colour from the brown of bare wood to a leafy green corner.

"Siamese Fighters," Carter said. He pointed to a row of jewel-toned fish stacked in tiny bowls like individual apartments. He lifted down a red one and held it at eye level. "Pretty, but completely antisocial," he said. "They can only look at others of their kind through glass."

"That'll do," Clea said.

"That's a very small house," said Minnie when the new resident was set up on the kitchen table. "Are you sure that's how the man said to keep it?"

"They like it like that. And they like to be separate, or they kill each other."

"Not always," said Minnie. "Otherwise, there'd only ever be one. This would be it. It's the last, great Siamese Fighting Fish! And it's living in our house! Call the Guinness Book of World Records! Edit Wikipedia!"

"Min, there were dozens of them like that, all doing perfectly fine." The fish took up most of the space in the bowl, its red so bright it looked artificial, like soon the dye would leech out, staining the water.

"Hmm," Minnie said, "we'll see."

Clea didn't know what woke her—the traffic on the street, someone shouting, a bit of rain against the window. When her parents had slept in this room, it had been dark and cozy, sheltered by the huge oak at the curb. The oak was gone now, the streetlight interrogationally close. A car passed and the bars of an old birdcage fanned across the room.

In Vancouver, the lights and noises from the street never bothered her. Her building was on an even busier road, right by an intersection. There, she slept just fine. Once, she'd even slept through an earthquake. It was true that while people talked about it the next morning, on the bus and by the coffee machine at work, she had wondered about her ability to respond in a crisis, but the next night she had laid down on the pullout couch and once again drifted off to something dreamless.

Maybe it was the time difference. Maybe, over the last two months, the three hours each day had accumulated and were finally asserting themselves. At first, she'd had no trouble sleeping. Not even the night they'd arrived, too late to visit the hospital, and she'd had to clean off a bed for each of them.

Really, it hadn't been like being home at all. It was somewhere else entirely—a place she hadn't known existed, like hearing for the first time the name of a country and learning of its centuries of plight. What else was she supposed to feel? Only the layout of her home remained, as if the earthquake had happened here. Every room was rubble, and even the surrounding blocks were altered.

Even her dad wasn't her dad. How could she explain to Minnie Granddad's sudden shifts from precise conversation to incomprehension, his mouth moving but nothing coming out, as if he were struggling to make sense of the air? But Minnie never seemed to question. She read to him and patted his hand and, when he seemed to retreat behind vacant eyes, Minnie read to herself. And now, Minnie slept as soundly down the hall in this big and foreign house as she had in her bedroom in the tiny apartment.

Maybe it was Minnie's accidental beginnings that had gifted her with this flexibility. Clea seemed to lack it entirely.

Clea's mother had died. Was that it? Or, was it the career she'd been unable to jump-start? The marriage that hadn't happened? The pregnancy that had?

"No, Dad, I don't think I'll come home this time," Clea had said, blaming the inconvenience of taking a baby on a plane, then, in the years that followed, the cost of two separate seats. When he'd offer to pay, she would say that Vancouver was where Minnie was comfortable, and holidays back east just wouldn't seem like holidays to her. "Why don't you come out instead?"

The times that he had, she'd thought his look of incomprehension was a response to the life she was living: the one-bedroom apartment, the high rent, the daycare costs, the low pay, the poor opportunities for

advancement—never guessing that the confusion stayed
with him when he went home, made him fill the empty
spaces with things that were broken and rotting and
would never be repaired.

Out there, the murky seasons let Clea fool herself into
thinking that she was merely suspended, just taking a small
detour from the path toward something better. But at
home, there would be no pretending. She would stand on
the beautiful veranda of her father's pristine home where
he had retired gracefully, refinishing antiques and buying
art, and everyone would see what she was. Teachers and
classmates would measure the distance between her promise and her life not in inches, but in miles. She would be a
cautionary tale. Even Melanie Geary would sneer from
behind the counter at the doughnut shop, while handing
Clea a brewed coffee that cost no more than $1.25.

Her pillow bunched and twisted, atomizing puffs of
must into the room, but it refused to be shaped to support her. Through her eyelids the light shone on as if it
swung from a wire on the ceiling, the accumulated furniture morphing into border guards repeating questions
she had no answers to. *What is your real name? What are
you doing here? Where are you trying to go?*

"Stacey needs to come for a sleepover," Minnie said. She
was packing her lunch.

The fighting fish was lying motionless at the water's

surface, as if it had surrendered to some invisible oppo-
nent. Clea lifted the bowl from the table and deposited
it, discreetly, behind a stack of crosswords, half finished
in her father's hand. The fish's tail shimmied like last
night's party clothes, tossed into the bay.

"I don't know, Min. Her mom might not want her
to," Clea said.

"Why not?"

"Well, we don't really know her," Clea said. But it
was Minnie she felt she didn't know. She had changed
so much and so easily, as if the new Minnie was the one
that had always been there and Clea had only imagined
the Minnie that came before. There were puffy breast
buds under Minnie's shirt. Clea could only look away so
long. On the weekend, they'd have to buy a bra.

"She's my best friend," Minnie said.

"What happened to Agnes?" Clea said. "And Terrence?"

"They're in Vancouver," Minnie said, "and we're not."

Clea waited her turn in the line of idling cars.

"Have a good day," she said, but Minnie seemed as
if she hadn't heard, as if she had already stepped out
and closed the door behind her. When it was finally
Minnie's turn, she waved over her shoulder with more
habit than feeling, and then she was absorbed into the
throng of children with nearly identical backpacks and
sweatshirts and jeans.

Before the turnoff down the mountain, Clea pulled into a giant Hellman's Building Supply store. Inside, she gathered an armload of black garbage bags. Most of the other early morning shoppers were men in workboots who shuffled purposefully along aisles of drywall sheets and shingles. There was only one cashier on, and Clea let her eyes lift to the ceiling, big enough for industrial equipment to move below the lights, storeys above. The line inched forward.

"Ma'am, are you ready?" the cashier said to Clea.

"Feeling industrious, I see!" In the next aisle, Stacey Hellman's mother was tucking a store card into her wallet and picking up a small shopping bag.

"Oh, just doing some tidying," Clea said, putting the first of the packages of garbage bags onto the conveyer belt. Suddenly, there seemed so many of them.

Stacey Hellman's mother waited while Clea paid and tucked the receipt into her pocket.

"I drove by the house, Clea. There are other options, you know. There are people who specialize in junk removal. People who will come and take it all away."

"Oh, it's coming along, you know," Clea said, walking ahead and pushing out the doors.

Stacey Hellman's mother's heels clicked across the pavement beside Clea, but she stopped in front of a black SUV. "Okay, if that helps you."

"Well, you'll see for yourself," Clea said. She could

already feel the regret mounting in her, like something she was compelled to collect. "You know, when you bring Stacey for a sleepover."

"Oh," Stacey Hellman's mother said. "Oh, right."

"I know the girls are really excited about it."

"Well then," Stacey Hellman's mother said, opening the driver's door and placing her package on a contoured seat, "we'll see if we can make that happen."

On the way back down the mountain, Clea stopped at a light. The heater had refused to accept the changing weather and kicked out hot air no matter where she set the dial. Clea rolled down the window and watched the hot air shimmer as it met the cold. Across the street, a real estate sign blew in the spring wind. On it, Stacey Hellman's mother smiled and nodded. Clea drove forward through the green light, but the image was inescapable. On lawn after lawn it repeated, a whole city of Stacey Hellman's mother, watching, judging. If you went up to any one of the houses, it would be Stacey Hellman's mother who'd come to the door and decide if she would let you in.

Clea stuffed papers into the bags by handfuls, her hands itching as the disintegrating particles worked their way under her skin like fibreglass. By noon, black bags clustered in the centre of every room like rival factions of mourners. Clea walked past them to her parents' room, where she saw that she had covered even the bed with garbage bags. When had she done that? she wondered. She lifted a bag and carried it to the stairs, then shoved it down. The bag caught the banister edge at the landing and broke open three steps before the bottom. She filled it where it had landed and shoved it out the door and onto the veranda.

Once, her father had known what could be salvaged and what wasn't worth saving. When she was small she had followed him through flea markets, loving the way he had said *Regency* and *Empire*, how he could pinpoint a thing's origin by the joists or the grain of the wood. On weekends, he'd take the battered pieces down to the turpentine-scented workshop and return with patinaed treasures. He'd give most of it away, selecting only the best pieces to keep, and trusting her mother to move the household around so that everything appeared to belong.

Moving through the house after her father had died, Clea had looked on the accumulated mess with her old expectation of order and wondered if there might be some meaning here even among the broken radios and piled news clippings and boxes of salt and pepper shakers, clues she should be careful to preserve.

But there was nothing to explain anything. Here was a magazine from the year her mother died; here was one from 1952. A tarnished but beautiful samovar was in a corner with a brittle plastic picnic set. Family photographs were mixed in with sheet music and buttons from

Expo '67. Dumping out a tray of gaudy costume earrings, she'd found her mother's engagement ring. It was all the same to him, as if he'd been building a barricade against the neighbourhood's toxic groundwater. Or perhaps it had all arrived in a flood, piling itself in haphazard stacks. Or maybe, Clea thought, looking across to the gas station and the empty lots where there had been a series of Victorian townhouses, just like the houses directly across from Clea now, but without the windows papered over in flyers, maybe it was the house itself that had spilled something poisonous out into the street.

"You're sure the water is fine?"

"It's perfect," Carter said. He dumped the sample into the sink in the store's backroom. He shook his hands then dried them on the seat of his jeans. Clea looked over to the birdcages. The parakeets were landing and taking off, alighting and then moving to another plane, the cages a whirr of blue and yellow and green.

The myna scraped at the metal bars. "Don't forget to vote," it said.

"I should be able to do this," Clea said.

"Sure," Carter said. "Why not?"

In the fish aisle, she said, "It's not like this is tricky. People have pets. I mean, for more than a day." Fish swam at her ankles, her knees, above her head. "I'm an evolved being."

Carter raised his eyebrows and then smiled. "Didn't you have a pet when you were a kid?"

"My father said we were 'not a pet family.'" Talking to Carter felt like treading water, an action that she could continue indefinitely—unless she thought too much about it, and then she'd forget how and sink.

"Well, that explains it."

Clea watched angelfish swim over Carter's shoulder. "I think my mother had a dog when she was a kid. Maybe it was a cat."

"Did it meet an untimely end?"

"How about those?" Clea said. The fish were tiny with a stripe of red and a stripe of blue on each side.

"For tetras, you need a filter and a pump," Carter said.

Clea thought of the bubbling, the air into the water, the sound of oxygenating. An operation she could monitor and count on.

"Okay," Clea said. "Let's do that."

The filter's drone took its place in the kitchen among the house's other noises, the refrigerator hum, the banging rads, and the buzz of street traffic that picked up and dropped off every time the light, one intersection away, turned green. All night, Clea thought she could hear the filter. Was it keeping her awake, or lulling her back into a fitful sleep? She couldn't tell.

As she poured her tea the next morning, she

wondered if the fish could hear it too. The half-dozen of them were darting up and down, one of them turning and the others following, the blue and red stripes along their sides flashing.

"That one's my favourite," Minnie said, pointing.

"Which one?" To Clea, they were indistinguishable. "There?"

"No! That one."

"This guy?" Clea put her finger on the glass, but the fish all swam away.

"Here." The fish Minnie identified flicked its tiny tail and merged back into the group. "He has the most personality," she said.

The fish were fine when Clea took Minnie up the mountain for school. But half an hour later, Clea saw one weaving a bit, taking too long to catch up to the others. Maybe she was imagining it, she thought, as she pulled the cardboard tongue on another box of garbage bags.

She propped the front door open. Stuffing and hauling the bags made her warm, but the air still felt crisp, even though it was late April. In Vancouver, everyone would be out of their jackets. Soon the rhododendrons would be in bloom. Here, spring was so hard-won. She had forgotten. Off the edge of the veranda she could see one lone daffodil poking through, a remnant of her mother's garden.

The garden was full of them, the last time she'd been home. She hadn't paid much attention to her mother's talk about flowers, but standing on the curb beside the cab that final day, she'd remembered that daffodils were the kind of flower you didn't have to plant each year. They'd come up again, she thought, though her mother wasn't there. Maybe that's what triggered the tears. Or maybe it was the smoke in her father's jacket, reminding her of when she had been young enough to crawl into his lap. The tears soaked into the rough tweed. "Tut," her father had said. "Now, now. There, there." As if he had to steady himself on a word before going on to the next one. "Daughter," he said. "Daughter." And then he opened the cab door and ushered her in. "I'll be all right," he said.

Through the smeared window glass, she'd watched him walk back to the veranda, stoop to pick up the morning paper from the step and place it under one arm before he raised the other in salute. And then he watched her go away.

He had said he'd be fine. She had believed him, assuming a full and dignified existence, with friends and interests, even with her mother gone. Had he imagined the same for her? Maybe it was easier for them both, believing the lie. But no, Clea thought, hoisting another garbage bag over the edge, he hadn't said anything about her at all.

She pulled out the doorstop and the hallway darkened. In the kitchen, two of the fish were still and floating. Their fellows circled beneath them, counting and recounting themselves, as if only their math was wrong.

———

Another fish was dead by the time they got home, but Clea managed to dispose of it before Minnie caught a glimpse of its tiny body. Over dinner, Clea tried not to let her eyes stray to the remaining three. At least Minnie was distracted. Stacey was coming to sleep over on Friday. It was only one night away.

"Do we have a night light?"

"Since when do you need a night light?"

"Well, maybe Stacey would like one."

The fourth fish succumbed before bedtime. Clea was folding laundry in the basement and came up to see Minnie staring at it while she poured a glass of juice. Minnie put her head down on the table and looked over her crossed arms at the fish's grey body.

"Are you okay?" Clea asked. She wanted to pull her daughter into her lap, but she seemed so solid, so separate. Clea sat down beside her, ran a hand through Minnie's hair.

"I'm just glad it's not Wilbur," Minnie said.

"Me too," Clea said. Two fish moved through the water. Was it Clea's imagination, or had they given up their fixation on proximity, struck out in opposite directions? One of them seemed to be scouring the pebbled floor, the other favouring the top, right near the surface.

———

Clea woke at three. She woke at four. At five, she got out of bed. The light from the street was too much to sleep through, but not revealing enough for any waking activity. Crossing the floor to get to the light switch, Clea felt her legs and arms go limp, as if the blood had drained from them. Her sides ached. Was it the lifting? Clea cracked her neck, bent forward. No, it was as if, in her sleep, she had been up to something. Something physically demanding that in her waking hours would be completely beyond her. The way, as a child, she had dreamed she was flying, and awoken with a certainty that she could do it again. Clea looked for a clue to her actions in the sheets—a cotton equivalent of tire tracks hardened in mud, a fossilized outline of herself—but there were only the usual wrinkles. She lay down again, wanting, at least, to remember. But whatever it was, it was gone. Only the ache remained.

In the dark kitchen, she flicked on the aquarium light and took the next dead fish from the water—an action as routine as putting the tea water on to boil. She sat at the table and stared at the tank. Maybe she slept and maybe she didn't. When she looked at the clock again, it was seven, the kitchen was light, the tea in her cup was cold. And Minnie was shrieking.

The remaining fish swam back and forth. Apparently it wasn't Wilbur.

———

"Do you want to stay home, honey?" Clea asked, looking at Minnie's eyes, which were dry now but starting to swell.

When Minnie was younger, how she had wailed. So hard sometimes that Clea had been afraid she would burst a blood vessel. Colic, pain, anger—whatever it was, Minnie had expressed it, her baby face screwing up, the sound coming out of her in louder and louder sobs, as if her infant self was crying not just for whatever irritant was passing through her system, but for the injustice of being so misunderstood. Day after day, night after night, for months and months, nothing had helped. If she wasn't asleep, she was crying. Eventually, Clea had given up trying—trying to return to a career, trying to keep up with friends, trying to integrate the two of them into the rhythms of other mothers and babies she spied from the corner of her eye, nursing discreetly in coffee shops or heading to library programs—and just walked: circuits of the apartment, the more brightly lit streets at 2 a.m., and in the daytime the miles and miles of seawall, all of it with earplugs buried deep in her ears. Until one day, passing the statue *Girl in a Wetsuit*, she glanced down and realized that Minnie had stopped. She wasn't asleep, just looking up at her with big and curious eyes, as if she had posed a question that could not be repeated.

"Are you joking?" Minnie said, the catch almost out of her voice. "Remember? It's Friday?"

Clea smiled and inclined her head, hoping it would come to her.

"Stacey?" Minnie said. "The sleepover?"

"Right," Clea said. "That."

In the car, Minnie pressed an ice pack to her eyes.

Back in the kitchen, Clea watched the last tetra veer from side to side, as if it were drunk or reeling in grief, as it came up to the surface again and again. It was still moving when she scooped it out, dropped it into the toilet, and flushed.

"It's not insomnia," Clea said. "It's more like a feeling."

"What do you mean?" Carter said. "Like, you're sleeping but you wake up tired? Like, you're sleeping but you don't feel rested?"

"More like, when you wake up in the morning and your foot stays asleep. More like, when you go to bed you feel just fine, but when you wake up your neck is all cramped to the side." In the other room, a rodent tongued a water bottle, its plastic canister banging against the metal of the cage, making it rattle.

"You mean like when you sleep funny?"

"Kind of like that," Clea said. She remembered reading "The Princess and the Pea" to Minnie. Twenty-two soft mattresses and in the morning this inexplicable bruise.

"Have you had this problem before?" Carter asked.

"No," Clea said. "But then again, I've never been the angel of death before. Come with me, little fish: drink the Kool-Aid."

"It's better that I think of it as bad luck," Carter said. "Otherwise, I'm an accomplice."

There were catfish sucking the side of one aquarium, an eel-like thing wiggled past in another. "I think we need something bigger, stronger," Clea said. The tetras had been too small, too pretty. You could almost look right through them. "I'll take one of those." She pointed to a tank full of black and hearty-looking fish.

Carter raised an arm over the tank, then hesitated, net in hand. "Are you sure, Clea? Mollies can be tricky."

"Okay," Clea said, "okay." She took a breath and saw the breadth of her choices, the variety of opportunities for failure. "Well then," she said, "I better take three."

"Oh my," Stacey Hellman's mother said, "it's growing."

After the garbage bags, Clea had pushed and shimmied objects and furniture through the rooms to the door and up and out onto the veranda. It was a step, she thought, though she had no idea toward what, because she hadn't been able to move them any farther. Instead, she'd organized a subtle triage, separating the lifeless from the merely wounded, and grouping the items by kind. Chairs with chairs, tables clustered together, rugs separated from blankets, genus and species. To keep the rain off, she'd covered much of it in garbage bags, duct-taped into makeshift tarps.

She shrugged her shoulders in what she hoped was a playful defence. "No point just cleaning around it," Clea said.

"Come on," Minnie said to Stacey as they made their way along the corridor from the porch steps and in through the front door, "I want to show you my room."

Something opened in Clea, like springs poking through a battered chair. Maybe Minnie was lucky not to know how this would end.

Stacey Hellman's mother stepped around the piles, keeping her nyloned legs well away from exposed nails and cracked wood. "If you want to sell this place well, you want to make sure that people don't get the wrong impression," she said.

"Which would be what, exactly?"

"One phone call," Stacey Hellman's mother said. She shook her phone as if she were clearing an Etch A Sketch. "One phone call gets you back to your life."

What did she imagine that to be? Clea wondered. Work had stopped sending e-mails after she hadn't answered the three or four that came from HR, marked high, then higher priority. Her paycheque had stopped arriving in her bank account. The messages on her voice mail from Minnie's after-school care had reminded her that "subsidized spots are in high demand." Last week, she'd called her apartment and found the line disconnected, returned to the anonymous file of phone numbers waiting to be reassigned. Only her postdated cheques kept the rent going through. There would be dust. There would be cobwebs. She vaguely remembered the contents of her fridge—tuna salad, a head of cauliflower. She pictured these things growing larger and mutating, knocking on the fridge door until it opened and deposited them in the chair in front of the TV.

Stacey Hellman's mother dropped her phone into her purse. "Just—a suggestion," she said. "I'll be back tomorrow, to bring Stacey home."

Clea watched her go, her heels thumping the waterlogged boards of the porch steps, and then teetering ever so slightly when she reached the cracked pavement on the walkway.

"Because that's what you'd do," Clea said.

"Pardon me?" Stacey Hellman's mother said.

"That's what you'd do," Clea said. She leaned on the railing, even though it wobbled. "That's what you're saying. That's what you'd do—if you were me."

"Well, yes," Stacey Hellman's mother said. "That's true. I would, if I were you." She faltered a little, but then she smiled, like a set of security lights coming on, tripped by motion in the bushes. "But of course, I'm not."

The mollies sat opposite Minnie at the table, as if they were smaller family members sharing a plate and a chair. Minnie refused to look at them. She squeezed the ketchup bottle over her hot dogs and it sent out a spray of red goo, along with the punctuating sounds of escaping gas. Minnie smiled across the mess at Stacey Hellman. Stacey Hellman returned her look, but altered. Go ahead, Clea thought, play along. It was obvious that Stacey was only tolerating the customs in this strange, uncivilized place. But underneath she was poised, she was attentive, just as friendly as was necessary, a miniature saleswoman in the making.

"I like the fish," Stacey said to Minnie. "We're not allowed pets on the table."

"No, I don't suppose you would be," Clea said.

Minnie looked at Clea and shook her head ever so slightly, as if this were only a warning and there'd be a longer discussion later. Clea looked at her lap. Maybe any good that was in Clea had gone into Minnie, and when she was born it had gotten out, grown up and away. It was Clea who was childish and petty, who'd stayed out west when her father had needed her, who'd used the loss of her mother, and then her responsibilities as a mother herself, to justify her own inertia. No, Minnie was generous and confident in a way that Clea had never been.

Clea reached out to clear the plates. "Is it time for dessert?" she said to Minnie.

But it was Stacey who caught Clea's eye and held her

gaze. Stacey seemed to be sizing Clea up, the way she would an equal. It was as if Stacey Hellman carried inside her a knowledge of who Clea was and what she'd been, the way mice pass on to future generations the way to get out of a maze.

"Ms. Osler," Stacey Hellman said, "may we be excused?"

Clea woke, her chest tight. Even sitting up, she struggled for air. Heart pounding, she flicked on the hall light and went to Minnie's room. She'd forgotten about the sleepover. Minnie was a mound in the darkness, displaced to an air mattress on the floor. It was Stacey Hellman in Minnie's sheets, her blonde hair spread like Goldilocks's across Minnie's pillow, her breathing slow and steady, as if she would always find waiting the bowl, the chair, the bed that was just right.

Clea wrapped a blanket around herself and went downstairs. The phone was sitting on a newly cleared table in the foyer. What had Carter said? "I'm always here for fish emergencies." He'd scribbled his cell number across the bottom of the receipt for the mollies. "Call anytime."

She clicked the button to talk, and listened to the tone. She would say—what? "It's dark"? "I'm alone"? "I'm sorry to wake you"? But it was her own number she dialled, waiting for the dull reassurance of the recorded voice, "This number is no longer in service," that had, like so many other undesirable things, been first a shock, then a comfort. Instead, the phone rang. And rang. The phone company hadn't taken back her number. *Ring.* The sound was blowing the dust across the top of her ancient TV, rattling the venetians over Broadway, falling out across the kitchen linoleum. *Ring.* Her father hadn't died. Clea had only come home for a visit, she was just going to check her messages, and they'd be on their way home. *Ring.* Soon, her own voice would knock at that darkness, three thousand miles, three hours away.

"Hello?" said a woman, groggy and annoyed. "Hello? Who's there?"

Clea was still holding the phone when she staggered through the dining room, past the piano, into the kitchen. On the table, the tank was blue in the dark. And it was empty. The mollies lay scattered on the table, like someone had detonated a bomb.

"Coroner's Office. Do you have a body to report?"

"That's not funny." Clea shifted the phone to her shoulder and dumped pancake batter into the pan. Minnie and Stacey were dancing around the kitchen in their pyjamas. She motioned at them to go upstairs and get dressed. "Besides, it's not one. It's three."

"At once? That's got to be some kind of record!"

"Don't say that. I feel bad enough." Clea rooted in the drawer to find something to flip the pancakes. The drawer was stuffed with utensils that would be useful in entirely different situations.

"Hey," Carter said, "I told you mollies were tricky. Ick—ick is a big thing with mollies."

"It wasn't like that," Clea said. "They were outside the bowl, Carter. They jumped out."

"Did you see it?"

"No." Clea tried to remember how they'd looked last. Just three fish, swimming in their clean and burbling tank. "They were fine at dinner." But even to her, her testimony sounded suspicious. As if there'd been a sign that she'd failed to interpret, as if she'd had a chance to intervene, and hadn't.

"I don't know what to say," Carter said.

In the pause, Clea wondered whether the bubbling sound she heard came from the store or from her kitchen table.

"I think you are some sort of special case, Clea Osler."

"I'm no case at all," Clea said. "I'm finished with pet ownership."

"No, don't say that. You just need to go indestructible. You need guppies. They take over everything. Come over. I'll explain."

"No, I've got Minnie's friend, I—"

"I'm here till six. I'll pick you out a dozen."

"I don't think I can," Clea said. "Thank you, though."

"Tomorrow then."

"Goodbye, Carter," Clea said. She put the phone on the counter. The pancakes bunched and crinkled from the frying pan to a wooden spoon to the plates. She put one out for Minnie, one for Stacey, then she bent down below the table and pulled out the plug to the filter. The last of the air bubbles floated up and went still. Clea thought of the mollies, swimming there opposite her, between Minnie and Stacey Hellman, nosing the water's surface even after they'd been fed. It was like they had been reaching for something just beyond the bowl. Something they had been promised, but couldn't yet imagine.

Clea settled herself in the bed beside Minnie. "Do you want me to read to you?"

"Tell about how you used to sneak the toilet paper from work," Minnie said.

It had been ages since she'd asked. When she was younger it was all she wanted, stories that cast them as a couple of slapstick comedians, making their way through life's perils like drunks weaving through traffic.

"There were extenuating circumstances," Clea said.

Minnie rolled her face close to Clea's. "It was wrong, but we had to," she translated.

"We were impecunious," Clea said.

"We were poor."

"Not quite destitute."

"We were not flat broke, but almost. And me?"

"You were incorrigible."

"I was a brat," she said, and Clea pulled the comforter up over Minnie in the room that had once been Clea's room, beside the room that was now Clea's room, in the house that seemed like it would always belong to someone else, though her mother was gone, though her father had grown smaller and smaller, though he had gone to the hospital, though he had died. And she thought that, even so, it was almost enough.

"Does that seem like a long time ago, Minnie?"

"Eons," Minnie said, and she curled in close to Clea, up to most of the places that no one ever touched.

"Mom, there's a man at the door."

Upstairs, folding sheets into the linen closet, Clea froze. She should have known it would happen. She couldn't keep the street out forever. "Don't answer it," Clea called, her feet sliding on the stairs. It was too late. Minnie had the door flung back.

Carter was standing among the debris. In front of him, the hallway looked empty, only an umbrella stand and an Art Nouveau lamp of a lady holding a sheaf of flowers, a worn Persian carpet. And then there were Minnie and Clea, just standing there.

"Can I come in?" Carter said. "I'd like to come in."

"Who are you?" said Minnie.

"I'm a friend of your mom's." Carter looked at Clea. "Right?"

"Carter," Clea said. "This is Carter."

"Are you the fish man?" Minnie asked.

"Not today," Carter said. He bent down and seemed to reach into the piles to the side of the door. He lifted a cage into the hall before him. "I brought you a present," he said.

"It's for me?" Minnie turned to Clea.

"I guess you'll have to come in, now," Clea said. Carter stepped inside and Clea made her way around him to shut the door. "What are you doing? Is this so I can kill bigger and bigger things?" she whispered.

"Is that a hamster? It looks like a hamster. My friend Stacey has a hamster." Minnie was pushing a finger inside the cage and stroking the thing that was curled in the corner.

"It's not for you, it's for her," Carter said. "I've got this figured out. In your case, good pet ownership skips a generation."

Minnie cooed at the rodent. Eyes opened in the fur. A nose twitched. Minnie looked up at Carter and grinned.

Clea clung to the radiator as though she were holding herself against a current that threatened to carry her away. She said, "The next animal that comes through this door, Carter, is going to be gutted and on Styrofoam."

The next night, Carter brought a chicken. He cooked it with spinach, carrots and sweet potatoes. While it was in the oven, Carter showed Minnie how to feed carrot tops to the hamster. Then he got her to set the dining room table.

"We eat in the kitchen," Minnie said.

"Okay," said Carter, "but not tonight."

Carter lit a small candle and put it in the centre of the table, then they sat. They stared across at each other.

"Do you say grace?" Carter asked.

"No," Clea said.

"Bon appétit," he said. "Please, go ahead."

"Have you ever been married?" Minnie asked.

Carter put his fork down and chewed more times than seemed necessary. "No," he said.

"Neither has my mom," said Minnie. "That's something you have in common. You might want to talk about that after dinner. You know, when I've gone to bed."

"Thank you for the suggestion," Carter said.

"Where did Granddad sit?" Minnie asked Clea. "Did he sit where Carter's sitting?"

"No, Minnie," Clea said. Could Minnie be more obvious? Until now, Minnie's directness had always seemed an admirable quality. "No, he didn't. My mother sat there, so she could be near the kitchen. Are you eating or just talking?" But Minnie was eating, even the spinach.

"Well, where then? Here? In my spot?"

"No, I sat where you are." Clea remembered her hands folded neatly over a cloth napkin, how every meal had had three courses and was eaten in small bites and with a straight back.

"And Granddad?"

"He sat here," said Clea. "Where I am."

Minnie nodded, as if, with this information, it all made sense. Minnie would be all right, Clea thought. With or without her, this girl would be okay. Clea took a quick breath in, the kind that precedes a sound that you won't even recognize as your own. She bit down against it and pushed her chair back.

"Excuse me," she said.

On the porch, the air was warm, and the sky over the gas station, the abandoned houses and the flyer-covered lamppost, was still bright. Clea wound her way into the section where the chairs were clustered, and sat.

Carter poked his head out the door. "Everything okay?" he said.

"Sure," Clea said. She drew her feet up under her and felt the centre of the chair sag.

"Clea," Carter said. He tried to walk forward, but he was trapped behind a sewing machine. "I'm going to come over there, okay?"

"There's no need," Clea said.

She watched him weave through the corridors until he found a chair close to her that still had a seat.

"Carter," Clea said, "I can't figure it out. Do you like me? Or are you just here to make sure no one gets hurt?"

"Hmm," Carter said. "Let's think: how's that going?"

"Oh God," said Clea. Over Carter's shoulder she saw an SUV turn into the driveway. Clea slithered her belly over the chair back. On the flat surface, she hurried across the porch and down the steps. She met Stacey Hellman's mother at the edge of the walkway.

"I had a showing a few blocks away. I thought I'd just come by to check on your progress. See how you were doing with the junk. Find out how close you are to a listing."

"I'm thinking about keeping it," Clea said.

"Keeping what? The house, or the junk?"

Clea threw her arms up as if she could toss a curtain over all of it and make it disappear. But it remained: definite and undeniable.

"The house." Clea threw a quick glance back at the porch. "And the stuff, actually. Some of it."

"What for?"

"I could fix it up." She was talking quickly now, the words forming in front of her like cartoon speech bubbles, surprising her with their solidity. "You said it could be zoned commercial, right? Well, I'll open a store and sell the stuff, right here." Stacey Hellman's mother's face was doing something strange and in slow motion, her eyes scanning the porch and the property, the whole collapsing mass of it. "You think I'm crazy."

"Clea, I'm going in before the pie burns," Carter called out. "Are you staying, Melanie? There's lots."

Clea didn't answer Carter. She didn't look at him. She looked at Stacey Hellman's mother, saw her take in Carter on the porch, start, and then recover, then wave to him as he went into the house. But really it wasn't Stacey Hellman's mother at all. It was Melanie Geary, grinning.

"Nicely done," Melanie said, when Carter closed the door behind him.

"What?" Clea said.

"Do you know how many of the mothers have been eyeing that cuddly pet? Good for you, Clea Osler."

Clea stared at Melanie Geary, her new teeth, her new hair, her new clothes. Was it possible that she'd really forgotten? Or had she chosen to forget? What have I done, Clea thought, to deserve such kindness?

"Melanie, don't you hate me?" Clea said. "I mean, just a little bit?"

"What for?"

"I was so sure of myself, so sure I was better than everyone."

"You weren't better than anyone."

"Obviously. Obviously, I know that now."

"Oh, Clea, I knew that then," Melanie said. She pressed her key fob and the SUV bleeped. "Call me tomorrow. I'll find you a Dumpster—you can't salvage all of it—and I'll give you the name of someone to call about the zoning. Oh yeah, and next weekend, Stacey wants Minnie to sleep over."

Clea watched Melanie wave and drive off, as if it had always been that simple, to go away, to come back, without dragging it all behind.

Then Clea walked up her father's steps—that might be her steps. She walked through the path of old furniture—that might actually be inventory. Inside, the house smelled of roast chicken and baking, clinging to the tang of the hamster's wood chips and the scent of old upholstery. It was a smell that was different and familiar all at once—the smell of family. Clea drew it into her lungs. It caught there, but she breathed again, letting it in, just a bit at a time. Maybe, she thought, this was something she could learn. The way mountain climbers trained themselves to breathe the air at high altitudes. Or runners built up their lungs. Or the way, long ago, some fish had stopped just dreaming of land and woken to pull itself out of the sea.

Carter and Minnie were sitting across from each other. There was a rhubarb pie at Clea's place, waiting to be cut.

Carter smiled up at her. He looked like he would follow her anywhere.

"Finally," Minnie said, "you're here. Now we can start."

ACKNOWLEDGEMENTS

My thanks to the following people and organizations:

The Ontario Arts Council, for providing me with two Writers' Reserve Grants. To *The Dalhousie Review*, which first published "Petitions to Saint Chronic," and to the marvelous Kim Jernigan and her team at *The New Quarterly*, who first published "Rise: A Requiem (with parts for voice and wing)".

To the jury of the Writers' Trust/McClelland & Stewart Journey Prize for awarding my story that honour and to Cecile Ryder who kept me from jettisoning the story that eventually won that prize.

Ted Barris shared his knowledge of WWII. Alexa Dodge, Chris Ralph, Laurie Monsebraaten, Jeff Keay, Catherine Graham, Molly Peacock, Marion Quednau and Susan Swan provided encouragement and inspiration, as did Ania Szado, whose parallel journey kept me going. My parents Sandra and Bill Hawkins banned television when I was five years old, leaving books the only option, and later made my writing possible by providing years of loving childcare for my own children. Sarah Knox helped clear the way for this book's publication and Gayle Waters offered me a place to finish it in solitude. Krista Foss provided wise feedback on many of these stories, and did it with sympathy and laughter. My fabulous agent, Samantha Haywood cajoled the stories from me, and then put her strategy and good graces to work on my behalf.

Thanks to everyone at Doubleday Canada, especially publisher Kristin Cochrane, publicist Nicola Makoway, designer Scott Richardson and to my editor Lynn Henry, whose work I had admired for many years before I became the happy recipient of her attention.

My thanks to Andrew Gray and the Optional-Residency MFA in Creative Writing at the University of British Columbia, especially my fellow students Jessica Block, Buffy Cram, Rhonda Douglas, Una McDonnell, Lori McNulty, Carey Rudisill and Zoe Stikeman, for their insight and camaraderie. I am incredibly grateful to have studied for three years with the inimitable, exacting and generous Zsuzsi Gartner, whose instruction triggered the crucial turning point in my writing and made this book—and any that may follow—possible. Thank you, ZZ.

Thanks to my children, who grew and made me aware that time was passing, and the writing could not wait. To Genevieve for appreciating (and defending!) my sense of humour; to Caroline for sharing her birthday and her clothes for photo shoots; to Andrew for teaching me to patiently watch dominoes fall; to Eve for furthering the writing urge and providing excellent material; to Beatrice for endless pep talks and pats on the back and for her fine ear for a great line.

Finally, my most profound thanks to my beloved husband, Lawrence Hill, my greatest fan and supporter, who inspires me with his own hard work in all circumstances; who read the stories when asked and paid me the best compliment by telling me when he didn't think I'd got it right (and was never offended when I disagreed); who kept me from sending things out too early and then pushed me to submit when I was hesitant; who juggled finances and his own work to make my writing time possible; who believed I could do this, and would have loved me even if I hadn't. Thank you, darling. Here's to many more, for both of us.